Death LEAVES A SHADOW

A *Marlowe Black* MYSTERY

GABRIEL F.W. KOCH

outskirts press

Death Leaves a Shadow
A Marlowe Black Mystery
All Rights Reserved.
Copyright © 2019 Gabriel F.W. Koch
v2.0

This is a work of fiction. Names, characters, businesses, places, events, locales, and incidents are either the products of the author's imagination or used in a fictitious manner. Any resemblance to actual persons, living or dead, or actual events is purely coincidental.

The opinions expressed in this manuscript are solely the opinions of the author and do not represent the opinions or thoughts of the publisher. The author has represented and warranted full ownership and/or legal right to publish all the materials in this book.

This book may not be reproduced, transmitted, or stored in whole or in part by any means, including graphic, electronic, or mechanical without the express written consent of the publisher except in the case of brief quotations embodied in critical articles and reviews.

Outskirts Press, Inc.
http://www.outskirtspress.com

ISBN: 978-1-9772-1567-3

Cover Photo © 2019 www.gettyimages.com.. All rights reserved - used with permission.

Outskirts Press and the "OP" logo are trademarks belonging to Outskirts Press, Inc.

PRINTED IN THE UNITED STATES OF AMERICA

By Gabriel F.W. Koch

Science Fiction
Paradox Effect

Fantasy
Emma and the Dragon's Tooth Sword

Mystery
Marlowe Black Mysteries
Beholden
Death Leaves a Shadow

Michael McKaybees Mysteries
And Come Day's End

Acknowledgements

This is my fifth book published with Outskirts Press. The team led by Lisa Buckley was professional as always. The cover design was spot on. The editor's work was superb. These are people I recommend for any writer not willing to slog through the endless maze of old time publishing. With Outskirts Press everything was done, as I wanted. Their, suggestions were well thought out, and helped me complete the publishing project successfully.

For Mac Titmus - there are no words.

As always my wife and daughters.

Chapter One

June 1951

A .32 caliber round robbed Lois of her life and me her.
I stared numbly at Detective Paul Dunbar, while something my father said years earlier ran through my head: *Death rides on all of our shoulders from the day we are born as if to inform us that only it knows of its appointment.*

The abrupt end of Lois' life burned like flames under my skin. The worst feeling since I first experienced death during war.

Seeing someone die will never get easier. For some reason the thought surprised me. I'd come to believe that untrue after years of being a private cop.

In Europe, GIs watched death strut boldly through battlefields and wade blood-splattered through the trenches, leaving broken and ruined lives behind it.

As a cop back home, I witnessed death as it swept the streets of the city, snipping off pieces of humanity where and when least expected, leaving survivors to wonder at their good fortune when they witnessed the results.

And to hell with them all, I thought with misery, exhaled a burst of air to smother the moan I felt in my throat, shook my head, and wiped my face with both hands. The tremor running the length of my fingers wouldn't stop, so I jammed my hands in my pockets.

Paul Dunbar, a New York City homicide detective working out of the Thirteenth Precinct spoke with a calmness I found offensive. I shouldn't have but I damn sure did. Something he said did not make sense, or maybe nothing could make sense after his announcement.

"Tell me again…how did you say she died?" I squinted, voice flat but normal, yet bitter, and angry too. Rage knotted my hands then. My fingernails dug moons into my palms. No way I could relax them.

"It's like I told you, the M.E. said her death was a simple act of suicide." He spoke monotone, had deliberately removed his hat, something he never did normally.

He held the snap-brim in his right hand, worried the brim with his left, and then used the back of his exposed white shirtsleeve to wipe sweat off his brow.

"What the fucking hell do you think is simple about suicide?" I demanded, fighting the need to shout. When he did not respond, I cut him a sharp nod to let him know how I felt about his silence.

To hell with you too. I glanced at the door once I caught his attention.

"Tell me the rest of it, and then get the hell out of my office," I said curtly. "I'm really not feeling comfortable with you in my place today."

"M.E. told me she put the barrel of the .32 they found at the scene in her mouth and pulled the trigger. The guys at the lab matched the gun barrel rifling to the bullet that they found with her body. It was her prints on the gun. Only hers.

"The boys at the scene saw signs of bruising on her left forearm and calf, her hip, but a few mild bruise aren't enough to indicate a struggle. They also found a half-empty whiskey bottle with her prints, no one else's, on it next to her opened on the floor. She smelled like she'd been drinking heavily for a few hours at least."

I knew he saw displeasure spark in my eyes as I felt its heat boil under my skin.

He looked at the window, staring out at the rain.

"Look, if it helps you any, I'm sorry, Marlowe, really I am." He spoke fast and glanced at the floor or his soiled and scuffed brown shoes. "I honestly couldn't think of a way to tell you that might make it any easier on you, pal." He mopped his brow again.

Well, isn't that fucking swell. I pulled in a slow, deep breath.

"The way you broke the news isn't what's got me teed off, Dunbar,"

I said, no longer caring how he felt or what he thought of anything.

There was enough animosity between us from our recent past. When I worked under him on the New York City police force for three-plus years, he'd been a miserable son of a bitch on the best of days. Nothing was ever good enough or done to his satisfaction. He smothered me in paperwork to keep me off the streets after I served justice to the bastards who escaped the courts. I didn't kill them, just did enough to let them know how their victims felt.

In my opinion our friendship during the war and before was beyond a point where any remnant of camaraderie stood a chance of revival without serious effort.

I was not about to make the attempt nor, I thought, was he about to try to recoup any of what we'd lost.

However, my throat felt tight with grief. I coughed twice, cleared it, which did not help much.

"Lois didn't have a reason to kill herself, and hell, she didn't even own a gun. She told me she hated the sight of mine, so I left it home when I visited her. I never took it with me when we went out someplace together." I stopped, and wondered why I was explaining anything to him.

Slowly, he lifted a small pistol from his jacket pocket. Fingerprint powder remained stuck among the gnarls of the grip like a rabid dog's dried spit.

"You ever see this before?" Arm outstretched he extended the handgun toward me with his forefinger in the trigger guard. It rocked as he held it out.

I walked across the room and accepted the .32 revolver, holding it by the end of the barrel. The weapon was not heavy. I turned it over and carefully examined it as if I might find something the cops had missed to identify the shooter, who I knew could not be Lois.

I sniffed it, smelled cordite and gun oil.

"Serial numbers are rubbed off," I said and scrubbed my thumb over the abraded surface where someone had used a file or grinder to scrape off the digits.

Dunbar lowered his hand to his side as if he did not want the weapon returned to him.

"No, I've never seen this gun before." Intentionally I dropped the pistol on the corner of my desk. It made a loud crash that we both ignored. "They find a note with her body?" Instinctively I again reached for the pistol and then pulled my hand back as a picture of Lois' small, delicate fist wrapping the grip popped into my head.

I sighed quietly and tried to concentrate on his words.

"They didn't find one." He frowned and gave me a look that told me he knew more than he had revealed, but would wait until I gave him a good reason to share the information. I didn't plan to give him one.

"I'm telling you that she didn't kill herself, Dunbar. I don't give a damn what Pat Solok told you or what you think. Pat didn't know her the way I did and neither did you." I spoke slowly and emphasized each word, but it took effort.

"Marlowe, the only prints we found on the gun belonged to her. Hell, the only prints we found in her apartment belonged to you and her."

"So whoever shot her wore gloves," I said and sounded as if I thought I needed to defend Lois.

Finally Dunbar took the pistol as if it was a tainted throwaway. He dropped it into his pocket and turned to the door.

"Case is closed on this one, pal. All you can do is bury her and mourn her." He did not sound like he really cared about how I felt. He stopped with his hand on the doorknob and glanced over his shoulder. "She have any family in town do you know?"

"They're all dead. Her brother bought it on Tarawa. She said his death hit her parents hard, and the grief killed them. She was the only surviving child."

DEATH LEAVES A SHADOW

And we had planned to get married in a few weeks, I reminded myself unnecessarily, wanted to shout it in his face, but he knew and, hell, now it didn't matter.

Moving uneasily, he cleared his throat. "You two getting along lately?"

"What? What the hell are you implying, Dunbar?" I frowned and stopped my hand as I reached toward my jacket.

"I'm doing my job, so answer the damn question." He stared at my face.

I felt my hands relax and pump into fists again. Blood dripped off my right palm and splattered the floor noisily.

"We'd discussed marriage, remember, Paul? I told you about it two or three weeks ago. Do you remember?" I took a few steps in his direction and stopped short of getting in his face, where I wanted to be. Hell, he was still a cop. I couldn't slug the son of a bitch.

"Despite what you think it's always possible she had a change of heart." He stared, flat brown cop eyes not revealing emotion.

"If she had changed her mind, she didn't let me know." I pressed one shoulder to the wall by the window, glanced at the streaked glass, and thought about putting my fist through its center.

"The last time we were together she told me she loved me. That was two days ago. We talked about her moving into my place, laughed about me not liking dogs and her having one."

He spoke quietly. "Where do you think she got the gun? Bought it or borrowed it?" Now he turned and walked away after asking one of those questions no sane man would ask a grieving fiancé let alone an old friend. An armed old friend.

However, I still did not think he cared, and only wanted to avoid seeing my reaction or catching my fist. By then, I really wanted to hurt him bad.

"Lois didn't own a gun." I answered with a rough edge that should have warned him to back off. "No more of this crap, Dunbar. Tell your goddamn captain you did your fucking job. Now get the hell out of my office, and shut the door after you leave."

"Sorry," he said again and closed the door with no more than the click of the latch after he stood in the hallway.

I listened to his footsteps as he descended, and then returned to the window. The fog from my breath had cleared off the glass. The rain slowed, so each drop pelted the panes like insects trying to burrow their way into the warm room.

Something bad happens inside when you lose someone important so abruptly, as sudden as a stray lightning strike on a cloudless day. It erodes memories and leaves behind shadows drained of color they might have held before. And you know eventually those memories too will fade like dried autumn leaves blown by winter's first storm until all that remains is a haunting wisp of who she had been when alive, and a fading framed picture bleached by time.

To fucking hell with all of that too, I thought. *Mourning her will have to wait until I can find her murderer, and torture and kill the bastard slowly.*

When I sat behind my desk, her photograph confronted me. Her smile reminded me of the warmth of her love and an invitation for a future together.

Then I thought of the night about three weeks ago I spent with her that had been so special, her words had melted my heart. We were sitting in the living room of her apartment with the rust of sunset sparkling across the polished oak floor.

"I'm pregnant," she had said softly, touching my face with her fingertips.

"Marry me!" I had blurted without forethought.

She did not hesitate to answer as tears shimmered in her eyes. "Oh, Marlowe, you don't know how much I'd hoped you'd say that."

"So you'll marry me then?" I asked, astonished to learn that I would be a father.

"Of course I will, darling." She leaned in my direction. I kissed her.

Now she and my unborn child lay dead in the city morgue.

With care I lifted the photograph by the top edge of the gold frame, slid open the bottom drawer on the left side of my desk, and placed her in it face down.

"Now what?" I said, felt the wedge grow in my throat, and knew I'd find and serve her killer the justice he deserved. Suicide was out of the question.

Chapter Two

The drawer slid shut with a dry, quiet squeal. Suddenly the office felt too small. I needed to get outside. I stood, retrieved my hat, pushed it on the back of my head, and nearly ran out of the building.

After two quick phone calls from the pay phone at the corner deli, I grabbed a cab downtown to the morgue, paid the driver, and stood in the rain outside the building, but did not look at the old weather-stained brick facade. Rain dripped off the brim of my hat. I felt it slip beneath my collar like chilled, wet fingers seeking warmth. Then the urgent desire to turn and leave without seeing her body felt like shattered glass carving the bottoms of my feet.

Clenching my teeth, I pushed through the entrance door, shook rain from my jacket and hat, and met Pat Solok outside the viewing room.

"You don't have to do this, Marlowe," he advised quietly as he had when I had called him earlier. "You know that, right?"

"And you know me better than that, Pat. If I don't get this done, I'll never live with myself." I stuffed my hands in my pockets again as if I no longer knew what else to do with them.

Otherwise, I'll never know if it's Lois in there, I told myself with the awareness of encouragement.

Pat put his hand on my shoulder, squeezed once. The movement was a gesture expressing something deeper than years of friendship. I knew he felt my pain because he'd been there. Pat had lost a sister a year ago. A hit and run on Madison Avenue in the middle of the afternoon. None of the witnesses could recall more than the color of the midnight blue sedan.

A moment later, a light went on behind the glass partition. Lois' still form lay shrouded under a white sheet. She seemed shorter, as if death had somehow drawn her in, deprived her of an inch or two. Her belly was flat, pregnancy not yet visible.

I nodded at Pat. He pressed an intercom button and said, "Okay."

His assistant lifted the sheet slowly, which revealed the left side of her face, but nothing more.

I felt surprised that she appeared normal, and then noticed that her head seemed off kilter, leaned to the right while her face pointed almost straight up at the ceiling. Her light brown hair had a matted appearance caused by dark, dried blood.

"We haven't had a chance to clean her up yet," Pat said quietly as if he noticed my reaction.

Hot bile singed the back of my mouth. I swallowed several times to drive it down, fought to keep the horror from carving my face, and glanced quickly at Pat.

He pulled his head back slightly and I knew he sensed, if not saw, my rage.

"There's no doubt in my mind that the body is Lois'." My words hissed out and I nodded at it.

Not her, it, I thought. *She's gone forever. The bastard took her from me.*

I couldn't possibly tell you what happened after I left the morgue, except that I got out to the street as fast as possible. Next thing I knew, I stood in the Battery feeling stiff, wet, cold, devoid of emotion and examined cargo ships move slowly toward the Westside docks with tugboats assisting.

The rain stopped abruptly. The sun burnt through crackled gray clouds like signals from a superfluous herald. The air smelled like an invitation to a spring day long in the past.

Two young teen boys rode by on bicycles. They laughed over something only boys cared about as spray from their wheels rooster-tailed water behind them. When I glared at them, they must have caught sight of the grief and horror twisting my expression. They stopped their bikes as if afraid that the dread I felt would reach out and send them to a place they had not imagined might exist beyond the lessons they recited from memory on Sunday mornings.

"Castillo," I said aloud to ventilate anger. I wasn't really aware of them beyond the first moment of their passing.

Vinnie Castillo ran the mob in south Manhattan. The last time I had confronted him, I'd seriously humiliated Castillo before his bodyguards, henchmen, and others in his neighborhood. He detested me, and Lois' murder was his style of retribution.

"Yes, sir," the oldest boy responded with nervous laughter and glanced quickly at his friend.

"Castillo your name, boy?" I asked sharply, hoping it was so he could carry a personal message to Vinnie. I stepped off the sidewalk so the kid might come closer. Water soaked through the bottoms of my shoes.

"No, sir," he said and pedaled fast, skidding around the bend in the sidewalk and disappeared while yelling, "Let's get outta here fast," to his friend. "That guy's a nut case."

"Time to pay up, Vinnie," I said, disregarding the boy's remarks, and rode a cab back to my office.

Night dropped like a curtain of mercy across the windows. Lights outside sparkled lively distraction that fractured in the raindrops still clinging to the window. I did not know how long I sat staring without seeing the activities beyond. Then, a sharp and sudden noise yanked me back.

My feet hit the floor hard as I swung them off my desk. The door window glass silhouetted a person moving in the hallway.

Lifting my 1911 Colt, I thumbed the safety off and jacked a round into the chamber. There was no doubt that I would shoot if threatened.

I didn't think about how paranoid my reaction seemed. Desire rode my nerves hard for me to kill someone as if that might restore some kind of balance to my life. Eye for an eye, as an old-time preacher once said during his sermon.

DEATH LEAVES A SHADOW

Lowering the .45 to my side, holding it behind me, I unlocked the door. When I pulled it open, Stella Vichery faced me.

I had assisted the police indict her for criminal, aiding, and abetting activities a year earlier. I had thought then that my written testimony would have put her behind bars for two to three years. Apparently, she had escaped punishment.

As I studied her face, I found what I saw there confusing. She seemed calm, like she was glad to see me. Her light hazel eyes examined my face before meeting mine. For a second, I saw a stab of emotion pinch the corners of her eyes. Then she shook her head slightly and smiled, but I couldn't tell what lay behind her expression. By rights, she should've at least despised me.

"Hello, Marlowe," she said in her cultured soprano and entered without invitation. She smelled like expensive perfume, looked older somehow, changed, but still strikingly beautiful. Her face was slightly oval, nose a bit narrow, lips full and colored bright red. She seemed to have a few creases starting to show on her forehead. Her hair was cut in a pageboy.

The last time I saw her she wore a worn pair of my blue jeans, a red-and-white checked flannel work shirt I'd loaned her, and not much more. The night before that she'd worn only moonlight that embraced her with a shimmering gentleness I'd found irresistible.

Now, she wore an expensive dark blue dress, matching shoes, purse, and feathered hat. The color contrasted her eyes and light auburn hair. Her complexion showed signs of emotional stress in the tiny lines next to and below her eyes. I did not recall seeing them the previous year, and we'd been real close together a couple of nights. Of course, the illumination was dim moonlight.

I closed the door and turned to study her progress as she walked to the desk. It seemed that the obvious question between us would remain unspoken for the time being.

"You heard about Lois?" I asked and wondered why she would care.

After a brief nod for an answer, she changed the subject. "My father's being sent to Israel for trial and punishment."

"Did you kill Lois?" The question rushed out without forethought.

"You think I would murder someone because you set up my father?" She sounded stunned. Her eyes sparkled with angry moisture and then narrowed to slits that hid whatever else she thought about me at that moment.

Which made me remember that the first time I saw her, I thought her eyes were brown.

Trick of the lighting in Cohen's office, I thought.

"He did it to himself by aiding the enemy. He was a traitor to his country," I said. The words sounded too resentful, emotionless, but right then I didn't give a damn.

"And his family lives to suffer the sins of the father. Isn't that the way people like you think?" She sounded tired, not angry, and sat carefully in the chair before my desk the way she had the first time I'd met her. She placed her purse on the desktop, used it to push aside the mail from yesterday I'd forgotten. One letter slid and hit the floor with a noise that almost sounded wet.

"I didn't kill your girl, or have anything to do with her death. By now I really do understand grief better than most people," she said bitterly, and then added with surprising gentleness, "I'm truly sorry about your girl, Marlowe. My brother-in-law got a call from a friend at police headquarters this afternoon. He thought I should know about her death. He phoned me about two hours ago." She glanced down at her gold wristwatch as if she needed to check.

I nodded. "The feds told me they'll put your father in prison for two to five years and then let him walk. These Jews aren't murderers. They're victims and seek justice for their dead. A need I understand quite well," I stated to make a point I did not think she'd miss.

I put the safety on and stuck the .45 into the holster under my left arm, walked around, and sat behind my desk.

"Needless to say, but I believe I'm familiar with that type of grief too." She sounded remorseful now, but her eyes seemed shaded with knowledge she would not reveal easily. Then she said, "My mother died unexpectedly a few months ago right after they took Father away." She visibly wrestled with the emotions that reshaped her features, which made me feel like an ass. For an instant I wanted to get up, walk over, and put an arm around her, but didn't believe that would work for either of us. Instead, I folded my hands on the desktop.

For the second or third time since Dunbar told me about Lois, a sob filled my chest. Looking down, I suppressed it with effort. Then there wasn't anything left to say about our past, how it had played into the present.

"I'm sorry to hear that. You're free?" I asked to change the subject into something that might hold a future.

"Yes. I told you my brother-in-law is a good criminal attorney. Other than that, I've had enough time to seriously reevaluate my feelings and actions once they arrested my father and Mother died.

"On one October afternoon, the day after the court absolved me for my involvement with the coins and the list of names, I sat in Central Park feeling sorry for Dad and me too.

"Several children ran by playing a game of tag. They stayed in the section of the park near where I sat. One girl hid behind me after begging that I not give her away. Of course, the girl who was IT discovered her, but she made a genuine effort to escape before her friend might tag her. She twisted and ducked as she ran hard laughing the way only young girls do.

"By the time they ran off, I started thinking I needed to stop playing tag with my emotions, my mistakes, own up to them and get a fresh start, help people in a way that might make me feel, well, cleansed or revived at least. So, with my brother-in-law's assistance, I got my PI ticket and here I am."

I ignored the last bit of information as too difficult to believe, and looked at the time: 7:13 p.m.

"Okay, but why'd you come to my office?"

"Because you need my help, Marlowe." I knew she wanted to say "this time," but was glad she did not feel it necessary.

"There won't be much for you to do. As far as I'm concerned someone will die for killing her, maybe more than one." I tried to keep the anger out, but failed. I felt it build in a flash of heat that stabbed out to my fingers.

"And death by gunfire is no place for a dame like me?" A strange, crooked smile plied her features in an odd way that made her quite appealing. However, the look that flashed through her eyes got me thinking she could and maybe would kill if she wanted, without much hesitation or mercy.

"Death is a place we all get to learn about no matter what life we live."

"Then how will this be different?"

"Who said different? I said someone or more than one will die, meaning the gunman who killed Lois and anyone who gets between me and him or any bastard that might've helped him." I spoke quietly while examining her eyes. She didn't look away.

She stood and walked around the room; touching objects with a deliberate casualness, she ran her fingers over the edge of the windowsill. Lifted her hand, examined her fingertips, and wiped them on a white lace-edged handkerchief she removed from her purse.

"I came close to falling for you in a bad way." She spoke quietly, which almost sounded like despondency, and glanced quickly over her shoulder. She folded the handkerchief, put it in the purse, and closed it with a click.

"Good thing you didn't, Stella."

Lois did, I added to myself. *And look where she ended up.*

Stella returned to the chair, but didn't sit. She pressed one hand on the chair back for support, lifted her purse strap off the desk, popped it open, and removed her wallet. With two fingers, she extracted a folded sheet of paper and placed it on my desk and pushed it toward me.

I unfolded it and stared at a new private detective's license, looked up at her, met her appraisal, and nodded to show my recognition.

Her brother-in-law has to have great connections and lots of cash if he helped her pull this off.

"Having this in your wallet and doing what I do are two radically different things." Flattening it on the desktop with my palm, I slid the license to her.

"Who are you planning to kill? Do you know who shot Lois?" She took her license, folded it, and slid it back into her wallet.

I liked that she had not yet mentioned suicide.

"Vinnie Castillo." I folded my arms, did not want her to know having her there made me feel a bit better, more human maybe, or just not alone. Whichever, it was enough for the moment.

"Castillo's been out of town for a month."

"His whereabouts don't matter to me. If he wanted to he could put out a hit from anywhere in the world."

"He didn't have her killed," she said with finality.

"How the hell can you be so sure of that?"

"Castillo's been locked up in an Italian jail, their version of solitary confinement for about two weeks now."

"Vinnie could have ordered her death before he left the States."

"I've read a lot about Mr. Castillo in the papers and talked about him with my brother-in-law, who knows Vinnie's attorney. They play golf together on Sundays." She shook her head. "No, Vinnie acts like a fool, but he's too clever to get on your wrong side, and you know that much."

"That's the first thing you've said about him that makes perfect sense."

"Then who else hates you enough to want Lois dead?"

"Where else would you like to start?" I asked and felt like it was time to end the discussion.

"The corner diner while we get something to eat. I'm famished." Apparently, she did too.

I came close to laughing with pleasure that she could manipulate me as if she knew my thoughts and habits the way an old friend might after years of being around each other.

"Let's go, doll," I said, but did not let her see or hear how her casualness made me feel.

Lois' body and our unborn child remained laid out in cold storage waiting for me to arrange their burial. That idea drove a hot spike of loss through my heart, and the realization evaporated any feelings Stella had stimulated.

Chapter Three

After adjusting my snap-brim, I opened the office door and held it for Stella, flipped off the light, then closed and locked the door. Within seconds, I heard heavy feet pounding up the stairs, which made me wish we had remained in the office.

Personal experience had proven more than once that anyone running up steps carried with them the burden of bad news, or that they intended to be the bad news.

Before I was able to turn around and jam the key back in the lock, I heard several bullets whistle past my shoulder as they burrowed into the woodwork like ravenous termites gnawing at fresh heartwood. Sharp splinters sprayed the landing, but fortunately missed both Stella and me.

She started shouting words I couldn't understand, which sounded like panic and made me think she was fighting to control the raw terror the possibility of unexpected death always created in the uninitiated.

I wondered if she would lose control and do something foolish like run down the steps to escape whatever waited below.

Then, I caught a glimpse of her as she clawed at the clasp on her purse, missed, and tried a second time. She started cursing like a longshoreman when she failed to yank it open, succeeded on the third try, and then squeaked a painful gasp followed by a cry of "Oh God, what was that?" A fist-sized spray of blood and tissue blew out from in front of her.

Her opened pocketbook clattered at her feet and dumped its contents across the floor. Her small handgun dropped and bounced off her right foot. A gold lipstick case rolled to the edge of the landing, went over, and clattered down the stairs like a handful of tossed coins.

I dove in her direction, tackled her right above her knees, and knocked her to the floor. Her breath and a groan of serious pain exploded from her opened mouth as she hit the wooden surface with a bone-jarring thud. I'd managed to get one hand behind her head to keep it from slamming the wood.

Single-shot gunfire continued while I struggled to free my Colt. The gun was wedged between me and Stella. By the time I held it in my hand with the safety off, the shooter had fled back to the street. His feet slapped down the steps rapidly.

I leaned over the top railing and fired six quick shots at his silhouette. He hissed, "God damn you, you bastard," which let me know I had at least winged him, but not seriously enough to slow him down or to kill him.

I heard him slam into the door and push it open as he reached street level. Sounds from outside briefly leaked into the foyer. Then I heard a car door slam and an engine's roar receding as the auto raced down the block with a cacophony of car horns following him.

Son of a bitch. I released the catch on the .45 to let the slide close, buckled the hold down after I jammed the empty gun in the holster, and then braced myself to turn over another cooling corpse. I took a long, slow breath and exhaled hard before I reached for her.

Stella still felt warm, but that meant nothing. Less than one minute had passed since he had fired the first shot up the stairwell.

This time tears squeezed from my eyes, and stung me with the horror of knowing that I was too damn selfish to send her away when she'd re-entered my life an hour earlier. Part of me had needed to be with a woman I knew I once cared about seriously.

Caring for her was before I became aware of her criminal complicity in grand larceny and conspiracy to hide evidence revealing the names of war criminals residing in the city. However, I had cared and right then, I learned that I still felt the same attraction, the same concern.

Gently, I rolled her onto her back, pressed the side of my face against her chest, and felt like shouting with joy at the sound of her beating heart. Not giving a damn who might witness it, or how she would react if she learned what I did, I ripped open her dress and located a wide, round exit wound burned in her gut below and to the right of her liver. Blood oozed out and puddled beneath her.

That was a close call, damn close call. Sweat beaded my brow. Angrily, I swiped it off and wiped my fingers on my trousers.

The wound looked as if the bullet tore through flesh and muscle only. A clean liver shot would have been fatal and would have bled profusely. Blood continued to leak out, but not fast enough to kill her anytime soon, or ever if I got her to a hospital soon.

Using my belt, I strapped my handkerchief over the exit wound, tore a strip of her blouse, and used that on the entrance wound. Inside the office, I phoned the cops, told them I needed an ambulance, and gave them my Flatiron Building address. Then I hung up and returned to wait with her until the cops and the ambulance arrived.

If she dies, I thought, *she'll not die alone. Nobody deserves a lonely death like the one Lois had while she stared at the face of her murderer.*

Picturing Lois made me feel appalled, and terribly alone. I placed my hand softly on Stella's shoulder. Then didn't know what to do. Helplessness stinks.

Chapter Four

A half hour later, for the second time that day, Paul Dunbar leaned with his back against the wall at the head of the stairs in the corridor outside my office. The uniformed cops he brought with him used wide-beam Eveready flashlights as they went over the area where Stella fell, gathered evidence, pried bullets from the wood, and took samples of the drops of blood downstairs where my .45 round and the shooter met without a resolution I could find satisfying.

"Sorry this happened, Marlowe," Dunbar said and sounded like this time he really meant it.

I accepted the cigarette he offered me, used the lit stick match he held out, and watched his eyes as I lit up and then dragged the hot smoke deep into my chest.

"Any thoughts as to what the hell this is about?" he asked without animosity. Neither his eyes nor his voice expressed anything but professional cop. Nothing unusual there, but strangely I felt relieved by his practiced demeanor. It did little to lessen my concern for Stella.

"He must've waited until I shut off the lights and locked the door." I turned my head to exhale. "I didn't hear him until I finished and started to head to the stairs."

"So the light was a signal, you think?"

"Bastard must have known that Stella was up here with me, and he didn't give a good goddamn if he killed her too." I glanced down and stared at the cigarette's orange-red ember, the tendril of smoke curling off.

The landing area still smelled like blood and burnt cordite.

"Seems someone wants you dead in a bad way, friend." He slipped a fresh Pall Mall between his lips and struck a match on the sole of his shoe.

"I'll be damned if I know who," I admitted without hesitation.

"That's because most of your enemies are dead," he said and chuckled with a cop's dry humor many of us don't find very funny. "Except for this guy, from the looks of it. Who'd you miss? You have any ideas?"

Jesus Christ, I thought rather than reacting to his prod the way I knew he wanted—in a display of anger. Instead I slowly shook my head, ignored his overused ruse. We both knew my reputation. I shot the bastards if they gave me a reason like them shooting at me first. Or taking a shot at someone innocent. Otherwise, I just kick their asses if I figure that's what they need. Of course once in a while that doesn't play out, and I get mine kicked, but I can take as well as I give.

"Those other bastards are all where they deserve to be, but not Lois. She shouldn't have died the way she did. Stella should not've been shot." I knew he was still thinking Lois committed suicide, but I planned to change that idea soon. My gaze dropped to where Stella fell after I tackled her. I examined the fresh bloodstain. The red smear had spread like a splayed hand.

She shouldn't die this way either, I thought, and ground out the cigarette in the sand urn to my left.

Women and guns. Clearly, I had a problem with the combination or maybe only with women.

A week after I closed the Vichery case, the federal boys had rounded up and deported the Death Head SS Nazis from the list Stella and I found in Himmler's sterling silver Death Head belt buckle, a trophy Gregory Twiggs took of Himmler's body and smuggled into the country after the war.

The feds used the information I gave them about Stella's father too. He worked as a banker in Germany for the Nazis during the war. Perhaps that was not his intention when he started out, but greed made him delay removing his family from the storm troopers' path, and they got run over by and absorbed into the enemy's machinery.

I doubted this shooter had been one of their survivors, because I didn't think any still lived or were free. I had shot and killed several of them while they hunted me, and Stella.

If what Stella claimed about Vinnie proved to be true, that eliminated my two most recent problems and left me without a suspect or a reason why some bastard might want me dead and six feet under.

Sometimes a wise guy might read about a private cop like me in the papers and then decide to test him, but this didn't feel like that either. This felt more personal.

"Are you going to need help with this?" Dunbar asked casually.

"I'd prefer to leave your boys out of it. This is too close to home." I left out "for the law's involvement," knowing he understood exactly what I meant. I also knew he would not keep his men from investigating.

"We've got to investigate the shooting, but basically the evidence is nonexistent from what I can see. A couple of my boys will interview your neighbors and we can type the blood, maybe get a print or two from the door downstairs, but without a suspect, hell, none of this will matter all that much." He flicked hot ashes on his palm the way he did back in basic training, ignoring the sand urn by his left leg.

"Regardless of that, Paul, I'd like to look into this without interference. I won't do anything without talking to you first, and if I find the shooter, the bastard's all yours." I inhaled some of his exhaled smoke, and lit a Camel using my Zippo.

After I've finished with him, I added mentally.

"I wasn't talking about using my boys from the Thirteenth to help you personally," he said. "I've got some leave time coming, and I think I need a vacation since I haven't taken any time off in two years."

"And you'd enjoy a little Wild West type action?" I repeated what he'd called my work a year after I quit the force. His wanting to help me seemed odd, but maybe the old friendship wasn't dead after all. Still, I felt leery, and wondered over his motivation.

His face expressed amusement and remorse as he nodded. "You and that damn memory of yours, Marlowe. I've got to learn to think twice before I speak around you. Never was any good at that kind of shit, you know." He hesitated as if thinking about what he wanted to say and then asked, "Have you ever gone fly-fishing? It's nice and quiet upstate in the country this time of the year."

"Anywhere upstate is too damn quiet for me except Albany, and I'll be damned if I'll go to that slum," I said emphatically, hoping he understood my seriousness and would drop the subject.

Again, he flicked ash on his palm. I remained silent and stoic, and watched his face.

"You know I won't break the law and I can't allow you to do it either while I'm around you," he said almost casually.

"Who said I'd be breaking the law? You ever know me to break the law?" I looked away so he wouldn't see my eyes, which I knew would give away what I felt and what I knew he knew.

"Marlowe, you come so damn close, but somehow you always know right when to pull back. Up until now, you've not broken any that I'm aware of or your ass would be in a sling."

Again, I studied his face while he took a long drag on his cigarette, and still could not read a reaction. I could not even make him nervous. Damn cop. He knew something he wasn't prepared to discuss right then, but I figured whatever that information was, it had caused him to bring up the topic of vacationing far outside of the city.

"Give me a couple of days to figure things out, bury Lois, and then I'll let you know? Okay?"

"Fair enough by me. You got my number, Marlowe." He crushed his smoke in the brass urn, dusted his palm over it, and descended deliberately as if waiting for me to change my mind right then.

"Thanks, Paul," I said to his back before he had gone more than three steps.

He lifted his hand and wagged his thumb and little finger in a wave like the old days while we fought in Europe. That was the kind of greeting we gave the flyboys when they went overhead after strafing enemy soldiers and saving our asses.

I did that once to a low-flying fighter heading south in Jersey, tail number 819. He wagged his wings in response, which made me feel pretty good, as if some of the best things about the war had not changed with time. I've always wondered who he was after that day, but I figured I would never find out.

Dunbar and I fought what history is now calling the Battle of the Bulge. We watched a lot of guys, many of them good friends, die before we beat back the Jerrys. The memory made me feel better than I thought it should, and I could not help but wonder why. Dunbar, if I accepted his offer, would get between the killer and me if I didn't find enough hard evidence for a jury to convict and sentence him.

On my own, unimpeachable evidence was not always necessary before I passed judgment and sentence occasionally. You know in your gut when a person is guilty, when reasonable doubt is nothing but the clutter of delay, and then you serve justice befitting the crime. In those cases, there's no reason to be screwing around waiting for a witness to get killed or to back out, or evidence to get thrown out or misplaced, or a judge to receive cash under the table, or a juror to get bribed or threatened. You get the idea.

Me? I gave them the opportunity to confess and turn themselves in to the cops. Yeah, I pushed the bastards as hard as I could. Some pulled a gun in response and died where they stood. Occasionally they took my advice and went to the cops. Other times we finished it man to man.

When the police were done on the landing, I locked up the office and went home feeling more empty than I wanted to think about.

After a quick bath the following morning, I left my apartment in Brooklyn. I grabbed a coffee and buttered hard roll for breakfast from the deli down the street and then caught the train into town and went directly to Saint Vincent's Hospital to check on Stella.

After removing my hat at the reception desk, I waited for an elderly couple dressed in their Sunday finest to finish quizzing the accommodating volunteer who worked behind the desk answering the phone and their questions too.

The candy striper smiled at me when it was my turn. Her light brown hair lay coiled up in a bun under a white-and-red cap. She had alert hazel eyes that highlighted a round face I found to be pretty despite the obvious signs from the stress of her job, or the life she lived when away from the security of work.

Sometimes a troubled home life can feel like a heavy burden, and make a steady job feel secure and safe regardless of what you did for a living, which included what I did. Though I had nothing like a home life. Just a troubled life from what people like Paul Dunbar claimed.

"How may I help you, sir?" she asked with concern lacing her contralto voice.

"I'd like the room number for a patient named Stella Vichery with a vee."

She raised the lid of a wide oak filing card box and fingered through a row of three-by-five index cards, nodding as she dug deeper into it. Her mouth moved silently as she read names. After a minute of flipping through them with a snapping noise as if she popped chewing gum between her back teeth, she lifted one out with two fingers. Carefully, she propped the card ahead of it on end as a marker, and raised the one she'd selected so I might see the name typed on it.

"Here she is. Miss Vichery is in room 215." She picked a pass from a pile alongside the telephone and placed it on the desk between us. "You'll need this pass to get by the nurse's station. Please return it to me when you leave."

"Thank you," I said, took the pass, and headed for the stairs.

The sounds of survival and the medicinal aromas that made me want to turn and run every time I visited a hospital, especially when

I'm the patient, filled Stella's room. She needed flowers and I had not thought to bring her some and decided that I would the next time I visited.

I stopped at the foot of her bed and studied her face. She appeared to be asleep, looked a lot better than I had thought she would so soon after taking a bullet, and wondered if that was because she didn't care about life's battles and past grief while dozing, or maybe she had excellent recuperative powers. Most likely her doctor prescribed a sedative. I grinned at the thought.

After my mental jigsaw puzzle of guesses, without scraping the legs on the floor, I moved a straight-back wooden chair to the side of her bed, lifted a two-year-old copy of *Life Magazine*, May 9, 1949, from her bedside table, and paged through the periodical.

The cover had a picture of a doll of a college girl from Missouri with the kind of smile that made shy men turn away discouraged before they spoke a word of greeting.

Inside I found a color, artist rendering of a new red Oldsmobile 98 for 1950. I didn't care for it as much as my '49 two-door coupe. Halfway through the magazine, I located the story about the cover girl, Jane Stone. She was a sophomore at the University of Missouri in '49.

Looking for a husband, I figured and started reading the story.

Stella made a quiet snorting noise as if she had awakened abruptly. I dropped the magazine on the table and reached for her hand when I saw her watching me.

"How are you feeling, doll?" I asked, squeezing her fingers and then releasing her. She felt normal, not hot or too cool.

"I've felt better. How long have you been sitting there reading?" She rubbed her eyes, yawned, and then pressed her fingers against her temples as if she had a mild headache.

"Not too long," I said. "I thought I'd stop by to check on you before I took care of Lois' arrangements." It sounded strange to say something like that while sitting bedside in a hospital, and the thought ignited my anger and grief, but I bit it back along with a strong surge of unspent angst.

"My doctor is due in shortly." She glanced at the wall clock and again rubbed her temples.

"I'll drop by this evening." I stood and kissed her cheek. "I'm real sorry I got you into this mess."

Her eyes flashed emotion that I found hard to read. "I came to you and volunteered. When I'm healed and feel better, I'll be ready to help you in any way that you want or need me to assist."

"That sounds terrific," I said with as much enthusiasm as possible, smiled, donned my hat, and left her room.

"Not on your life, doll," I said once outside her room and halfway down the hall so she could not hear me. I did not want another innocent death on my hands. The blood I wore already had sunk below the skin like acid and stained indefinable elements of my soul. Nothing I could do about the past, but hopefully plenty I could do about the future.

A couple of years ago, I buried my mother alongside my father, who died right after VE Day. Back then, I had an uncle who helped out, but he moved off to Jersey down in Monmouth County somewhere right after the war. This time I would take care of the arrangements on my own, hoping I would not need to make plans for another burial for many years to come. Unless it was mine and then I'd not be around to witness the result.

After a couple of phone calls, I managed to get most of the arrangements finalized. Bible Funeral Home up in the Bronx couldn't pick up Lois' body for two days, but Pat Solok told me with his own brand of black humor, "There's no need to hurry on my account, Marlowe. I can hold her here for any of a number of reasons. Let me know when they plan to come around for her and I'll get her ready for transportation."

I gave him the information I had, and said good-bye before he could pass on his condolences again.

An hour later back in my office, I stood to walk around my desk, felt something like a large flying insect plow across the top of my head, and then heard glass shatter, and lastly a gunshot.

The floor seemed to fly at my face when I dove for cover, hoping to avoid the next five rounds as they blasted holes in the thick plaster wall and the old schoolhouse clock hung behind my desk. The fifty-year-old clock gonged once, then the mainspring broke and the metal ribbon shredded the side of the thin mahogany case.

I hadn't noticed my rapid breathing until I felt that the gunman had finished shooting and prepared to search for him.

Glass crunched under my knee and foot as I half-crawled to the window to scan the buildings across the street. The decision was unwise, perhaps, but I knew I would never catch him if I hid under my desk.

Of course, I suspected he would be long gone by the time I reached the window, but not necessarily. Some of these bums liked to wait for and see results. One window on a building on the other side of Madison Square Park stood wide open without a visible screen, but that was not irrefutable evidence. We were at the start of summer, and the air felt warm enough for office workers to want to invite a breeze into their space.

I knew I could call Dunbar again, but I didn't feel like telephoning him and reporting the crime. This time, I would deal with it without his or anyone's help. Then a silhouette slid past the opened window, and light sparked off metal at the same location. Dropping to the floor, I crawled back across the room and exited my office as if I was on the lam.

Taking the stairs three at a time, I hit the street running, dodged traffic and blaring horns as I raced into the park around a dog chasing a squirrel and a mother pushing a navy blue baby carriage.

DEATH LEAVES A SHADOW

Less than a few minutes after the final shot, I stood in the lobby of the building where I believed the shooter might have hidden after he emptied his weapon. I waited to catch my breath before climbing the stairs to start my search. The elevator would've been faster, but I hated giving a machine that kind of control over my life, and the shooter might be waiting for its arrival.

Four stories up, walking slowly down the hall. I located what I believed to be the correct door and pounded a fist against the wooden panel. The sound echoed inside the office behind the door. The hollow noise was a good sign that the room stood unoccupied. I had stepped to the left side of the doorframe for shelter. You really never know when a fugitive might decide to fire a couple of lucky shots into the door in response to a knock if he felt trapped inside.

No one answered, and no bullets blew through the door panel. I moved back a yard and kicked the door right next to the lock with the sole of my foot. Three blows and it flew open, and long wood splinters from the ruined doorjamb hit the floor by my feet.

With .45 in hand, I entered as if I owned the place, scanned from corner to corner, and discovered an empty office. There were no furnishings, but on the floor by the window lay several brass rifle cartridges that reflected sunlight.

Odd he didn't take them with him, I thought. *Maybe he is trying to tell me who he is, or for me to understand that he knows who I am.*

Using a pencil to lift them, I dropped them into my pocket. The room smelled of sweat and cordite.

Dunbar can get them printed, and maybe I'll get lucky.

While I stood staring out the window at foot traffic around the intersection, my life started to feel as if it might end long before I thought I'd be properly prepared to meet my Maker. The proverbial crapshoot from hell, beginning with Lois' death, seemed as if it might continue unabated, and I couldn't visualize a satisfying conclusion. I decided that the three shootings might well be connected, and if so, I was in seriously deep shit.

Maybe I should take that fishing trip upstate, I thought and knew the only thing I would be fishing for was the man who wanted me dead, the bastard who had killed Lois and shot Stella if the shootings all proved his doing.

My reflection in the upper window glass showed that I had a new part through the middle of my hair. The first bullet he fired scorched it but didn't cut into my scalp. I ran my fingertips across the singed hair and shrugged.

Kind of crooked, time for a cut, I thought and headed back to the street. Hell, I was getting tired of combing it anyway.

I remembered the bums who tried to poison me the previous year first grabbing my hair to slam my head against the floor to render me helpless. Then they died. Not so helpless after all.

In many ways, New York was an odd place to live and work. People on the streets could be either friendly or cold and uncaring or just plain oblivious. Even after the sounds of six gunshots echoed through Madison Square Park and off the surrounding buildings, not one person that I saw paused to look around and/or thought to take cover. Traffic continued to move endlessly with its normal stuttering slowness and blaring horns. Pedestrians strolled, stopping occasionally to stare into a storefront window, or talk with a companion.

Young mothers and kids roamed the perimeter of the park without a care in the world. Several mutts ran after tossed sticks or hard red rubber balls like those we used as kids when we played stickball in the neighborhood streets. We called the manhole cover home base. We scrawled the other bases on the street with chalk we snatched from the blackboard trays at school.

If the gunman had blown off the top of my head, those same people would not have slowed enough to notice my demise beyond the arrival of an ambulance to remove my body, or by reading my obit if anyone thought to publish one. It was as if the sounds they must've heard were ordinary occurrences, events like a car backfiring or firecrackers on the Fourth of July.

Mine would be an existence cleanly severed from life in a town that waded through its own versions of preoccupation. Except for the unfortunate janitor or street sweeper—had I been outside—who would've cleaned the mess and gotten paid for his labors, city life would not have done more than pause, if that.

In a town of millions, each person was a stranger, solitary, unattached to all but family, a few close friends, and business associates.

Maybe that's the reason Uncle Lou moved down to Jersey, I thought. *Make a better life for him and his family, and be more important to the people in the town where he lived and ran his deli now.*

But me? Hell, despite it all, I liked the anonymity offered by city life. I liked that people let me live how I needed to live and did not attempt to push their brand of expression or their interpretation of existence down my throat.

In return, I helped keep the scum, swindlers, and recidivists off the streets and from getting in the middle of the average city dweller's personal affairs. Although most of them would never know of my activities, it seemed like an equitable tradeoff to me.

Then, out of the blue, I recalled Lois' black spaniel Gabby, named after the actor Gabby Hayes, and wondered if he'd been left behind at Lois' apartment over in Brooklyn. I'd never been much of a dog lover, never seemed to have much time for pets, but I owed it to Lois to adopt the mutt and care for it. Besides, right then, I felt like I needed a guard dog to watch my back.

Instead of heading back to the office, I went down to the subway, deposited a token, and rode the train out to Brooklyn.

Lois' key still hung on my key ring, so I went straight to her front door, raised my hand, and stopped dead when I realized that part of me wanted to knock as if she might still be home. An unnatural stillness filled my chest with a sensation like stepping into a puddle and discovering too late that I walked into a flooded, open manhole, whose strong currents might sweep me out to sea, where I'd drown in a whirlpool of grief.

After a long, slow breath, I jammed the key in the door lock and discovered the door was unlocked.

"This isn't right. The cops would've locked up after leaving. Not a goddamn thing is good about the way this feels." I spoke as I lifted the Colt from the holster, flipped off the safety, and used the barrel of the .45 to push the door inward.

From somewhere inside her apartment, I heard the floor creak and snap as if someone walked extra fast to escape my unanticipated arrival.

With one foot inside, I stopped to listen. The air felt hot and carried the sharp sweetness of perfume, a brand I could not immediately identify.

Lois' apartment did not look the way I expected to find it with a dog staying there alone for a couple of days, *but then maybe the cops took him*, I thought hopefully.

The alternative was that he died in a corner, but I didn't smell the odors of recent death, and did my best to ignore the dried blood still splattered across the wall and floor where Lois died.

To surprise any unsuspecting burglar despite the possibility that he must have heard the door open, I entered fast, swinging the gun left and right. I saw no one and then nearly shot the damn dog when he leaped out from behind the sofa and jumped up to let me know he was glad I arrived finally, or was hungry or needed to be walked; undoubtedly the latter. I guessed he had hidden there and the cops never knew he was around. That was when I smelled urine.

Stupid animals are why I never have pets, I thought with my heart racing after his fast appearance.

"Gabby," I started, and then hesitated when I heard noise in the kitchen like shoe leather scuffed across the linoleum floor. My heart skipped as my mind played games and informed me maybe the body I saw at the morgue was someone else and Lois now stood in the kitchen preparing dinner. My mouth felt bone dry, and my heart pounded in my ears loud enough that I wasn't sure what I was hearing.

I ruffled the dog's long, silky neck fur and walked slowly to the back of the apartment toward the kitchen. The back door leading from the kitchen to outside swung open with a creak as I crossed the threshold, which made me hesitate long enough to avoid stepping into the line of fire as two quick reports sent bullets screaming in my direction.

Burglars rarely carry a gun. This is a man with a mission beyond theft. I dropped to the floor and rolled so I could see into the kitchen.

As far as I could tell, nothing was missing. I looked around and felt like I needed to understand what he searched for and why he returned to look for it. *What might be so important that he'd risk coming back here? What did the cops miss?*

I sighted as best I could and emptied the Colt, heard a scream among the repeated concussions, and knew I got lucky. *Again.*

Absentmindedly, I brushed what felt like a cold palm off the back of my neck, glanced at my hand, and saw that my fingertips were coated with sweat.

Not blood this time, I thought gravely.

Then, I took time to reload the magazine before I entered to investigate the kitchen. Inside a room where Lois and I laughed, talked late into the night, shared meals and warm affection, I discovered a woman's body half propped against the exterior doorjamb.

Goddamn fucking damn it!

The door stood open, wedged by her weight. She sat in a fast-spreading pool of dark arterial blood. A small hole in the center of her sternum rhythmically pulsed out her life. After walking to her, I squatted and saw a jagged fist-sized hole that showed that the bullet hit bone and fragmented as it blew through her chest and out the center of her back.

Her long, thin fingers clutched a stubby .44 with a tendril of smoke leaking from the end of the barrel.

What the hell are you doing here? Using one hand, I lowered her onto her back, and examined a woman with a plain but attractive and unadorned face. She had a short, squat nose that sat over wide lips and a protruding chin like my great-aunt Tilly. Stupid damn thing to remember right then, but my mind wandered when I couldn't sort out logical answers for events that interrupted my life without a clear reason or a satisfactory conclusion.

She wore no makeup of any kind, no jewelry, but did wear soft cotton gloves. Carefully, I removed the glove from her free hand and held her hand in mine. She squeezed feebly as if to let me know she appreciated my show of kindness. I wondered if she would have returned the courtesy were the shoe on the other foot and I took the bullets she'd fired.

Then her ice-blue eyes went flat, and I watched her frightened examination of my face turn into a lifeless death stare focused on something far beyond me and the earth.

Damn it, I hated watching her die, but no one should die alone.

I damn sure didn't like shooting and killing a woman under any circumstance, and knew I might never learn why she'd been in Lois' apartment, or why she attempted to kill me, though I suspected that her reaction was fear-inspired, defensive in nature.

Was she Lois' killer? Had she left some evidence behind and thought the police would return, locate and remove it if they came back for a second look? Decided she should get there and retrieve it first? If so, how could she know they didn't find it?

Hell, the cops missed finding the stupid dog, I thought. Of course, he undoubtedly did a good job of cowering silently between the back of the sofa and the wall.

I looked at the dead woman and did not see anything obvious, or a place to store an object bigger than what might fit in a pocket. If she returned for evidence and placed it where I could not see it, then I knew the cops might find it, and if they did, they could have whatever it was.

After checking for a pulse and not finding one, I left her and in the living room discovered that Gabby hid behind the sofa again.

"You'll make one hell of a guard dog," I said and he ran over for another scratch and rub behind his warm, floppy ears.

"At least you're not a poodle," I told him. "Now there's an animal out of place among human beings."

I dropped onto the sofa and with a feeling of dread and resignation phoned Dunbar.

Chapter Five

Although the shooting happened far outside his precinct, Dunbar arrived around thirty minutes after the first black-and-white. By then Lois' apartment had filled with the official investigative sideshow that would find nothing but the obvious left by me, and that most likely would prove only slightly more useful than what they'd find from the dead woman.

She'd worn gloves. Therefore, she left no prints to indicate what she touched. Maybe they'd discover what if anything she removed from the apartment and hidden, but I was starting to think that was not her reason for returning.

While they processed the scene, I stood on the sidewalk with Gabby on a leash and a half-smoked Camel between my lips. The wavering smoke made me squint. The dog lay at my feet after using the nearest streetlight to relieve himself for about five minutes. Now he acted as if he'd spent the last of his energy and needed to recharge.

Dunbar approached with a tackle box, a creel—what anglers called their shoulder-slung fishing basket—hung over his shoulder, and a fly rod and reel in his right hand.

"You'll be needing these where you're going," he said and shifted the creel as if its weight caused unanticipated discomfort.

"I'm not leaving town," I replied emphatically, struggling to keep the anger from my voice. "Not now. This has become too goddamn personal for me to ignore it."

"Like hell you're not leaving town. You either go or I have orders to put you in protective custody for your own safety. It seems you've become a target, and the people around you might unfortunately become collateral damage. The captain told me to inform you that you get to choose which opportunity you'd rather pursue."

He grinned as if enjoying my discomfort, but I thought it looked like an act. No matter how much bad blood there was between us from past encounters, he was a good man and would feel the pain of what he knew I went through during the last couple of days. But as a cop, he'd never obviously reveal those emotions to anyone, including me. At least not while on the job.

"That woman," I nodded at Lois' house, "didn't know I'd be here," I said slowly, still fuming inside, which felt like something acidic burning in the pit of my stomach.

"Maybe not, but she must've known that Lois lived here, and she came ready to kill. If she knew Lois was dead, and I think it's fair to assume that she did, then it's a good possibility she was waiting for you to show up." He glanced at Gabby. "The dog was in the apartment, right? He's not dead. Who else would care for him?"

"Okay, yeah." Everything he said sounded right, too much so.

"I won't bother to ask what else your captain said about me." I nodded at my place diagonally across the street. "Might as well put all it on my front stoop for now."

After he returned, he filched a cigarette from my pack and lit up. With smoke leaking from his mouth, he said, "The woman you killed is rather special to certain government people in Washington. We've all been on notice about her for over a year."

"She related to someone I know about?"

"You mean like a politician or an actor? Hell no, at least none that I'm aware of." He scratched behind his ear and examined his fingernails.

"Then how's she special."

"She's a rarity would've been a better choice of words, I suppose." He nodded at Lois' apartment as if the answers to his riddle might lie hidden inside. "The woman's got a file at headquarters, and the feds wanted her too."

"What'd she do to attract that much attention?" He had my interest.

"Who'd she do and how many of them is the real question here." He looked at the end of his cigarette, flicked the growing ash, seemed to study it as it dropped, and then took a long drag.

It dawned on me that he was talking about a known killer. "You saying a good-looking dame like her did professional hits?"

He nodded, but the smile creasing his mouth got me thinking there was a lot more to her history than that.

"Who'd think it was possible, right? She worked undercover in Europe for us during the war."

I'd heard about women who volunteered for duty that involved going behind enemy lines and getting close and personal with Nazi brass to learn their battle plans. I never heard of a survivor before. Fleeing Krauts killed most of the women, or local residents; they felt betrayed by the women, shaved their heads, paraded them through the streets, and then killed the ones left behind. I'd heard some were stoned to death, but who really knew?

Some of the women blended into society and stayed in Europe after the war. This was the first one I'd heard of who returned to the States, and she had a serious bone to pick with someone.

"Tell me more about her. She works for the mob boys?" I said, squatted, and scratched poor Gabby's head.

"Nothing to do with the mob. She was a freelancer." Then, Dunbar explained her wartime activities in detail, which pretty much matched what I'd been thinking.

"She was smuggled out, came home, and went bad after she failed to put her old life back together," he said. "Seems that her new husband, after he learned of her wartime activities, considered what she did for her country the behavior of a glorified prostitute. Although I imagine his language was a bit rougher than that. Stupid bastard doubtlessly called her a whore and then some."

"And she killed him on the way out the front door?" I enjoyed the sardonic picture of it in my head. Her holding the same handgun, smoke spiraling up from the end of the barrel as she stepped outside.

"Feds don't know what happened between them. No one ever did find his body, but she did take out a couple of Nazi officers in Paris before shipping home. Slit their throats while they slept. Who knows what a person like that is capable of doing when under certain types of duress." He grinned a forced, sad smile and took a long, dramatic drag on his cigarette. "Whoever you've pissed off, pal, he's determined to use whatever resources he can find and is willing to pay good money to have you turn up a cold corpse."

"What was her name?" I asked, ignoring his last comment, and pointed to the front door of Lois' apartment. If I'd had any sense at all, I'd've left her anonymous, but I could not think of a good reason to do that considering that I'd put the hole in the center of her chest and then held her hand as she died. Besides, as I've been told often enough, I don't have a good goddamned lick of common sense.

"You sure you want to know?" he asked with a concerned frown.

I nodded slowly and watched his eyes.

"Her name was Melody Gibbson. She started her life on a corn farm in Iowa." Dunbar shook his head as if pitying my sentimentality, or thinking about the woman's life and how it might've been if not for the war and her desire to make a difference. Can't even think how many of us felt that way about ourselves, and others, especially those who died overseas. A lot of them never came home at all.

"And she died a very long way from home in more ways than one. You think her family will want her body returned to them so they can bury her proper?" I asked and snuffed out my spent smoke under my shoe.

"Rather difficult to say what any family member might want to do with a daughter gone bad like this one did. What would you do if you were her father?"

I thought hard for a minute, and then nodded brief agreement. "I'd bury her and let her and God deal with her activities. She helped us win the war, making a huge personal sacrifice more than any man might understand. She deserves better than Potter's Field. I think if I were her father, I might want to give her soul a place to rest; give her a chance for redemption if such a thing is possible for any of us after what we did in Europe."

He shook his head and answered with a crooked grin. "You're nuts, you know that, Marlowe? The woman waded hip deep in the blood of innocent people here in the States. She killed who she got paid to kill and as far as I know never asked questions about her victims—even their names. How could you or anyone expect redemption for people like her? Never was, never will be. That's why some guy coined a phrase like *burn in hell*." He shook his head slowly.

I waved him off with the hand holding my pack of Camels. I didn't believe in any form of hell beyond death after the lessons I learned during my years of combat. Hell happened right here on Earth in anyone's lifetime and at any given moment during it. Yeah, and death often arrived without a moment's advanced warning. Wherever she might be now, Lois knew that and so too did Melody.

"Nevertheless, she deserves a decent burial," I said and pocketed my cigarettes.

He stared at me as if I'd revealed a character trait or flaw he had not known about, and now that he knew of it, he felt uncertain of what to make of the information he possessed.

"We all deserve that much." I pressed the point.

"Yeah, I guess you're right," he finally said with a sigh, but didn't sound convinced. It's hard to change a good cop's mind once he's decided he is correct.

I glanced back at Lois' place. "I have to take care of Lois before I leave town." Then I pointed at the pile of equipment on my stoop. "Guess I'll be needing waders too if I'm going to do any fly-fishing."

"Waders are in my trunk along with some hand-tied flies I picked up and also a fisherman's hat and a vest specially for you. Thought about having your named embroidered on the vest, but didn't have the time." He grinned, which this time reached his eyes.

DEATH LEAVES A SHADOW

"Swell. You sound like you're enjoying my suffering," I said.

"Good guess, buddy. You should have stayed on the force. You worked hard at being a damn good cop."

"I know that, but I needed a change so I could stop crooks instead of letting the courts pander to them and give them a pass."

"Not that many of the bastards walked, Marlowe, and you know it's true." He looked away as if debating whether or not to continue and then shook his head once.

"You can take care of Lois, get her a proper burial, but you'll have a few of us shadowing you until you're done."

I knew there was no sense arguing, and nodded, to show my agreement.

"You interested in a dog?" I asked to change the subject.

"No, I have a Siamese cat."

"What'd you say, a cat? I never would've expected you to be a cat lover."

"They're clean, quiet, and terrific companions." He crushed out his smoke under the heel of his right shoe. "They never argue either."

"Guess you can never tell what a guy likes. I'm going home to put the dog inside, and then I'll have to go get dog food," I said to avoid a debate I thought would degrade quickly into an argument.

"We'll be around, so don't go losing any sleep about her or who hired her." He nodded at the covered body the coroner's people carried from Lois' apartment. Which was when I decided I'd be the one to bury her if her family didn't care enough.

Dunbar's formal announcement proved to be nothing less than an understatement. City cops drove and escorted me everywhere I needed to go. They provided a dozen men and their wives to attend Lois and my unborn child's funeral. Other than the cops and me, no one else showed up. I hated what that implied and struggled to keep from letting the thought become a worm of anger due to an indifferent

41

world. While fighting during the war, I believed we Americans were above the ordinary. After a few years home, I wondered why I ever thought so.

I wept alone with the dog after my place emptied of cops and I could lock and bolt the front door to be by myself finally. When I felt able to, I called Stella at Saint Vincent's and filled her in on what I planned to do.

"Please be very careful," she said. "I'll try to find you up there when I'm healthy enough to get out and travel."

"Take your time with that," I told her, still uncertain as to why she was so damned interested in my life and welfare. Perhaps she felt I was the only link to the past she once had that I'd taken from her. No matter what her reasoning, I found myself dealing with seriously conflicting emotions.

"If you're going to work with me, you'll need to be more than healthy enough to get discharged from the hospital and ride a train." I wasn't sure my words would matter to her, but knew I could not stand the thought of burying her too.

Chapter Six

The following morning, we left the city. By mid-afternoon, Dunbar drove Gabby and me down a narrow dirt road that ended at a cabin alongside Lake Orange. We were south of a small town named Modena located somewhere between the city, Albany, and God alone knows where the hell else. I could have counted the number of times I'd visited the country before that day on one hand.

With the addition of this trip, I thought, *it'll be one goddamn time too many.*

The cabin had two bedrooms and a living room with a large fieldstone fireplace. In the kitchen, I found a hand pump for water and no hot water. Down a short hallway was a bathroom that, thank God, had a toilet and shower with an overhead tank that needed to be filled with hot water according to the sign posted on its side. I stood looking, shaking my head. I squinted my eyes, but that changed nothing.

Using an outhouse during the night in bear country was anything but a pleasant thought. I felt sure I could not count on Gabby to chase wild animals off if they found me stumbling around after dark with my trousers around my ankles.

I dropped my suitcase on the single bed in the nearest bedroom and finished exploring the house while Dunbar unpacked as if he brought something breakable. I figured he carried a fifth of bourbon wrapped in his robe. Dunbar liked his drinks neat and strong. I liked cold bottled beer.

My bedroom smelled a bit musty, but it was nothing an open window would not cure with time.

Yeah, Paul stayed. I could not decide if he meant to act like a bodyguard, or if he really needed a vacation to get in a few days of flyfishing. Either way, it seemed as if we would need to deal with our differences before too much more time passed. Because god knows what might have happened if we didn't sort things out.

New and old paperbacks by Spillane, Stout, Christie, and others, including a handful of old-time classics, filled a small bookshelf next to the fireplace. A spine-creased copy of Spillane's newest book *Vengeance Is Mine!* caught my attention. I turned the front cover back and read, *To Joe and George, who were always ready for a new adventure, and to Ward... who used to be*, and I wondered what happened to Ward, decided he had been one of Spillane's war buddies who didn't make it home, or did in a flag-draped pine box like too many of mine made the return trip.

The first chapter started out with: *And the guy was dead as hell*. I grinned. I liked it already, carried the book into my room, and dropped the paperback on the night table, where I would find it later.

Dunbar worked at starting a fire in the kitchen stove. Then we grilled burgers to have for an early supper along with a couple of bottles of Schaefer Beer. The brand was certainly not my favorite brew, but I knew it would have to do under the circumstances, which meant that Dunbar bought the suds when we stopped on the way up.

By the time the burgers finished, the smell made me ravenous. After eating and downing the second beer, I went outside, walked to the edge of the lake, and saw a huge rainbow-colored fish leap straight from the water, which got me thinking that with that much spirit, it earned its life and didn't deserve death just yet, at least not by my hand. The verdict got both the fish and me off the hook.

To hell with fishing, I thought and went back to the cabin as the sun set behind distant mountains.

Chapter Seven

Several days later, I enthusiastically confirmed that fishing was not my sport when I hooked yet another tree branch about ten feet behind me.

I wasn't meant to use a fly rod. Maybe I should stick to hunting criminals, I thought, feeling quite frustrated.

As I turned to free the fly, feeling disgusted enough to walk straight back to Manhattan, I tripped on a submerged log and went into the water headfirst. Dunbar laughed so hard that I thought he might choke to death.

Fat chance of that, I decided sardonically as I came up for air between howls, just in time to witness the aftermath of a bullet as it caught him high in the chest, twisted him around like a puppet, and sprayed a cloud of red liquid behind him that enlarged as it expanded. Then the impact slammed him backward into the lake. Water splayed around him as if it meant to enclose him in death's watery embrace. The water turned red above him, and he sank like a stone. The sound of rifle shots reverberated in my head as they echoed across the lake.

Jesus Christ. I dove underwater to avoid dying, swam to Paul, and lifted his head above the surface while bullets splashed five feet away like ravenous jumping parasites.

I kicked against mud and rocks along the lake bottom, and somehow managed to drag Dunbar ashore. We ended up under overhanging branches that effectively screened us from the gunman. Now bullets zinged tree limbs, and rained chips of bark and shredded leaves.

Dunbar's breath came in shallow gulps as I hauled him out so his entire body rested on dry land and turned him on his right side. By then, I knew the bastard doing the shooting had finished with us and left. The final sounds of rifle shot bounced around the lake using the water's surface to amplify volume. Not like in Manhattan, where the buildings absorbed most of the sounds and traffic noise buried what escaped. The difference made me feel eerie, as if I now walked on another planet.

I stripped off my water-filled waders and tugged Paul's off too.

Dunbar shook his head and moaned. "Guess it wasn't all that funny after all." He showed a rare bit of a sense of humor and caught me off guard. I figured he tried to get me smiling by blaming his laughter and fate for what happened to him.

"Not funny as I see it." I removed my shirt, wrung it out, and used it to staunch the blood flowing from his left shoulder. "Now shut the hell up," I added as I fought the twist of emotion struggling to remold my face. "Or I'll leave you here to bleed to death and the fish can clean your mess. Call it fish revenge if you want." I kept my right hand on the wound, hoping the pressure would at least slow the bleeding.

He nodded, and passed out. At that moment, I made the first clear decision I'd made since learning of Lois' murder. The time we spent fishing isolated me enough, kept me from the city and churning bad memories and the killer who ordered my death. Paul and I found enough of our old friendship to get it started again. We both seemed to enjoy the renewal.

After three failed attempts by the gunman to put me—or have me put—six feet under, I knew that time had rolled around far enough for me to settle a score or two. In my line of work you're either the hunted or the hunter. I was ready to change places.

Only a few members of the police force and Stella knew that Dunbar and I had gone fishing, where we planned to go to waste bloodworms and lose expensive hand-wrapped flies in the trees—six to date. Paul had no family that I was aware of, and I wasn't certain he had any true friends off the job. I had no one to tell other than Stella, and I was sure she wouldn't betray us. She might've had a bone to pick with me, but not Paul. She truly liked him.

Whoever informed the killer we would be staying near Lake

Orange would reveal his complicity as soon as I located his whereabouts. The murderer made his first serious mistake.

One way or the other, I thought, *you, pal, are dead as hell*, and felt good using part of the line I read in Spillane's book, and then felt like an idiot for doing so. *But what the hell, who'll ever know?*

The thought that I might need to kill a cop or jail a woman who made me think differently about myself right after losing Lois, watching Melody Gibbson die, didn't feel good, but if it came down to them or me, there could be no other option. *It has to end now.*

Stella took a bullet. I knew she was not the shooter, and hoped she was truthful when she stated she had nothing to do with Lois' death.

However, I'd do whatever needed doing; no questions asked beyond the first two, which would be *Who did you tell where we went fishing and why did you tell him?*

Using a fireman's carry, I hefted Dunbar onto my back and slowly lugged him to the cabin. I found a telephone inside the living room, but when I lifted the receiver and jangled the cradle to alert an operator, I listened to the static hum of a dead line.

Having a telephone is bad enough, I thought, *but why the hell install one and not keep it in working order?*

The logic escaped me, but that's often the case when dealing with our increasingly modern society.

The first-aid kit I dug out of the bathroom medicine cabinet provided me with ample amounts of gauze and white cloth tape to patch up Dunbar's shoulder well enough that I decided it might be safe to get on the road before night set in. I'd be driving through unknown country and did not appreciate the prospect of getting lost with a severely injured passenger after dark.

Since I didn't know where else to go, when I spotted a traffic sign, I drove Paul across the Hudson River to Poughkeepsie. The Saint Francis Catholic Hospital turned out to be the closest large facility near Modena and Lake Orange according to the road map I picked up once within the Poughkeepsie city limits.

After leaving him at the emergency room, I filled in a form with my name and the telephone number for my city office. Then, I purchased a silver Saint Francis medal and a silver chain in the gift shop, and returned to the lake.

As I stepped from the car, the sun glowed a deep orange-red directly above the horizon. The water shimmered colors that reminded me of a bloodbath like one I witnessed during the war when we slaughtered several dozen SS who clustered together as if thinking that safety in numbers applied during wartime. They all died within five minutes of each other after firing a volley of shots at us first.

After walking Gabby, I locked us in the cabin, stoked up a fire with some good-smelling split cedar logs that I located stacked outside the back door, and put my .45 under the pillow. Then I spent a sleepless night trying to force myself to doze off, which I finally managed around 3 a.m. with moonlight shivering across the room from behind sheer white lace curtains that moved with the currents created by the fire.

Gabby's sudden and loud bark woke me at dawn. I rolled off the bed, gun in hand, jammed a round into the chamber, and flipped off the safety. I've always loved the sound a semi-auto makes when you load it. It's a loud and unforgettable clack and snap that's easily recognized by the dumbest crook.

Someone knocked quietly but with deliberation on the front door. The unwelcome arrival tripped my heartbeat high in my throat. Wanting to avoid accidentally shooting anyone, I lowered the Colt to my side and silently walked across the cabin. I stopped at the right side of the doorframe listening, hoping to hear a sound that might help identify whoever stood on the other side.

Chapter Eight

"Yeah," I said. "Make it good and make it fast."

"Marlowe? Is that you?"

Stella. What the hell's she doing here? I unlocked the door and pulled her inside, glanced out and saw a dark sedan, slammed the door behind her and threw the lock.

"Didn't know you'd be so happy to see me," she said with a weak smile as she struggled to appear unafraid of what I'd done.

"You alone?" I asked hurriedly.

"Yes, I came to find you."

"How'd you find the cabin?" I asked and went into the kitchen to stoke a fire under the coffeepot.

"Are you kidding? Last night everyone in Modena talked about two city slickers trying to kill themselves out fishing on Lake Orange." She looked around the cabin as if she thought about redecorating and moving in.

"Did those cowboys tell you about Paul?" I stared at her face not certain if I should or could believe her. I did not know her character well enough to have that kind of knowledge regarding her sense of humor.

"Detective Dunbar?" She shook her head. "No, tell me what happened to Paul." She leaned a hip on the edge of the kitchen counter. From the way her face pinched as she moved, I thought she might be experiencing some pain from her wound and wondered how she managed to be released from the hospital before feeling a hundred percent.

With a dismissive shrug to make it seem less dangerous, and a level voice, I told her about the lakeside shooting. Her shoulders rounded and sagged and her pretty features wrinkled with pain. She looked like she might faint as moisture rimmed her light brown eyes. She folded her arms across her chest as if she needed to hug herself for support.

"Goddamn it, Marlowe," she said and sounded sincerely upset. "I'm so sorry that he got hurt. Do they think he'll be okay?"

"Paul's tough, he'll live."

Carefully, so I did not hurt her, I guided her to a chair by the fireplace, helped her sit, and went to the hand pump for a glass of cold mountain water.

"Drink this." I watched her hand shake as she complied and drained the glass.

"Are you all right? You didn't get shot too, did you?" she asked a moment later and brushed strands of long light auburn hair behind her ears. Her earlobes looked pierced and she wore diamond chip, stud earrings.

Weird thing to notice, I thought and then shook it off.

"He missed me completely, so I'm as good as can be expected." Then I went and got impulsive and kissed her hard on the mouth. She smelled better than I remembered, like a fresh bouquet, and tasted better than expected too.

She pulled back at first, then softened and returned the kiss as I sat on the arm of the chair.

"I'm glad you're okay with me being here," she whispered and put her arms around my neck, held on as if frightened that if she let go she might lose her grasp on sanity or, worse, her self-control and break down completely.

I came close to feeling the same way, but couldn't let her know or read it in my eyes. Instead, I gently removed her arms from around my neck, held her hands, and turned my head so I could stare at the fire while I regained my composure. I knew I rode a rugged crest of turmoil that might crash either on the rocky shore of irrational behavior leading me to commit acts I might regret, or carry me inland like a tsunami, and clear away the debris of my past.

In retrospect, neither sounded different from the other, which explained my confusion and hesitation to react to her kindness. I knew that part of me wanted to use her to forget, if only for an hour, what I'd experienced over the previous week and a half.

I felt my jaw muscles tighten as I quietly ground my rear teeth after a minute or two passed and then I asked, "How are you feeling? Did your doctor release you from the hospital or did you walk out without permission?"

"They bandaged me up, but since nothing significant inside me got injured badly, he allowed me to leave provided that I promised him that I would get plenty of bed rest at home. Naturally, I agreed."

She smiled weakly and looked at my eyes.

"And you drove all the way up here to get some bed rest." I didn't know whether to be annoyed by her willingness to cause herself serious harm or be happy that she cared enough to find me in her condition. Maybe I missed Lois too much and just wanted female comforting, which might be the worst of the three options right then.

I swallowed a sigh since truthfully I felt pleased she'd found the cabin and me. However, her arrival resolved something more important that made me feel confident there was no way she could be connected to or involved with the killer. Maybe it was unfair to think she still might be involved in Lois' death after the shooter on the stairs put a bullet in her, but until that moment, I felt it best to err on the side of caution.

Gently, I lifted her warm, soft hands, and felt her fingers move under mine as if she wanted to turn her hands over and entwine our fingers. I knew it was not the time to become more intimate with her, despite the strong feelings I harbored that demanded I do otherwise.

"I'm planning on heading home tonight—after I find the place across the lake where the shooter hid out yesterday to take pot shots at me and Paul."

"You know where you want to start looking?" She seemed more alert, but did not release my hands. Her growing possessiveness felt good and bad.

"I've got an idea where I want to look first. I saw a muzzle flash on the other side of the lake after I pulled Paul onto dry land." Vividly, I recalled the scene and inwardly winced when I thought of Dunbar going down with his shoulder torn up. At the time, due to the amount of blood loss, I thought the round had caught him in the chest or neck or, worse, nicked an artery or punctured his heart.

"Okay, I'll drive you there."

"Drive me around the lake?"

"Yes, I passed a badly rutted dirt lane on the way in." She stood and pulled me to my feet. "Besides, I need some more driving practice with my new car."

"I need to eat something first and then I need to take care of poor Gabby. The dog must be hungry by now."

"I'll cook for you. What do you have?"

I went to the kitchen and worked on fixing a pot of coffee while she fried bacon and eggs. I fed Gabby as she finished and let him out to run and take care of his business.

After cleaning up the breakfast mess, I took a quick shower, using some hot water to make it feel tepid, and then dressed.

Stella sat alongside the fireplace reading an Agatha Christie paperback about that Belgium detective with a ridiculous waxed mustache, from the looks of the cover, propped on her lap. When she saw me, she slid the paperback into the gap on the shelf and said, "Must remember that title and pick up a copy when we get home."

"Do you think she's a good writer?" I opened the door, shook Gabby's leash to get his attention, and when he sauntered over, clipped it to his collar.

"She's one of the absolute best writers who ever lived," Stella said with conviction, walking slowly ahead of me as if struggling to hide a limp, which told me that she suffered more pain than she wanted to reveal.

I decided to avoid upsetting her, climbed into the passenger seat of her car, and let her drive. Gabby jumped in back as if he knew what I expected of him.

Her auto was a showroom 1951 Chevrolet Coupe Deluxe with power glide, what they called the automatic transmission. In other words, there was no clutch to push between gearshifts. The plush two-tone tan upholstered interior smelled the way new cars do, which I considered an odor that a couple of smokes would quickly neutralize and improve.

Automatic tranny is a lazy damn way to drive a car, easy way to forget what you're doing. You have to be physical with a good car, let her know who's boss. Well, I suppose Detroit is building cars for women now, so they have to be easier to control, I thought as I studied her movements.

However, Stella drove like a pro once she steered us onto the dirt road. Calling it rutted might have been a kindness, like giving an insignificant street hooker the moniker Uptown Call Girl. The roadway made the worst of the city's deepest potholes a comfortable ride.

After driving about a quarter of a mile behind the lake, I spotted an overgrown side road or wide path leading in the direction of the water.

"Let's have a look down there," I said and pointed as she drove by the opening between hardwood trees.

Stella jammed on the brakes, skidded about fifty feet, and then threw it in reverse. Somehow, she got us back in one piece without leaving piles of busted gears strewn across the dirt.

"Whew," I said as I opened the door and swung my feet onto solid ground. "Feels good to be standing again." Gabby jumped out and wagged his tail as if he totally agreed with my assessment.

Stella laughed a soft, sexy laugh that sounded great. "Sorry about that, Marlowe. I'm still getting the hang of driving the car. It handles a lot differently than my old forty Ford coupe."

"How long have you had it now?"

"I picked it up the day before I drove up here to find you."

I looked at her, determined from her expression that she was serious, and closed the door without shaking my head in disbelief.

The air outside smelled distinct and unique for a city boy, like forest and wet dirt. I started to miss Brooklyn and the salt air breezes that blew onshore at night.

Together, we walked into the woods, following a double track the width of a car. It seemed obvious to me that someone drove there recently. Tree branches, leaves, and brush hung bent, broken, and smashed. Gabby made an effort to sniff each tree trunk. He peed on several as if to leave a marker behind. Maybe he thought I would get us all lost and he'd finally have the chance to come to the rescue.

Twenty feet from the edge of the lake, I spied fresh-cut wood that appeared sawed with a handsaw and stacked to prop a rifle for stability. The pile lay under the low boughs of a tired and worn-out apple tree and two sugar maples. The bastard must have watched us for some time before he decided to kill one or both of us.

"Sawing off the limbs instead of chopping," I said, "would've made it impossible for us to hear the shooter's activities, until he decided to fire the first round."

As I squatted to examine the gunman's work, shiny brass sparked in the sunlight within arm's reach. I lifted a spent cartridge, checked the bottom, and saw it was the same brand and caliber as what I found in the office building across Madison Square Park. The strike mark from the firing pin looked the same too.

"It's a thirty aught six," I told Stella as if sure she might understand the significance, and held it up so she could examine the casing.

"Should that mean something special to me?" She reached, placed a fingernail on the brass, and tapped it lightly. Her manicured nails glowed with light pink polish.

I glanced at her face and realized she had painted her lips to match her nails, which got me wondering about her toenails. She wore shoes, so I could not tell right then. Stella continued to look at me with an expression of expectancy. I had a feeling she knew what was running through my mind.

"Yeah, it could've," I said. "But I failed to tell you about getting shot at while I was in my office after you got hit."

Her eyes widened, and then they flashed with sudden anger. "Why the hell didn't you tell me? What, you don't think I'm a strong enough woman to take it, or is it because I'm not a man?"

Whoa, doll, aren't they the same thing?

"I didn't tell you because you had your own problems. There was no way for me to quickly tell how seriously the shooter wounded you. Wouldn't have been right to add to your or anybody's troubles under those circumstances." However, that wasn't the only reason. I did not want to have to deal with the thought that she was honestly concerned over my welfare.

I dropped the cartridge into my pocket, examined the ground, found ten more, collected them all, and put them with the first. They clinked together, which got Gabby's attention for a moment. Then he quickly ran off to sniff and pee some more.

How much liquid can that little dog hold? I shook my head.

Stella, I could tell by looking at her, was still annoyed, which bothered me.

Women, I thought. *Just can't win.*

"I don't think you need to shelter or patronize me like that, Marlowe Black." Stella put her hands on her hips. She sounded disappointed and hurt. She walked to the lake, leaned over, and splashed water on her hands and arms. That was the first time someone had used my full name to express dissatisfaction since I was a kid back in the days when my mother did it several times a week. She told me more than once that I was difficult to control.

"I wasn't trying to protect you and would never consider patronizing you for any reason. I really didn't know if you—" I stopped before finishing what ran through my mind.

She glanced back without standing. On her face, I read surprise and knew she immediately understood what I did not say better than if I had shouted the words in her face.

"You thought I might be involved in a plot to kill you or to have your girl killed?" She stood and again planted hands on her hips. "I thought we'd straightened all of that out already." She sounded hurt and confused.

"You have to admit that you did have a good reason to want me dead. But I didn't think you had anything to do with killing Lois." I moved closer to her, clasped her hands in mine, and pulled her to me. Small wet palm prints decorated her hips. She smelled better than the fresh air lifting off the surface of the lake carried by a light breeze.

She resisted. "No," she said and shook her head. "I have a reason for wanting you to stay alive." She did not move away or closer, but stared into my eyes.

"And that reason is?"

"It seems that someone wants me dead too." She pulled on my hands and I stepped closer to her. "And despite what you might want to think of me, Marlowe Black, and all that has happened between us, I find that I am still strongly attracted to you. It's a dangerous way to feel when it comes to a man like you who seems to enjoy violence so much, I suppose, but for now at least, I'm stuck with it." Her eyes did not tell me anything more.

Like a moth to a candle flame, I thought grimly, closed the space between us, and felt the strength of her body heat. I recalled the night about a year ago when I watched her undress with liquid moonlight silvering her movements, and then felt her soft, warm flesh quiver under my touch.

"How does your stomach feel?" I shook my head and lifted her hands onto my shoulders, let go of her, and put my arms around her waist. She felt even better than she smelled, and the situation made the growing tension difficult to bear.

"I'm still a little tender, but in a few days I'll be healed completely."

"That sounds like an invitation to me." I wanted to kiss her right then, but a picture of Lois lying in the morgue vividly popped up in my head.

Sorry, doll, I thought and glanced away.

"You're thinking of her, aren't you?" Without waiting for an answer, Stella used one hand to turn my face to her, leaned, and kissed my lips with a tenderness whose meaning was unmistakable.

The same powerful urges she ignited the first night we spent together came alive, blew down my defenses like a battering ram, and made me want to…

I pulled back enough to speak.

"I was thinking of her, but Lois is dead," I said quietly, not knowing what other response to give or expect in return.

And I intend to kill her murderer, I reminded myself.

Then her lips moved against mine, fired something electric through my gut, and I found myself struggling for self-control. I did not want to stop what was happening, but felt as if I should make an effort no matter how feeble that effort might prove to be. I pulled back only enough to break contact.

"We should get your dog and return home," Stella said, staring straight into my eyes with the kind of look a woman gets when she knows she has ignited serious and lasting attention: half smile of pleasure and half dare.

I returned her grin without the dare, took one of her hands, and led the way back to the car, opened the door for her and went around and climbed in. After a sharp whistle from me, Gabby beelined over with his leash trailing behind him like a captured snake, and jumped onto the rear seat.

"Who wants you dead?" I asked, desperate to change the conversation from a subject that ran like wildfire through my body. My thoughts progressed way beyond the color of her toenails.

"I have no idea who, and that scares the hell out of me." She started the car and backed up, turned around, and headed to the cabin.

I considered telling her that I would protect her, but so far, that had not panned out. Hell, I had a hard time protecting myself right then.

"Do you know who wants *you* dead?" she asked, obviously trying to sound casual.

"He could be one of several men. You thinking it might be the same guy?"

She shrugged indecisively. "I think he could be, but since you don't know who wants you dead and I don't know who wants me dead, how could I answer that?" She glanced in my direction.

"If it's not Vinnie, no, I don't know who. But Castillo has enough money and power to hire all the help he needs." I told her about the woman I killed in Lois' apartment, stared out the windshield while I did, and tried to focus on a thought that chose that moment to appear and disappear like a blurred face in an express subway as the train rolled through the station. There was a second of recognition hidden behind a heartbeat of anticipation and then it was gone. I heard my rear teeth grind again and forced myself to relax.

"We'll find him," I said finally, and patted her forearm.

"Yes, we will." The car bucked along a series of holes. With white knuckles, she gripped the wheel tight to maintain control.

Gabby seemed extraordinarily pleased with the ride. I felt saddle sore. When we got out, Gabby gave Stella superficial attention. As we went into the cabin, Gabby stayed near the front door, sat, and glanced at me expectantly. I reopened the door, removed the leash, and let him run so he might get some exercise before the drive back to the city.

Stella kept busy cleaning the kitchen. I went and packed my bag, and then did Dunbar's suitcase. On his night table, I found his keys and a book titled: *The Wisdom of Confucius*.

I stopped and fanned the pages, randomly selected a line, and read it aloud.

DEATH LEAVES A SHADOW

"The true man has no worries; the wise man has no perplexities; the brave man has no fears."

I have too many worries and perplexities and a couple of outstanding fears. None of this crap applies to me. I tossed the hardback into his suitcase, didn't think to look for his bottle of bourbon, carried my gear out to Stella's car, and put Dunbar's case in the trunk of his Ford.

When we finished, I closed and locked the cabin's front and rear doors, rounded up Gabby, got him settled on the Chevy's rear seat, and looked for Stella.

She watched me and glanced at the dog with a wry kind of smile, as if she knew something she did not want to reveal, yet felt she wanted to discuss the knowledge.

I nodded to let her know I read and understood her expression. *Guess, I'm a sucker for animals after all and she knows it.*

"I'll need to drop Paul's car at Saint Francis Hospital across the river in Poughkeepsie where he's recuperating."

"No problem. I'll follow you." She climbed in and started the engine.

I did the same with Dunbar's black-and-white Ford sedan. Inside, it smelled like his Old Spice aftershave with a hint of cigarette smoke layered in the background.

When I dropped off his keys and suitcase, I found Dunbar sitting up reading another book on Chinese philosophy.

"Didn't know you enjoyed that kind of stuff," I said and pointed.

"Best to know who your enemy is, or will be when things turn bad." He showed me the cover. *The Art of War*.

"I think our enemy is communists, not a country that can't feed people who procreate more often and have children faster than rabbits."

"Their country is communist, Marlowe, and there will come a day when they'll try to rule the world." He took a drink of water, and condensation dripped off the glass. "Look," he said after setting the glass half on the water ring on the bedside table and then wiping water off his chin. "I need you to do me a big favor."

"Anything, just ask, Paul." I refilled his glass from the pitcher.

After he drank again he opened his key ring, selected a brass key, and handed it to me. "Keep an eye on Betty for me."

"Betty? You've got a girl?" I held the key between thumb and forefinger, not sure if I should accept it and the implied obligations.

"My cat." He smiled, but looked extremely tired. "I didn't think I'd be gone this long so didn't get anyone to look after her. She's usually good for a week alone, but this might prove to be a lot longer."

"You named her after Grable?"

He nodded, and his smile twisted with irony. "What made you think of that?"

"You carried a pinup of her taped to the inside of your helmet liner during the war."

"You know how it is, Marlowe. There are a few women in life that are kind of hard to forget."

I did, but didn't want to discuss it right then.

"I don't know anything about cats, and before you tell me there's a time for everything..." I wanted to refuse, but the way his eyes shifted, as if he knew without my help something he cared about might die, stopped me in my tracks.

I grinned and nodded, knew it did not show much enthusiasm, but it was enough expression to get by.

"Okay, Paul. I said anything you need and I meant it. Betty'll have to get used to me, that's all there is to it."

"Thanks. She likes it if you scratch her behind her ears and under her chin, and I keep her food in the cabinet under the sink. You'll need to scoop out her waste pan and dump it outside."

I shook his hand and left before he could ask another favor. Like, don't forget to walk the Morgan horse I keep stabled out on the north shore of Long Island somewhere. With Paul, you never knew what might happen next in his private world. Maybe that's why he was divorced.

Two hours later, we rode together in Stella's Chevy, heading south with Gabby pressing his nose to the partially opened window as if he could smell something he might want to chase if he could only get outside.

He'll chase it as long as it's not alive, I thought as I recalled his cowering behind the sofa.

The road trip proved uneventful, which made me as nervous as I would have felt if a car filled with armed gunmen shooting at the tires to force us to stop and confront them had chased us the last five miles.

It made no sense to me for the killer to give me an opportunity to escape, but of course, he must've known that I would have only one destination in mind. What he did not know was that my plan included placing the tip of the .45's barrel against the side of his head and watching his eyes as I sent him to the hell he wanted to deliver me to given the opportunity.

All I needed to do was find him, or let any of his possible hirelings lead me to him. Either way, unless he got to me first, his life expectancy grew shorter by the hour.

I glanced at Stella's profile and read the determination in the set of her chin and inviting lips.

She must have sensed my attention, as she glanced over and smiled in a way that lit her eyes and then looked back at the road. Her right hand left the wheel and patted my knee tentatively.

"You'd best keep both hands on the wheel, doll. I might cause you the wrong kind of distraction."

She laughed a light sound like a giggle, nodded, and said, "You might at that, and I might enjoy it too."

When we drove onto the approach to the George Washington Bridge, I studied the skyline as it grew before us. There's a special feeling I got whenever I entered the city. It filled me with a sensation of joy and foreboding both. My hometown was loaded with good memories, but it was changing too fast for me to hold onto what created those memories.

Headstones and memorials did not keep the past alive. The buildings, the streets, individual shops and stores, neighborhoods and the people who filled them robustly made New York the distinctive town it was.

After I returned from Europe in '45, I walked around for days refamiliarizing myself with the special places of my youth, from Coney Island to Orchard Beach in the Bronx a few blocks north of the IRT Pelham Station.

However, back then, too, it changed like the city always had and always will. I wondered when the changes would lock out a regular guy like me.

Just over an hour later, I watched Dunbar's cat hide when I entered and called for her. The apartment smelled like an outhouse. I spotted a pan of sand the cat used as a toilet and a bucket of clean sand placed on the floor next to it by the back door.

I dumped the refuse in the garden outside the rear of Dunbar's building and then scraped and refilled the pan with sand. As I filled the water bowl and food dish, I heard scratching. A glance in the other room showed me that Betty apparently wanted to mess the sand. She was a long-legged Siamese with fawn tan fur and a dark brown mask and boots. Her appearance somehow seemed appropriate for Dunbar's oriental interests.

I swore she felt my observation, quickly covered her mess, and ran from the room making a howling noise like she needed me to think I was unnecessary, my presence nothing more than an unwanted intrusion.

"I'm a private cop," I said. "But I can tell that becoming your friend will require some serious effort on my part. Hope you enjoy your dinner." I locked the front door behind me and went back to the car.

Chapter Nine

Stella's place on Dyer Avenue off 35th looked different than I remembered from my last visit. Of course, that time I'd confronted a hired gun paid to take Stella's life, or kidnap her and do God alone knew what to her afterward.

The shooter missed her by several minutes, but I did not run into the same problem with him. After he attempted to kill me for interrupting him, I managed to put a round through his rib cage, creating a sucking chest wound that would've killed him if I didn't call for help quickly enough. He told me the information I needed, and then and only then, I phoned the police for an ambulance so they might save his worthless ass, which I leaned later, they had.

As I closed the door, Gabby tugged on the leash to get free from me to quench his curiosity, or search for a hiding place should he need it in an emergency. I opened the clip and let him roam, watched as he acted like a bloodhound and stuck his nose into every spot where he must have smelled something suspicious or intriguing.

Fortunately, he did not lift a leg to pee on the furniture. He did attempt to claw some fragment from under the edge of the sofa, but gave up when he failed.

Five minutes later, Stella returned from the bedroom dressed more casually in a loose-fitting flowered housedress with buttons down the front. She had manicured bare feet, pink nail polish that matched her fingernails and lips. The idea made her more interesting and maybe more inviting. I didn't feel intrigued enough right then to attempt to discover the answer.

Gabby chose that moment to bark and dog point at the front door. Then he turned and hightailed it behind the sofa. A second later a loud knock echoed into the living room.

"Are you expecting company?" I asked as I lifted the .45 and checked the safety.

"No," she said nervously, looking concerned, and maybe a bit frightened. She went to the window and reached for the sheer lace curtain.

"Don't do that," I said more harshly than I intended. "If he doesn't know we're here, then you lifting the curtain will be a sure giveaway."

She nodded and backed into the room.

The knock came again but louder, more persistent. With a glance at the door, I saw that I had failed to turn the lock and knew that in moments, he might enter uninvited. Soundlessly, I wrapped my fingers around the knob, held my breath, twisted, raised the gun, and yanked the door wide open.

A pair of uniformed cops stood outside. They appeared unimpressed by my Colt after glancing at the gun, as if what I held was the stub of a number two yellow pencil with a chewed eraser.

"We're here to find out if Miss Stella Vichery is home," the broad-shouldered, brown-haired six-footer said as he again glanced at my .45. His uniform brass was highly polished. There were cut creases down the legs of his uniform trousers. The sheen on his regulation shoes looked like a mirror finish. None of that seemed right.

"You have a license for that Colt?" he asked, pointing to it.

"Yes." I stepped back and visually scanned his partner's uniform, their badges and hats. Both seemed legit, but you never know. Something still did not feel or look right.

"Then put it away," his short, rail-thin partner said with a sneer that curled his lips in a way that made me want to drive his teeth down his throat. He had small, dark, hard-to-read eyes set close together, high, sharp cheekbones like knife blades, and prominent oblong ears, acne scars scattered across both ruddy cheeks.

I left the safety off and dropped the Colt in its holster and let them read my PI ticket.

"Marlowe Black," the six-footer said and passed it back to me. "I've heard about you." He did not sound pleased by his revelation, but I didn't give a damn so stared at his face.

"Can't say the same thing for the two of you," I told them, hoping to learn their names. "I know most of the cops who walk a beat in this neighborhood."

When they did not identify themselves, I remained between them and Stella, glanced quickly over my shoulder, and saw she stood about ten feet behind me and to the right.

Neither cop seemed to notice her yet, but I felt sure that was only what they intended for me to think.

"What do you want from Miss Vichery?" I asked firmly.

"This is our new beat. The captain told us to drop by occasionally and see how she's doing. Miss Vichery's been away from home recently and there's been some crime in her neighborhood."

Bullshit, I thought, frowned, and shook my head. *That doesn't make a damn bit of sense.*

"Yeah, well, she's been with me, pal," I said and smiled in a way that should've got them wondering what I meant.

Stella came closer and put her left hand on my shoulder, looked over it, and said, "I'm fine. Please thank your captain for me."

The cops nodded. "We'll do that, ma'am," said the six-footer as he touched the brim of his hat.

When they did not turn to leave, I got a stronger feeling something was seriously wrong, slammed the door, and locked it.

Roughly, I grabbed Stella around the waist and pushed her to the floor a moment before several bullets ripped a ragged line through the upper door panel, digging into the ceiling over where we'd stood.

With the .45 in hand, I aimed at body mass level through the door, wrapped the trigger with my finger, and squeezed. I emptied the magazine.

Need a new front door, I thought and shook my head as I rolled away from Stella.

When the noise dissipated, I stood in a light cloud of gray smoke, cordite so hot in the air I could almost taste it. I went to the curtain and peered outside. Both cops lay on the sidewalk in a spreading pool of blood.

Shit, I thought. *What the hell was that about? If they're really cops, I've screwed up big time.*

However, I knew in my gut that they were not city cops. The bastards shot at us without provocation, intending to kill us. They had not revealed their identities, which was something I'd never run into before.

A beat cop is not going to pull his weapon unless he feels threatened.

And it was too late in the afternoon for those two to look like they just stepped out for the start of a new day after a shopping spree.

No scuffed shoe leather? Never happen walking a beat in New York.

"Are they dead?" Stella, eyes wide, asked fearfully as she stood, moved, stopped, but did not look outside to learn of their fate for herself. She had her hands clasped together in front of her as if she needed that to stop the shakes.

"Yeah, looks like it. Neither of them are moving," I told her and let the curtain fall closed. "They're not going anywhere until someone picks them up."

"Now what do we do." Stella ran her hands through her hair.

I'll be damned if I know, I wanted to say, but hell, it was my job to know.

"Let's leave your Chevy parked here. Whoever sent them might know by now that the car belongs to you. We'll take the train out of town. I've got a friend who owes me a favor. A few weeks ago, he told me he recently purchased several rental properties over in Brooklyn."

Stella's brow pinched questioningly as she asked, "Is he safe?"

"You know him, doll. Irwin Cohen."

Irwin Cohen, Manhattan's lone Jewish fence, occasionally took property for payment when cash was unavailable for someone who needed it without going to the bank and getting rejected.

"He's a lovely man and has a terrific American Flyer two-rail train layout that fills his basement. His pike, he called it and sounded like a pleased little boy." She smiled as if the memory brought her an odd kind of pleasure.

I knew her sharing the memory with me provided her with a way to escape what we then faced, and I winked at her.

"I'll ask him if he's got a place out there with toy trains in it."

"You're joking now, aren't you?" She looked confused but oddly interested as she brushed loose strands of hair behind her ears.

"No, I'm serious. Toy trains might give us a way to pass the time." I didn't really think that, but if it made her happy...

"I can think of other ways too." She tried to smile, but it looked weak and then her eyes held a touch of fear and pain as if at that moment she became aware she'd spoken without thinking and now worried about my rejection along with the two bodies outside her front door.

"I'll bet you can and so can I," I said as casually as possible, reached for her, looked her over, and saw her left hand pressed tight against the side of her abdomen where the gunman in my building hit her while attempting to shoot me.

"Did I hurt you before?" I dropped my arm and pointed.

"I'll be fine. Please call Irwin now. I'm afraid to wait here a minute longer than necessary."

I found the telephone, lifted the receiver, and then heard a distant siren. "We're too late for this, doll. Grab your shoes and purse and let's go."

Gabby—New York's finest guard dog—remained hidden behind the sofa. I snapped the leash to his collar and half dragged him to Stella. Finally, I picked him up and carried him out under my left arm with his tongue lolling and drooling.

We walked quickly down the alley, the way I fled detection the first time I visited her building months ago, and wondered if that was some kind of convoluted message.

A minute after we left her apartment, a black-and-white prowl car howled down the block and around the corner on squealing tires with two more cars close behind him.

Hope they're not recaps, I thought and grinned.

As we walked to the 8th Avenue subway station at West 34th and 8th, I concentrated on one simple fact. I could not turn to the cops, and I should not appear in any place I normally frequented, including my home in Brooklyn. The killer stalked me with a skill I found difficult to comprehend and impossible to avoid up until that moment.

This left me with the option of calling Irwin or returning upstate to the cabin. I felt reluctant about visiting Irwin's downtown office building. If the shooter followed us, then Irwin might be next to die.

Then I thought of his telling me over a second bottle of Ballantine Ale one Friday night about a nice used one-family house he acquired in Sheepshead Bay. It was on Homecrest Avenue about four blocks east of the 61st precinct. That would be a short, brisk walk from the Brighton Beach Line subway station. He thought the location might prove safer since it was close to the 61st.

I didn't know the house number, but decided that I could use a pay telephone once out in Brooklyn and call Irwin after we arrived. Worse come to worse, we could head back upstate if the place was not available.

I dropped a fiver on the token sales clerk to get Gabby on the train and then we ran to catch the next outbound.

Gabby made himself a couple of new friends during the ride, received several food handouts like half of a Nathan's hot dog and a rolled-up slice of hard salami, and gulped them down with one or two bites. He seemed to prefer prepared meats better than the canned

Alpo dog food I'd been feeding him. He might have been a lousy guard dog, but he was not a fussy eater.

As we stepped off the train in Brooklyn, I spotted a telephone booth, dug in my pocket, fished out a handful of change, closed the door, and called Irwin.

When he picked up, I said, "I'm trying to locate Irwin Cohen. He said to call this number between the hours of ten in the morning and four in the afternoon." I glanced quickly at the clock by the exit and saw I had enough time. The clock showed 3:46 p.m.

"Cutting it kind of close again, my friend," he said with a sardonic chuckle.

"Couldn't be helped this time, Irwin. I'm having some serious problems and I need somewhere safe and remote to give me the time to work through them."

"That's what the newspaper seems to be omitting."

"What do you mean?" I hadn't had time to look at any newspaper since leaving the city to go fishing with Dunbar.

"The news boys keep reporting about shootings, but these aren't you doing the shooting. These are about someone trying to shoot you, it seems. What's going on in your life, Marlowe?"

"To tell you the truth, I can't say I know right yet, Irwin, but I plan to find out and put an end to it as soon as possible."

"I knew that you would." He sounded more confident than I felt.

I wiped sweat from my forehead with three fingers and checked on Stella and Gabby. The dog busily sniffed around the base of a painted steel support column as if he needed to pee in a bad way.

Stella studied me with interest and turned away when a train approached as if the sound startled her. The train passed and the wind from it blew her hair back and lifted the hem of her housedress enough to show her knees. Stella held it down with one hand and smiled coyly after the train went by.

"Irwin, I'm kind of in a hurry and I've got Lois' dog down here with me. I think he's planning to piss on the platform."

"Sorry about your gal, Marlowe." He hesitated, and then asked, "Where's down here?"

After thanking him for the condolences, I told him where I stood and explained what I needed from him.

"Number is 2246 and the key is under the mat inside the garage. Enter through the side door, which is in the wall facing the house. The electricity is on in both the garage and in the house if you need to use it, which you will since you're staying the night.

"I had the outside spigots shut off in the basement. It seemed that the neighbors helped themselves to my water when their lawns dried up. Inside water is running, of course. And please don't go shooting up the place. It was freshly painted a couple of weeks ago." He chuckled and sounded as if he didn't really mind one way or the other if I shot holes in the ceilings.

"I don't much care about watering anything outside. We won't need to wash a car, and I don't go in for gardening. Stella wants to know if you've got any trains set up there; she told me how she enjoyed the layout in your basement."

"Tell my favorite duchess I'll bring a set of Lionel trains around tomorrow."

"Great. I'm sure you'll make her day, and thanks a lot, Irwin."

"My best to Stella," he said with a chuckle and hung up.

I waited to discover if I might get my nickel back, did not, but rattled the yoke several times, which did nothing to return my money either.

After a quick climb, we reached street level and daylight. Gabby sniffed, searched for, and found a suitable patch of grass with a no parking sign planted in the middle of it. He lifted a leg and relieved himself on the pole.

Swell, a cowardly dog with a wry sense of humor—that's really what I need in my life right now.

We strolled to 2246 Homecrest like a married couple on the way home after a day of work in the city. With my hand on her elbow, I guided Stella around the side of the garage and opened the door. Both of us entered and confronted an old Model A Ford sedan. She was a black beauty with polished chrome and brass, and headlights like Little Orphan Annie eyes. I could see our reflections in the finish on the curved fenders.

I located the key where Irwin said I would find it, opened the front door to the house, and stepped inside without hesitation.

The place looked clean, was newly carpeted, furnished, and smelled of fresh paint. However, most of all, no one other than Irwin knew that we would be staying in Brooklyn. For the first time in days, I felt reasonably secure, and glanced at Stella. She looked more relaxed, too, but I suspected that our feelings of tranquility would not last long.

Chapter Ten

While I searched the two-story house, checked the attic and basement, Stella rummaged around in the kitchen.

Finished, I joined her and found the GE refrigerator running and cold, but its shelves sat empty. In the small freezer compartment, I saw two aluminum ice trays with handles down the centers used to loosen the ice. Uniformly shaped ice cubes filled both trays.

The hot water felt hotter than warm but not scalding. I examined the Hotpoint four-burner electric stove. It had a double oven, a clock set with the correct time according to my Timex, and a row of push buttons controlled the temperature settings for the burners and the ovens.

Brilliant-colored Fiestaware dinnerware, apple green drinking glasses, and copper-bottom pots and pans filled the overhead cabinets. Everything looked and shone like new. None of it compared to the mismatched collection I used at home.

Inside the living room, I smelled a kind of acrid cleaning fluid, like ammonia and fresh-cut pine boards. New carpeting covered the center of the parquet hardwood floor. The place looked and felt like a normal home, but not for me. I'm not the Sears and Roebuck catalog type.

Stella dropped onto the plush velveteen red sofa, kicked off her shoes, wriggled her toes in the new light blue carpeting, and for the first time since she walked into my office days ago, looked and acted like her old self, relaxed and self-assured.

"It's been a rough couple of weeks for you." I released Gabby, sat on the opposite end of the sofa, and studied her as she stood and moved around the room like a newlywed. The housedress did not hide her curves, but instead accented them quite nicely each time she turned quickly.

"I went through worse during the war, but never got shot before."

She turned in a complete circle so the skirt rose to reveal her shapely knees and then she peered out the front window after pulling aside the lace curtains. This time, I did not interfere but watched with quiet pleasure.

"Let me take a look at that wound of yours," I said without thinking first and waved her to approach me.

"Marlowe, I'd need to take off my dress." She glanced over her shoulder, seemed to color some, and looked away quickly enough to make me wonder what thoughts slid through her mind.

Oh, well, now that's too bad, was what I thought, but said, "Then you should go in the bathroom and examine it. Decide if we need to find a drugstore to get you supplies to treat your injury. We've got to keep it clean so it doesn't get infected."

"I'll need clean gauze bandaging and adhesive tape, but I brought the ointment the doctor gave me before leaving the hospital." She nodded in the direction of her purse, which lay in the corner of the sofa.

"You can stay here with Gabby and I'll go hunt down a store." I pointed at her pocketbook. "I assume you've got your gun in there?"

"No reason not to." She returned to the sofa where she dropped the purse, sat on the arm, popped the purse open, and removed a nice little S&W .38.

With a nod, I left and found a Rexall Drug store two blocks away, purchased two cans of dog food, bandaging, and a pair of Dr. West's toothbrushes, Pepsodent toothpaste, and a fresh pack of Camels with a book of matches that advertised a dive of a pub called Alex's After Hours on Atlantic Avenue.

After returning, I closed and locked the door behind me, and heard the water running in the bathroom. Pressing an ear to the bathroom door, I listened to Stella singing in the shower. She had a rich, strong soprano and hit the high notes of "The Sidewalks of New York" like a pro.

When she killed the water and I heard the shower curtain slide back, I knocked and said, through the door, "I've got what you need out here," and heard her chuckle.

"Not right now you don't, buster," she said in a way that let me know what she'd been thinking about in the shower while I was gone.

"Maybe later, then." I went upstairs, walked into the rear bedroom, put the bandaging on the dresser, and then went down to the kitchen to light up a smoke.

I really felt good, better than I should have, but could not force myself to feel otherwise. For the first time in two or three weeks, I knew I'd made a decision the shooter did not anticipate before I could put it into action. That felt like a serious accomplishment right then, and I was not about to complain under the circumstances.

Hell, I did not even know who wanted me dead or if there was more than one who did. I had more questions than answers. Fact was I did not have any concrete evidence to back up my suppositions.

However, I trusted my hunches. There was only one son of a bitch gunning for me, hiring help as he went along. Why? I could not figure that part out yet.

Now, I thought, *I have to learn how the bastard knew Paul and I went fishing upstate. Once I have that information, I'll be one step closer to finding the shit-for-brains son of a bitch.*

Stella entered the kitchen wrapped in a large light green towel. She smelled like Ivory soap and clean female and left damp footprints on the black-and-white checkered linoleum.

"Where'd you find the towel?" I asked, and let my eyes take in the sight of her nice legs.

"There's a closet in the hallway with linens stacked in it. In the larger bedroom upstairs, I found an oak dresser filled with men's clothing. Maybe they're the right size for you, but they look to be a few sizes too large for me."

Stella stood about five foot four and weighed around 120 to 125. I'm five seven and weigh in at 165. I guessed those three inches meant more to her than to me. Of course, the forty or so pounds mattered too.

"What you located upstairs might have to do until Irwin comes by tomorrow. When he gets here I'll ask him to give me a loan for a few days and then I'll take you shopping."

"Sounds like fun to me." She grinned knowingly as if she understood how I felt.

Shopping is not my idea of anything but a pain in the ass if it goes on for longer than a few minutes.

"If you say so, doll. I'll take your word for it."

Spontaneously, I reached for the opened side of her towel, lifted it enough to look at her wound, and gazed up at her face at the same time.

Right then, I was not sure what I planned, but once moving, realized if I stopped, she might get the idea she caught me misbehaving, and be right too.

Her eyes briefly registered surprise, but her smile did not falter until I pressed my fingertips to the edge of the healing wound.

The stitches held, but the flesh seemed a bit too red and hot for my liking.

"That hurt you much?" I asked softly.

"Not so much, it's tender mostly." Her smile weakened, and I knew she was in more pain than she would admit.

There's nothing wrong with being tough after getting shot and living to talk about it unless the pain is indicative of a more serious condition like an infection, blood poisoning, or internal bleeding.

I'd had an ancestor who was a farmer in old Westchester County before it became the Bronx. He fell off a wagon and was run over by the rear wheel. He died from blood poisoning after refusing amputation. My mother told me that he suffered terribly from a nasty infection.

Casually, I smoothed my palm across the soft flesh of her hip and reluctantly released the towel before temptation pushed me too far. She felt awful good and I wanted more, but my timing was more than a little off.

"I think you'll heal fine," I said and went to the sink to drown my spent cigarette. "You'd better keep it clean, bandaged, and take some aspirin."

When she came down after dressing in men's clothing, I suggested we use the remainder of my cash to buy food at the grocery diagonally across the street from the Rexall.

We returned with bags of canned goods, cold cuts, bread, coffee, eggs, bacon, butter, and a six-pack of Ballantine Ale of course.

While we prepared sandwiches and drank beer, I switched on the green Arvin AM-FM radio that sat on the corner of the kitchen table.

The WNYC reporter discussed two uniformed cops discovered shot dead on a sidewalk in the westside of Manhattan after a neighbor called in a shooting.

"After a preliminary investigation, a source at police headquarters stated, it has been determined that the deceased are not, I repeat, are not members of the city police force. They did not carry any form of identification. Their badges are not official. Currently they're being listed as John Doe one and two."

There you have it, coroner creativity, I thought. *Will there ever be an end to it?*

I heard Stella sigh her relief and I spun the dial until I located a station playing soft Johnny Mercer music.

"At least I don't have to sweat that one out," I said aloud, but had not meant to admit that I'd been seriously concerned over the consequences of their deaths if they'd been legitimate cops. Of course, Stella would have surmised as much.

She set plates and flatware on the table with napkins, and placed a fresh bottle of opened beer in front of each.

"Thank God, they're not cops, Marlowe. Maybe this is a good sign for us." She poured her beer into a tall, clear glass after tilting the glass enough to avoid a thick head of foam.

"A good sign for what?" I sat across from her and swallowed a long time before putting down the bottle.

Someone hired the shooters, and whoever did the hiring must now suspect I killed both of them, I thought without sharing that idea with her. *I need to know who sent them and how the hell he knew I would be there with Stella.*

And then it hit me hard. *The phony cops didn't know I'd be at her apartment. Whoever sent them had another plan for her, but was it kidnapping or a quick execution to inflict maximum pain and duress on me? Or was it something entirely different that had nothing whatsoever to do with me? That's the question of the hour. I need to find this bastard soon and get Stella to someplace safe and remote.*

Stella interrupted my thoughts, and although I tried to hold onto the one that was forming, I lost it.

It'll come to me later.

"The news might be a good sign that things are starting to turn around for us." She smiled and bit into her sandwich as if she'd not eaten in days.

A superstitious optimist—now how do you deal with a person like that? Someone once told me there is a thin line between being an optimist and being a fool…a dead fool. I thought she was nuts, but did not want to hurt her feelings again. I'd learned by then that despite her demeanor, Stella reacted sensitively to my sarcastic wit, which she seemed to take as biting criticism occasionally.

On the other hand, maybe I was really under too much stress to think through what I said before I allowed it to vent. I vowed I would do better.

"Guess you can never tell one way or the other," I finally replied noncommittally, but did not look at her face. I didn't want her to read my doubt.

We cleaned up and went to the living room, where I discovered a situation I hadn't anticipated until that moment.

As I said earlier, a year ago, Stella and I spent two nights together, but somehow this felt a lot different. I buried Lois over two weeks before then, but still felt the loss deep in places I tried to avoid in my head, places filled with the memories of wartime buddies who died in combat or after returning home. They lived in a sacred zone where my thoughts kept them alive. Stupid, I suppose, but their sacrifices deserved remembrance.

On the other hand, maybe it was because I thought of Stella as a woman from money, who had expectations I didn't know how to meet. I was an uncomplicated kind of guy with simple desires and needs.

And too, there was the incident with me turning in her father after helping her save his worthless ass.

Hell, Stella, I felt sure, bore layers of personality far deeper than anything I was accustomed to in other people I'd known. She was well educated and had a quick wit that left a slower mind in the dust of her conclusions. Her sense of humor came off as both sarcastic and childish, depending on the moment and her mood.

I did not know how to explain my sense of humor beyond cut and dry, a sense of the absurd, if I still had any at all. The sense of humor that remained with me was what I used to survive daily life in combat while in Europe, but maybe it was nothing more than that and it was shallow too.

I think anything amusing about life and humanity bled out like an arterial wound the day I entered the Nazi death camp we stumbled upon in the heart of a beautiful, quiet, lonely forest. The snow made us all feel nervous, wary as if we'd entered some kind of surreal setting for a movie, and then we discovered the living dead, and the hundreds of bodies piled and rotting in long, wide ditches.

God, the horror of it never leaves a man's heart or mind.

However, Stella had another surprise in mind. She dropped onto the sofa and said, "Sit over here and let me give you a backrub."

I could not help smiling as I obeyed, felt her strong fingers dig into my shoulders and neck, and drifted off to sleep about ten minutes later.

She roused me enough to guide me upstairs into a room where I fell across the bed and went out before she finished removing my shoes.

I awoke fully alert to darkness and noise outside, rolled onto my back, and listened for a minute before deciding to investigate the mumbled words that drifted up and into the partially opened bedroom window.

Glancing around, I discovered Stella asleep next to me. Everything else looked like vague, shadowy shapes of unfamiliarity.

Carefully, I lifted the covers and found she'd undressed me to my shorts. With a wry grin, I stood and picked up my Colt.

Moving barefoot downstairs and through the kitchen, I watched a silhouette glide across the side yard. My heart pounded loud enough for me to hear it. When street lighting clearly illuminated him, I saw an older man and his dog, a boxer judging by its gait and the shape of its short muzzle.

I waited until they went around the corner of the building, slowly opened the kitchen door, and stepped outside. The air smelled clean with a tinge of saltwater.

After I searched around the building, I re-entered the kitchen and nearly shouted when a shadow crossed the threshold into the living room. Without hesitation, I flipped off the safety, yanked the slide to chamber a round, heard the round that had been chambered ring as it hit the floor, and then heard Stella's voice. "Marlowe, is that you?"

"Jesus Christ, Stella," I muttered softly and lowered the .45.

She stood beyond the doorway with a bedsheet draped around her shoulders.

"Damn it all to hell." I exhaled, closed and locked the outside door.

"You scared the hell out of me."

"You went outside in your shorts with a gun?" she asked and pointed at the .45, nodded at my boxers. She was grinning.

"Heard something and I wanted to investigate. We can't risk taking any chances right now. Anything goes until we find and stop the bastard before he finds and stops one or both of us."

"So, did you see something interesting out there?" She came into the kitchen. The sheet swept the floor behind her bare feet with a kind of ethereal elegance.

"Only some older guy walking his dog." The safety snapped closed as I rubbed my thumb across it. After placing the Colt on the table, I didn't know what to do, but wanted to add, *and you looking as good as an extremely pleasurable memory.* I located and retrieved the round I'd dropped, placed it on the counter by the sink.

"Must be his lucky night," she said with a touch of trepidation as she got close enough to read my expression. Close enough for me to sense her body heat.

"Yeah, you can say that again." I wanted to return to bed, and too seriously yearned to see what she wore under the sheet that draped from her shoulders. The hints of shadows caused by the lights leaking through the curtains looked promising and filled me with a longing I tried to stifle.

Stella took my hand and guided me upstairs into the bedroom.

As the sheet slipped from her left shoulder displaying bare flesh, I said, "I can't, Stella," knowing I could, but the desire did not feel right, not completely.

"I understand how you feel about her, Marlowe. Anyway, all I want is your arms around me, and nothing more than that right now. I'm so damn tired of feeling lonely and scared." She sounded sincere.

We climbed under the covers and she nestled against my side, kissed my cheek, and fell asleep seconds later. My hand rested on the silk of her upper chest. I stared at the blank ceiling wishing I could let go of the emotions churning inside, opening and closing portals into the past that gave me glimpses of cherished memories and, too, the sight of Lois lying in a coffin, ready for that uncertain journey to childhood's mystical beyond we can only hope is prepared to greet us in death.

Stella turned in her sleep and laid her arm across my chest. Her touch pushed tears from the corners of my eyes, which was like having a switch thrown that gratefully shifted my thinking back to the present.

I dozed and awoke to light leaking around the blinds and a dog barking as if he'd treed a squirrel. It all looked, smelled, and sounded like what I imagined might be the life of ordinary people. The kind of life I chose to avoid back in '48 and could never look back on if I changed my mind, got married again, and invested in a white picket fence I'd never get around to painting once a year.

Stella still lay pressed against my side. Her heat felt like a warm, loving embrace. I didn't want to get up, or move, wanted to stay there in that position until the biblical horsemen rode black flaming stallions from deep inside towering thunderheads to wrench human sanity from Earth and thrust its remains into the hellish reality of the apocalypse.

My thinking forced a low chuckle. I'm not what anyone might call a morning guy.

That kind of thinking is why you'll never live an ordinary life, pal, I thought and quietly went into the bathroom for a shower where I did not need to boil water first like in the cabin.

Chapter Eleven

"I need to call in a favor," I told Stella after we finished breakfast.
"What kind of favor?" She half turned to look at me. Her eyes moved as if she wanted to examine my face carefully. Beyond that I could not read her expression, but decided she looked more nervous or wary instead of curious.

She shrugged and smiled weakly. I decided that maybe I read her wrong. A few women express more than they want you to know and others not much at all. Stella seemed to fit somewhere in the middle, leaning toward not enough expression so I might easily figure her out. That got me wondering why she felt concerned, and if I should tell her everything I had on my mind.

"A friend of mine works at 240 Centre Street. He lost a bet to me on a ballgame a few weeks back."

"Wait a minute...240 Centre Street—that's... He's a cop? You bet on ballgames with a cop?" Her quick smile became a crooked, mocking grin, and she tilted her head slightly as if she believed I might be pulling her leg for the fun of it and hoped to catch her off guard.

I lifted a shoulder in what I hoped would be a hapless gesture and then grinned too. "Yup, that's about the gist of it. Normally, we play one night every week. Either Friday or Saturday depending on his schedule and what teams are playing. We've been making friendly wagers now for what? I guess at least two years or more, maybe as many as three. He and I used to walk a beat together before I resigned from the police force; of course back then we didn't bet on games."

"No, of course not, that might've gotten you into serious trouble," she said humorously, seeming interested in only the sordid details of our conversation. "How much do you bet?" Now she turned around, placed her hands on her hips as if she might be more than curious, yet still couldn't be quite sure if I was being straight with her.

Hell, I couldn't pull off a practical joke if you paid me, and I always forget punch lines.

"It was a friendly wager for a buck and a cold beer on tap." I raised an eyebrow in challenge. I did not really like the idea that she thought she could question me about what I did for fun, but what the hell—maybe she was pulling my leg.

"I know a buck sounds like a lot of money, but we started out with a quarter and then both of us felt that such a small wager didn't make it challenging enough. But hey, mostly, I do it out of friendship and for the beer, not the money. As far as that goes, I think we're about even for the last year."

She studied me for a moment, walked over and looked out the window as if she wanted to think over whether or not she should stay with a guy who wagered on baseball with a cop no less.

In turn, I studied her slim silhouetted form under the baggy blue men's shirt that she wore tucked into loose-fitting men's gray trousers.

Then, I realized she struggled to hold back her laughter, maintaining some amount of composure, and had her arms across her chest as if she needed the support.

"What's so damn funny about that?" I went to her and put my hands on her shoulders, but did nothing more.

"Oh nothing, Marlowe, absolutely nothing is funny about what you said." She paused and giggled like a kid. "It's just that you go and act all tough and law-abiding, yet you gamble with a cop, for God's sake."

"I gamble with a cop. So what's the big deal?" I patted her upper arms. "I mean how bad can that be?" I added to get her laughing.

Now she did laugh. "And that makes all the difference in the world to you, I guess."

"Of course it makes all the difference in the world to me. What the hell is he going to do about it—report me to his superiors or have me arrested? Who would he use for a witness? His reflection? Would he report me to his captain and get me locked up?"

"Well, don't let me stop you from making a phone call to your gambling buddy." She shook her head, laughed more, and pointed at the telephone. "No really, go ahead and make the call."

"Hey, we need dough right now. A buck is a buck."

"I know, Marlowe. I was teasing you."

Swell, I thought.

"I knew that," I said, but we both knew otherwise.

As I studied her, I saw her eyes reflected real fear, as she grew serious. "Wait a minute, you believe a cop told the killer about your fishing trip upstate with Detective Dunbar, don't you?" Surprise lilted her words enough to make me hesitate with the receiver halfway to my ear. I did not respond nor look in her direction, which was all the answer she needed.

"Jesus, Mary, and Joseph, Marlowe, that's a frightening thought." She glanced up as if to say a silent prayer with her eyes, and her fingers went to her necklace.

Stella was a Christian convert. Before the war, her family was Jewish, but after Hitler's Final Solution became a reality, she started wearing a small gold crucifix as a disguise. After the war, she and her family as survivors came to the United States, and she believed that Jesus watched over them for six years of Nazi rule, so she converted to Catholicism.

I'd never heard her use His name in vain before and considered it a sign of how genuinely afraid she must have felt.

Yeah, you finally figured it out, doll. I hoped she would not catch on to my motives for joking around, but she was intelligent and quick-witted, and that might've strengthened her growing fears. Hell, to be honest, my fear grew every time I confronted another of the killer's gunmen. It seemed as if his resources would not run dry before my time ran out.

"Someone did and only you, Dunbar's partner, and his precinct captain knew where we'd gone. Oh, and his cat Betty too." I decided to slice through to the heart of the matter and stop treating her as if she couldn't handle the truth. We both might die real soon, so she deserved to know as much as I knew.

"That really narrows it down dramatically, doesn't it?"

"Indeed it does. And I've got you here with me, so that counts you out."

"How about the clerk who handled the paperwork?" she asked. "I doubt Paul's captain does the precinct's paperwork, and he wouldn't assign Paul's partner the job."

"Now that's good thinking." I pressed the black telephone receiver to my ear while trying to recall if Brooklyn still used an operator.

"I'll go get the newspaper while you phone." She opened the back door.

"Be careful," I called as she stepped outside, watched her wave over her shoulder and pat her purse possessively.

Dunbar's captain, Louis Steiner, was a Bruno bucking for commissioner. A tough guy with a hard-nosed attitude, like one of those Joes who wore a chip on their shoulder and dared you to knock it off if you proved to them that you were brave enough to try. It was a temptation I often found hard to ignore and sometimes did not even try to resist. What the hell, temptation added excitement to life.

A week or so after I quit the force, three years plus since the day I joined, I ran across him in a downtown bar. He got pretty drunk and started mouthing off at me for being a quitter. He gave me a shove and I lost my temper, split his lip, blackened one eye, and played a round of chin music with him until he sagged to his knees and folded quietly at the foot of the stool where he sat.

I then poured the remainder of his beer on his head. Ballantine Ale on tap. Waste of a good beer, I know, but it felt great to shut him the hell up with a cold dose of public humiliation finally.

It turned out that the man had a glass jaw. I earned myself an enemy in the wrong place. I knew he would never make commissioner, so I needed to work around him ever since—not a real problem, truth be told.

This time might be a different story. Dunbar was his best detective, and I felt sure Steiner would believe he needed Paul as a liaison up there to help him find out who did the shooting. I was the best or most available man to meet and talk with Paul unless he wanted to send a cop upstate, which I didn't think would happen if it could be avoided.

Upstate cops didn't like city cops and would throw up a few roadblocks if Steiner attempted to push them around, as he had a reputation for doing in town.

I tapped the phone cradle and got an operator, told her the number I wanted, and listened to her say, "Is this an emergency, sir?"

If you only knew, I thought. "No, I'm calling to talk with a friend." I told her his name.

She thanked me and put me through, but not through to Steiner. I would deal with him if and when I needed to, but not before.

"Yeah," Phil Ball said when he picked up.

"Phil, it's me."

"What the hell are you involved in now, Black? Jesus, I hear Paul Dunbar is laid up in a hospital somewhere way the hell off in the middle of nowhere thanks to you." Phil Ball did not sound too happy to hear from me.

"That might depend on whether or not you lived up that way." I paused and, when he did not respond to the joke, knew he was serious.

"Someone in the Thirteenth gave out the information where Paul and I stayed, which let the shooter know where we went fishing," I said without emotion.

"How can you be certain of that?" He sounded calmer, but not by much, like he hung off the edge of a vital decision.

I explained my thoughts to him and waited for him to explode. To my surprise, he said calmly, "I'll look into it and get back to you.

What's the number there?"

"Keep it to yourself," I said, gave him the number, and hung up.

Ten minutes passed. I grew apprehensive waiting for Stella to return.

After opening the front door and stepping onto the stoop, I spotted her walking back toward the house with a newspaper tucked under one arm. She strolled down the sidewalk as if she was on top of the world and excited to be there, not like a woman on the lam wondering if she'd live to see tomorrow.

Damn, she looks great in men's clothing too, I thought. *Way too good-looking for a guy in mourning to have around all day and night. This is bound to end with trouble one way or the other.*

I caught her attention and she waved the folded newspaper over her head as if to let me know there was a story in it that I would want to read.

Swell, just what I need—another headline with my name in bold type under it.

Some reporters—one guy in particular named Peter Morgan with *The New York Daily News*—seemed to like to glamorize or sensationalize everything I did or said in public while working a case. He seemed to enjoy writing articles that made me sound like I lived on the edge of the law. He quickly became a royal pain in my ass, but hadn't done anything I could use to stop him.

Behind Stella, a shiny two-door black Studebaker coupe with a sharp chrome bullet nose rolled around the corner as if driven with determination. The sleek car moved much too slowly as it rolled up alongside her.

Finally, Stella heard the car, spun around like she was prepared to run like hell, and reached in her purse, but then she stopped and waved her free hand as if a lost friend had showed up unexpectedly to offer her a ride home.

The driver tattooed the horn and I knew he had to be Irwin Cohen.

I let out the breath I didn't know that I held.

The phone rang behind me, so I left them to their own devices and lifted the receiver.

"Yeah," I said curtly.

"Phil Ball here. The woman who processed the paperwork for Dunbar's vacation time quit early yesterday afternoon."

"Shit," I grunted. "Looks to me like we got us a winner, pal."

"Yeah, it does look that way. She only worked here for three and a half weeks. I've got to admit, though, that I thought you went way out in left field with this one, Marlowe."

"You have a name for me?" I asked without letting him know how I felt about his skepticism. He was a cop. Skepticism was part of his job, kept him sane and focused.

"Steiner's going to have a cow if I tell you, but what the hell do I care. You only live once, right?"

"So they keep telling me." I tried to laugh, but coughed instead, and lit a Camel with my Zippo. "Keep the money you owe me, Phil."

He chuckled. "Thanks, I can use it. Now, you ready?" he asked as if he knew I needed to prepare myself.

I opened the drawer under the phone and found a pad of paper and several sharpened number two yellow pencils.

"Yeah," I said. "I'm as ready as I'll ever be."

"Her name is Kate Twiggs. She lives over in—"

"Union City, New Jersey," I interrupted without hesitation. *Son of a bitch*, I thought. *What the fuck is she doing and who's she doing it with?*

"No, Marlowe," he said. "She's lives over in the Bowery according to this. You want the address or not?"

I told him the one I remembered in the Bowery from my last run-in with the Twiggs family. They'd proven themselves to be a nasty piece of work.

"That's the place. Care to fill me in on how you knew where she lived?" he asked.

"Not yet, pal. Not yet, but thanks. Now I owe you a cold one too," I said and hung up before he could push for more information.

Katlyn Twiggs set up me, and Paul too, to get one or both of us killed. She and I had a history that spanned the previous eleven months. I found her brother Gregory dead in my office chair after the July Fourth weekend last year. He'd been murdered elsewhere and deposited where I couldn't help but find him.

The men who killed Twiggs left him as a message to me to stay away from what they planned. However, I didn't know what to expect, and when it arrived with Stella as the courier, I waded in without paying heed to the warning.

Katlyn Twiggs' brother smuggled Heinrich Himmler's sterling silver belt buckle home from Europe to sell to a collector. He knew about the list of Odessa names hidden in a small built-in compartment on the reverse side of the Death's Head, and tried to sell the list to the highest bidder. He got the ultimate price, Nazi-style death by strangulation.

But what does Twiggs want now? What, if anything, did her brother's death have to do with Lois? And why wait until now to try to kill me? Hell, why would she want to kill me or have me killed? I could not come up with one solid reason, but nonetheless she was a place to start my hunt.

Stella and Irwin entered, chatting away like long-lost cousins, which interrupted my thoughts. Irwin had a box of Lionel trains under one arm with a picture of a steam locomotive with 671 on the cab, smoke billowing from its stack while it pulled a line of freight cars and a red caboose.

I did not listen to their words. My mind wandered back and then stayed busy with memories from a night in Union City, New Jersey, last July.

Without provocation, Katlyn Twiggs intentionally shot Stella. The only thing that saved Stella was a cigar box filled with extremely valuable Russian gold coins she had tucked under her waistband. She shouldn't have had the coins with her, but luckily, she did. The bullet struck the box and lodged in the center of one coin instead of tearing its way end over end through the final moments of Stella's life. Katlyn Twiggs had a killer's desire to act impulsively. I wondered again as I had last year if she succeeded yet.

A noise from behind turned me around. Stella slapped the newspaper on the counter. Alongside the *News*, I spotted the new issue of *Sports Illustrated*.

Absentmindedly, I lifted the magazine and flipped it over where I found a picture of Miss Rheingold 1950 on the back cover. Pat Burrage was a gorgeous blue-eyed blonde woman with a smile that might easily distract any red-blooded American male from the beer ad she promoted.

I glanced up when Irwin cleared his throat and caught Stella's amused gaze. The look faded fast as she examined the straight set of my mouth and jaw.

"You off in a daydream, Marlowe?" Irwin asked, placing the train set on the kitchen table.

"Something like that," I said and nodded in the direction of the side door. "Why do you have an old Model A Ford Roadster parked in the garage?"

Irwin stood an inch or two taller than I did, with broader shoulders, curly, short black hair, and dark eyes that reflected the wisdom known best by people who learned the hard way about man's inhumanity to man. His dark blue raglan suit appeared new as did his dark gray snap-brim hat and black lace-up shoes. He wore a dark blue tie with a gold clasp that matched his cuff links. Each piece of jewelry looked like he had it cut in the shape of the Star of David.

"The car came with the building," he said. "You interested in it?" His smile told me he thought I would not be, and his eyes said he wanted to ask questions that were more serious.

"Let's have a cup of coffee and coffeecake," Stella suggested, setting the train set on the kitchen counter.

"Great." Irwin sat at the kitchen table after lifting the knees of his trouser legs so he did not spoil the knife-edge creases.

When steam rose from three cups and Stella sliced the cake, he studied me as he sipped his coffee black.

I winced and dumped three cubes of sugar in mine followed by a good dollop of cream.

"What have you gotten yourself and Stella into?" he finally asked in his best matter-of-fact business voice.

"Irwin, I really don't know yet. Apparently, someone has decided to kill me and take out anyone that gets between me and him."

"Your old Italian friend, you think?" he asked and took a forkful of cake.

"No, I don't think Vinnie Castillo is involved this time." I ate too, sipped coffee, and added, "But whatever this is about, it's in some way related to at least one member of the Twiggs family."

Stella gasped audibly. She dropped her fork, which clattered on her plate, and raised the back of her hand to her mouth as if to protect her from a deliberate punch.

"Katlyn Twiggs?" she asked with tightly controlled emotion reflected fearfully in her eyes. "I hoped I'd never see her or hear her name again after last year."

"Yes, her. You know any reason she might be out for revenge?" I asked her without glancing up from examining my coffeecake.

"Not really. As you must've guessed from the night we met her in New Jersey, I was supposed to return the next morning at ten and—"

"Collect your share of the money?" That time, I cut her a sharp look.

"No. She wanted that damn cursed silver belt buckle." She frowned and looked away, shaking her head slowly.

"Why in God's name would anyone want Himmler's silver Death's Head belt buckle?" I felt more stunned by her revelation than I let on.

"She claimed it was worth a fortune and demanded it as payment for helping me bail out my father. It was either give it to her, or lose everything I'd fought to accomplish to keep Father out of prison, although I thought our government might lock him up if they found out what he did, not the Israelis."

"And then I came along and screwed it all up," I stated, nodding.

When she did not comment, I asked, "Do you know where the buckle is right now? We might use it to get her to come to us."

"The G-men from Sixty-ninth Street took it with them. I suppose the buckle is buried in a safe in the FBI building or is somewhere down in Washington." She finished her cake and drank coffee with one sugar and a splash of cream. Her actions seemed deliberate, intended to delay answering any other questions about the buckle or Katlyn I might think to ask.

Without looking away from her face, I nodded acquiescence to let her know that I wasn't interested in interrogating her.

"Okay. Then we'll need to confront her about why she told whoever about Dunbar and me fishing upstate and who she told, but not at a time or place she might—"

Irwin cleared his throat as if he thought I'd forgotten him and felt quite uncomfortable with the direction our conversation had gone in the last two minutes.

"I should be getting into my office before long. Anything else I can do for you two now?"

"Yes. Since neither of us can make a trip to the bank, how about lending us some cash?"

He stood without expressing any hidden or obvious emotions. A good fence can be as stoic as a twenty-year veteran detective can be. His right hand dug under his suit coat and returned with a plain black leather billfold. He extracted a few bills and placed them face down on the table unceremoniously.

"There's four hundred dollars. If you need more, give me a call and

I'll drop by with it."

I stood and offered him my hand.

"Thanks, Irwin," I said sincerely.

"I'll be expecting you to live long enough to repay that, but forget about any interest," he said with a wry grin. "Think you can set up the Lionel trains without my help?"

"I intend to try to do both." I watched him walk to the front door. "Take care of yourself, friend."

He waved and left.

When I turned back, Stella stood directly behind me, close enough to touch without reaching for her.

"I'm getting really scared now, Marlowe."

"Scared about what, doll?" I asked, although I felt sure I knew the obvious answer.

However, she surprised me. "How are you planning to approach Katlyn? And what will you do to get her to tell you how she's involved, let alone whom she told about the fishing trip? You know, or maybe you don't, that she's a tight-lipped bitch who won't tell you a damn thing if she isn't convinced she has no other option but to talk to save her ass." Stella was angry and it came through in her voice and her choice of words.

"I think I can come up with a way that will convince her," I said evasively, but could not help smiling.

"And you're not going to tell me what that way is, are you?" She studied my eyes with care as if expecting me to let her behind them and inside my head to discover the reasons on her own.

I shook my head. "It's better that you don't know right yet. I'm thinking that I'll attempt to approach her on the street and see if we can come to some kind of arrangement to discuss what she did, and who she talked to about our fishing trip." I lifted her hands in mine and looked at her soft palms under the sunlight shining through the kitchen window. She had a long lifeline like my aunt Betty, my mother's sister, would have said she saw in Stella's palms.

"I'd like these to stay clean for a while at least." I rubbed my thumbs across the base of her thumbs.

She shuddered, gently pulled her hands loose, and put them behind my neck. Before I could react, her lips found mine, and her body pressed tight against me with a desire that felt like hot, raw need.

What I harbored in my head, the pain and grief, released unexpectedly. I crushed her lips against mine, her breast flattened against my chest as I drew her close enough to feel her pounding heart. As I scooped her off the floor and carried her into the bedroom, I fought both the knowledge that I should stop and the thought that there was no way I could stop even if someone attempted to force me away from her with a gun at my head.

Stella tore off my clothing as I did hers, and we fell on each other like the lone and desperate survivors of a deadly calamity.

I lit a cigarette about thirty minutes later, and blew smoke at the ceiling as she lay with her head on my shoulder, my free arm around her, fingers resting on her breast. I knew my commitment to her had now developed into something deeper, but also knew I would never allow my feelings or desires to push or lead me into a relationship that might end somewhere near an altar or in front of a Justice of the Peace. Or worse again standing graveside.

If Stella wanted to be with me, she would have to do it on my terms or look elsewhere for another guy. One divorce and a murdered fiancée with an unborn child in her womb was more than enough for a lifetime, maybe two.

Stella snored lightly. Carefully, I worked my arm free, used the bathroom, and dressed quietly. She still slept while I wrote her a note to let her know when to expect me to return. She continued to sleep as I walked out the front door, locked and closed it softly behind me.

"You might not want to forgive me for doing this, doll," I said under my breath, "but I don't want you to get hurt again. I need answers and my gut says Twiggs has them. If you're mad at me later for leaving you out of it, so be it."

After walking two blocks north and four west to Avenue U, I rode the subway into the city. It was long past breakfast time when I arrived. I grabbed a sandwich and a hot coffee at the first automat I found with an empty table, ate while sitting as far back from the window as possible, and then left for the Bowery and God alone knew what path of destiny my decisions would thereafter create for me.

Chapter Twelve

Katlyn Twiggs, as I recalled her, stood about five seven and weighed somewhere around 125 and was a real looker. She dressed with style, and had the diction of an educated woman except when angry. Then, it seemed she reverted to the level of a street urchin scrounging for scraps and, finding none, cursing the world as if it alone might be responsible for her failures.

Katlyn was not the type of girl I would've expected to discover living in an area of the city that many small-time crooks avoided after dark.

Day and night, sections of the Bowery looked and smelled like an open sewer. I considered it a place for castoffs, rejects, and those who preyed on the desperate like turkey vultures circling overhead, while traffic ground down roadkill as if to ease their task of consuming carcasses.

I walked around the block to the Twiggs' apartment building, kept my head down, hat shading my eyes, and did not go too far in any direction away from her block.

Katlyn strolled casually up the street around 5:15 p.m. She moved with assurance and the determination of a self-possessed woman with an important destination. I planned to change that self-imposed evaluation forever before the next sunrise if she refused to cooperate and tell me who she gave the information I suspected she purloined from the Thirteenth Precinct.

From the corner of my eye, I watched her walk past the alley where I stood with a copy of the *News* opened so she could not easily see my face. I could hear her approach as her heels clipped the concrete sidewalk.

Then, as her quick stride took her directly to the entrance of her building, I stepped onto the street and watched her open the front door without looking back to where I stood. If she had, Katlyn would've easily spotted me spying on her. It seemed that she felt safe in her new territory, like a Park Avenue mistress on the way home from a highly profitable appointment.

"Katlyn Twiggs," I called out only loud enough for her alone to hear me before she closed the door.

She stopped abruptly, and I knew she'd recognized my voice. She stepped out onto the stoop, turned, and stared in my direction.

"Remember me?" I asked and waved a hand at her.

"No…oh, Marlowe Black. What the hell do you want from me now, you bastard?"

"You don't look too pleased to see me, Katlyn, but you do look rather shocked. Why might that be?"

"You caught me by surprise. What do you want? I'm kind of busy right now."

"You know what I want. Give me one minute of your time, answer a couple of questions, and I'll be gone for good."

She ran one hand through her hair, pushing if off her brow, stared at me as if thinking over her options, and then shook her head.

"Go to hell, Black. I'll never talk to you. If you come anywhere near me or my family again, I'll call the cops, and if they won't stop you, I'll gun you down myself if I need to."

"What are you so angry about?" She hadn't sounded confused, as if she were innocent. Yet there was no chance she could've known that I'd learned about her clerk job at the Thirteenth.

Maybe with a little commonsense deduction, she just figured it out, pal. You aren't dead and you're standing outside of her building of all places. She isn't stupid.

"You can stand there and ask me that question? After what you did to my family, you deserved to die slowly and painfully. We lost everything we owned because of your interference, and this is where we're forced to live now." She spit out the words and nodded at the building with a movement that reminded me of a slashing knife.

"I only need to talk with you. That's all," I said quietly, tucked the paper under my arm, and held up my hands in a gesture of compromise. "I'm not here to hurt you or to otherwise bother you."

"Stay the hell away from me!" she screamed loud enough for the neighbors to hear her. "Don't hurt me again or I'll have to call the police to have them protect me from you! You're a rapist, you bastard!" She fumbled with her purse and produced a handgun, cocked the hammer, and aimed in my direction.

Shit, I thought, *despite the planning, this isn't going well. But this is the reaction of the guilty.*

Even the drunk on the corner reacted to her scream. He raised his head and peered around, sniffing the air. She sounded as if she had really been raped and beaten by me. Yet, I'd never touched her except to shake her hand when I first met her last year.

"There's no need to do something you'll regret, Katlyn," I said, then again recalled that she'd shot Stella without provocation and escaped punishment since Stella never filed a complaint.

Keeping a watch on her, I started backing away. Katlyn knew how to use a gun, which got me thinking, *Maybe she shot Lois, but could she use a rifle too? Hell, why not?*

She lifted her arm higher, sighting along the barrel, turning her torso, shifting her stance to brace herself.

"I told you to leave me alone, Black. Get away from here or I'll shoot you where you stand. And if I don't now, you ever return, I'll kill you on sight. No one will blame me for defending myself."

She was shouting, but I didn't hear trepidation, I heard angry determination. She was acting like a person who knew that what she'd done which brought me to her home was an act that required a strong defense.

She cocked the hammer, aimed over my head, and squeezed off a round. The bullet slammed into the bricks ten feet above me. Red powder and pieces of brick rained down.

"That was a warning shot, Black. Get the fuck away from me!"

Guess I'll need to find a better way to get her alone where I can ask her questions without any more of her bullshit, and without an audience or getting killed.

"You've got the wrong guy, Miss Twiggs. I'm a private cop. We'll discuss this another time." I said loudly, waved, and left as quickly as possible without moving as if I was in a hurry, but waited to feel the sting of a bullet I would not hear being fired should it hit me.

Several minutes passed before I calmed down enough to observe my surroundings, and then I walked uptown and had a roast beef dinner in a small corner diner where I'd never eaten previously. However, I grew impatient, like a coiled spring compressed beyond tolerance, and worked at forcing myself to slow down while I formulated a plan.

I thought briefly of calling the cops, but didn't have evidence of a crime except for the bullet in the bricks. If it was a hollow nose, or lead, the round would be crushed beyond identification. Katlyn would continue to cry rape, and by the time I was out of jail, Lois' killer would be long gone.

Then I decided I needed to ride this one through to the end without the cops delaying me.

Katlyn might decide to leave town now that she knows I'm on to her involvement. I have to finish this tonight.

But involvement in what exactly? I wondered and felt in my gut that she was somehow involved with Lois' killer.

※

At 2:00 the next morning, I located a doctor's office on a quiet side street in the Upper Eastside. I knew what to look for and hoped to find it there. In the alley behind the building, using my pocketknife, I slipped open a window lock, lifted the window, and climbed carefully inside, avoiding the metal file cabinet to the left of the casing. I flipped on my Zippo and let the light guide me to a glass cabinet that held an array of medications. A medium-size brown glass bottle of chloroform sat on the top shelf toward the rear. With an unbent paper clip from the good doctor's office desk, I picked the lock and took the brown bottle, then closed and relocked the glass door.

In the examining room, I found lightweight rubber examination gloves. I winced when I realized what type of examination the doctor might have used them for, and located a box of cotton gauze. I took a fistful of gauze and jammed it and two pairs of gloves in my pockets. I wiped down the surfaces I touched and left through the window. It closed smoothly with a dry, rubbing noise, but the frame was marred from my pocketknife where I worked the lock open.

To hell with it. I left quickly.

At the parking garage downtown where I stored my '49 Oldsmobile two-door coupe, I spied a guy dressed in dark, casual clothing standing about fifty feet away from my car. By then, I expected trouble everywhere I would normally go.

He nervously looked around as if he anticipated unwelcome company.

Inaudibly, I wet some gauze, put the bottle quietly on the ground alongside a new black Caddy parked two cars from my Olds, slipped off my shoes, and came up behind him too fast for him to react. He went down after a brief and desperate struggle while clawing at my hand and arm. He was heavy, but stayed in place once I'd propped him in a seated position against the inside brick wall.

I checked my hand and found a superficial scratch that hadn't drawn blood and rubbed it on the seam of my trousers.

After collecting my shoes and the bottle, I slipped my shoes on. I climbed into my car, dug out the Saint Christopher medal and silver chain I'd purchased at the hospital gift shop, and hung them from the rearview mirror. You just never know. I was thinking by then that I would need all the help I could get, and a few blessings couldn't hurt either. Unfortunately, my guard dog didn't guard. He, too, could've used a few blessings.

The Olds started after one pump on the gas pedal and ran like a kitten as I returned to the Bowery.

I checked my watch and saw that it was almost 2:45 a.m. by the time I parked in the dark alley alongside the Twiggs' building.

Surprisingly, I found the building's front entrance unlocked. Using my pocketknife, I jimmied the lock on their apartment's front door. Katlyn, I saw as soon as I was inside with the door closed behind me, slept in the first bedroom. That was my first break in days.

Before she could awaken, I held wet gauze over her nose and mouth. Her eyes popped open and expressed surprised horror when she recognized my face.

I grinned, letting enough teeth show to make it more of the snarl she deserved if she was complicit in the crimes I suspected she committed…accessory to the attempted murder of a cop, and too maybe Lois and my unborn child. Not to mention attempting to shoot me earlier.

She struggled to hold her breath while she tried to scratch my face, squeezed my wrists, nails biting in, as if she thought she might use pain to force me to release her from events she must've suspected would unfold in ways she did not want to experience.

I understood her fear, but I also thought her desperate fight confirmed that she knew something she was afraid or unwilling to tell me.

As she grabbed her purse from a chair alongside her bed and dragged it onto her chest, the chloroform did its job finally. Clearly I hadn't used enough, but I really didn't want to kill her so had been cautious. She deserved prison time.

Her head lolled helplessly, eyes closed. I lifted the gauze before the chemical could kill her or damage her brain. I needed information and Katlyn was about to provide it if I didn't hurt her with the drug.

I quickly looked up and down the hall to make certain her elderly parents, who I suspected still lived there, had not heard us. The apartment remained quiet except for a low, steady snore.

Katlyn, I saw upon examination, wore a long flannel nightgown covered with small yellow sunflowers.

Lois' favorite flower. I took two cotton belts from dresses in her closet and tied her ankles with one, and her wrists behind her back with the other. After looping the strap of her purse over my head so it dangled in front to make it seem she left on her own, I hefted her over my shoulder with a grunt, carried her downstairs slowly, checked the street, found it deserted except for the drunk now asleep on the stoop next door, and slowly walked her to my car.

Once I'd settled her on the front seat, I slipped off my rubber gloves and drove to the destination I'd decided on while eating dinner as the best place I knew of to interrogate anyone involved in Lois' death. The best place to question anyone about anything.

The place was perfect for a quick and thorough grilling, as I'd learned once or twice in the past. Although both of those times I needed information from men. I hated trying to force a woman to do anything, but Katlyn hovered far outside my definition of feminine.

Lou Wilson was an old friend from my abbreviated school days. I'd dropped out to enlist at fourteen, lied about my age, and told the recruiter I graduated high school. I figured my country and freedom should be more important and that finishing school first would not matter much if we lost to the Japs and the Nazis.

My father, an Elizabethan scholar who taught at City College, disagreed. Since he named me for his favorite author, Christopher Marlowe, I guess he'd expected me to amount to more than a Battered Bastard of Bastogne, if I returned at all from the fighting in Europe in something other than a flag-draped coffin.

However, Christopher and I had one other thing in common, it seemed to me. We both knew that you could never bribe the Prince of Darkness, nor could an ordinary man like me outsmart him.

After the war ended, Lou Wilson purchased a butcher shop by the Third Avenue El. After parking in the alley next to it, I used the key he had once provided me so I could keep an eye on the place for him when he left town on business or pleasure. He never knew what I did there on occasion, and I planned to keep it that way if possible.

Five minutes later, I brought Katlyn inside his walk-in meat locker. I stacked sections of beef carcasses to form a rough chair, put a folded old beach blanket I kept in the car trunk down, and sat her on it.

I figured it would take about an hour for the temperature to give her serious frostbite and thought we'd be done long before that might happen.

As I thought of Lois dead by gunshot and Katlyn shooting Stella, aiming down the barrel at me, pulling the trigger, burying a bullet in brick a few feet above my head, something snapped inside. It filled me with a primeval anger so powerful I felt as if I watched someone on a newsreel as I reached for her throat, fingers grazing her pallid flesh like a wolf scenting prey.

Then, as if awakening from a nightmare induced by dreadful battlefield memories I'd suppressed, I felt deeply shamed by my actions, released her immediately, and turned away feeling horrified by what I'd nearly done.

None of this is any good, pal, I thought sadly. *Remember, she might be the only link to whoever shot at Paul and me. It makes sense that either she's the shooter who killed Lois or she knows him. Unless someone else could've told him where we went fishing, but there is no one else.*

Doubt began to eat at me, and I hated the reaction. I knew the image would never leave me. My fingers reaching for her throat bunched into claws of hate as if I wanted them wrapped around her neck to snap the life from within.

"Trust your gut," I said softly, nodded, turned, went outside, and pressed my back against the warm brick wall of the building where it seemed it still held some warmth from the previous day. As I lit up a smoke and exhaled, the moon broke through a layer of clouds between the buildings across the street and grinned at me like Mephistopheles' henchman.

Another shudder ran the length of my spine. I felt deeply troubled that everything in my life turned bad. I wondered if I'd be unable to stop events now cascading out of control. Maybe this time it was me with one foot in the grave and no way to escape death.

"Finish this and learn what she knows. Then you can make different decisions if needed. Like where to hide from the killer or the cops she sends to arrest you for kidnapping her. Shit." My choices were slim before I took her and slimmer afterward if she proved to be innocent.

"Desperate people do desperate things," my mother once said. I felt distressed, despondent, and knew that they made for a bad emotional combination when I added in grief and anger.

I went through two cigarettes' worth of thought before returning inside, where I discovered Katlyn groggy but awake. When I flipped on the overhead lights, she squinted and then glared at me. You might consider her blue eyes startlingly beautiful and you'd be correct. Except for what I knew resided behind them from my experience with her. She housed an evil streak of some kind that threaded itself through her mind like a mental tapeworm, and left her with no feelings of guilt when she decided to fire a loaded gun, taking a shot from less than fifty feet away that she must've known would killed Stella if she didn't miss. She did not miss. Stella got lucky.

"I'm awful thirsty," she said quietly in a voice free of fear.

"I don't really give a shit what you are," I said with intended indifference.

She glanced down at herself and her eyes narrowed, but I could not tell if the look was the result of pain caused by her discomfort or something else.

"What the hell did you do to me, Black?" she asked sullenly.

"Took you for a ride. How do you feel?" I asked without any concern for her response.

"My entire body hurts like hell, and I'm freezing, but you don't care, so why do you ask as if you want me to believe that you do?"

"Sitting on frozen carcasses will do that to a person."

"You dragged me unconscious out of my home in the middle of the night. That might do it too, don't you think? Kidnapping me in my nightgown? What do you think a judge might say about it, Black?"

Her strange sarcastic humor reminded me of someone, but I could not recall whom.

"Sorry, I didn't have the time to dress you for the occasion first, so this will have to do for now." I waved a hand at her.

"Did you like what you saw, Marlowe Black? Did you want to have sex with me too?" She attempted a smile, but her lips quivered with anger or pain.

At least she did not say rape.

"It was dark at the time we left your apartment. I couldn't see much except for sunflowers."

And my hands a few minutes ago, I thought grimly and looked away.

"I think my shoulder is bruised badly." She winced briefly.

I went to her and felt both shoulders. She tried to bite me, failed, kicked me in the left knee, slid down the frozen meat, and landed on her back.

I backed away, rubbed my knee, and then put my hands on my hips.

"The guy who owns this place won't be in today. It's Sunday. I can leave you trussed up like a turkey ready for dressing until you either cooperate or freeze to death. I prefer that you answer my questions, but truthfully, after all you've done, at least what I know of, I don't care if you don't answer. However, if you answer me honestly, then I'll take you back. It's your decision, Katlyn, so choose."

"Tell me why I'm here," she said as if she really did not know, which I supposed she still did not unless she figured out that I learned about her clerk job.

It's about time you asked that one.

"You killed a friend of mine and have been trying to kill me. You told someone where Paul Dunbar and I went fishing, and whoever you told attempted to kill both of us, or you tried to kill us."

"Who is the friend that I allegedly killed?" She didn't react in any other way as if she was at least guilty of something related to my second statement, or was indifferent as a casual observer was to a traffic accident. Katlyn acted as if we sat in her living room conversing about weather.

A slow chill not related to the room temperature crept down my spine as I told her who died and stared at her face. Her eyes pinched enough to let me know that she knew Lois, and led me to believe that she really was involved in Lois' death.

Damn glad she doesn't have a gun right now.

"Never heard of the name before this minute." She looked away.

"Bullshit, Katlyn. I just saw it in your eyes."

I walked across the freezer to the thermostat and tapped the glass that covered the thermometer to get her attention. When she looked at me, I said, "Not freezing…yet."

I made a show of adjusting the dial down to twenty-eight degrees.

"That should do it though," I said and fought a shiver as frigid air blew hard across my back from the large overhead refrigeration unit.

"I'll return in a few minutes and we can talk more then." I went outside into the early June predawn morning, lit a Camel, and smoked it all while worrying at the idea that I still could not be certain of her involvement. It felt right, but misgivings manipulated my thoughts.

Let's get this done now.

When I returned ten minutes later, I found her staring defiantly, but starting to shiver from the increased cold.

"You ready to talk? Ready to tell the truth?" I asked and squatted before her.

"Fuck you, Black. Your whore's dead and I don't give a goddamn about her." She spit at my face without any other acknowledgment that she had right then admitted her guilt.

Careful examination showed a light blue cast to her flesh, and I knew she was as tough as nails. However, the biggest spike bends under the right pressure, and my anger felt like a ten-pound sledgehammer. I needed to force a full confession, and then decide how to make it work in court.

I shook my head in disgust, dropped the temperature to fifteen degrees, and tapped the glass loud enough that she could hear it over the fans.

"You'll freeze to death in three minutes or less, Katlyn, unless you want to talk to me first. I understand that it's not such a terrible way to go. First, you shiver violently without control, and then you get sleepy. When you finally doze off, that's the end of the game. You'll never wake up again. You will be just as dead as the cattle you're sitting on, and maybe they'll plant you in Potter's Field.

"You'll have nothing on you that the cops could use to identify you. They'll assume you're a damn prostitute and you got locked in accidentally. Your purse is in my car, so I'll toss it off the bridge into the East River."

I turned and walked to the door of the freezer and reached behind me to close it. Part of me was ready to give up on her, leave, and head back to Brooklyn and Stella.

"Okay, you son of a bitch!" Her teeth chattered her shout. "I know who shot your ex-prostitute of a girlfriend, but I didn't kill her. Why would I do that? She never double-crossed me the way Stella Vichery did." She spoke more rapidly, as if more afraid of being left alone than of dying.

After adjusting the thermostat to its original temperature setting, I lifted her onto my shoulder and carried her outside.

"Lois was never in prostitution," I growled.

"So you think, Black. Ever consider asking her why she did not have a day job, where she went the nights that she wasn't home to fix you dinner? She was in bed with some John or in the backseat of his car in an alley giving him pleasure with her mouth and getting paid cash for it. You're a typical man. You don't think, you just act."

Lois went to work every day. I used to watch her leave and watch her return home after me. I hated the seed of doubt Twiggs burrowed into my memories, but shook it off.

Then, she opened her mouth wide as if to scream.

"Scream and so help me God, I'll put a bullet between your eyes," I told her with deadly calm. "Not a soul lives anywhere nearby. This neighborhood is all shops like this or mom-and-pop stores. The cops rarely patrol these streets at night because there's no crime around here."

"I believe you would kill me." She still shivered, teeth chattering louder.

"Shit, woman, you tried to kill me yesterday."

I put a lit cigarette between her lips and watched it bobbing as she sucked in the hot smoke.

"Now tell me who shot Lois and why he killed her. Is it the same person you told about Paul and me fishing upstate?" I asked, not wanting to dwell on her claim about Lois' employment. I'd never asked Lois about her income, never even thought to question her about it. Hell, her source of money was not my damn business then. The possibility she was a hooker did not lessen my feelings for her one iota.

"I don't know why he killed her. Said he wanted to get rid of another whore, and, yeah, he's the same guy I told about your fishing trip. His name is Bobby Palmer. He was a Marine sniper in the Pacific during the war—a hundred and fifty-two kills, he claimed when I first met him." Her tone of voice made me think she was impressed by his accomplishment, and maybe in love too.

His name sounded familiar, and his involvement explained the shooter's marksmanship if he never intended to kill any of us, *but why wouldn't he have?*

"He shot at Stella too in my office building?"

"Said he only wanted to wing you and her both as a warning for you to butt the fuck out of his personal affairs."

"Warning me to do what? What affairs…killing Lois?"

"He wouldn't tell me more than that, but I think it had to do with your girlfriend being a hooker, or maybe had to do with something in his past, or maybe he decided that any man who loves a whore should suffer for it. The only thing I know for certain is that he wanted you to ignore him, leave him alone just like I wanted and still do."

"He could've asked me politely." I struggled to ignore the last of what she'd said because not all of her information made sense right then.

Why kill my girl and then expect me to ignore him? Especially after he tried to wound Stella and me, and kill Paul? Make me suffer because I loved Lois? I doubted that too.

"That's really why he told you he killed her?"

"That and he hates you, but really, I don't know why he hates you."

"He fired the shots at Detective Paul Dunbar too, right?"

She shrugged, looked at my face, and then added quickly, "He said something about you dragging a cop into it and making the situation worse for him. I didn't know what he meant by that either. Bobby is not an easy man to understand. He had me tell him where the two of you went fishing upstate. Hell, Black, he arranged for me to get the clerk's job with the cops. He knows a lot of people in town, important people he works for occasionally. But Bobby isn't much of a talker. If you start asking him questions about himself, he shuts right up."

"Where can I find your friend Bobby Palmer?" I had a strong feeling that she held back information I needed to learn, but what and why were beyond me right then. Pressing her too hard might only make her lie about everything she told me just to get me to back off. That type of information was, more often than not, deadly or ineffective, either way useless.

She shook her head and spit out the spent cigarette. Sparks exploded around and over my left foot.

"You don't find him. Bobby finds you, Black. And next time he does, he'll likely put a single bullet in your head." She sounded sure of herself as if she also believed that the killer would protect her from me.

What the hell's he got against me? I thought and crushed her spent butt with the heel of my scuffed shoe.

"Describe him to me."

"He's tall, about six one, weighs around two thirty, all muscle, dirty blond hair and gray eyes. He has a slight limp and a recent scar high on his left cheek shaped like a hook. He's also incredibly unpleasant, so you two should get along just fine, if you live long enough to meet him and discover that for yourself."

Obviously, she felt recovered in more ways than one, and thought she now had the upper hand. I knew I could not return her to her apartment. Did not want her calling Palmer and telling him that she'd revealed his name and description to me. I did not like the way her involvement felt either, yet didn't want her dead if she told Palmer about our discussion and he turned on her.

Hell of a damn mess and getting worse.

"How'd you get tangled up with a son of a bitch like him in the first place?" I asked to make her think I cared.

"He knew that you helped Stella with the coins, turned in her father, which cost me the buckle by the way. When he came around to collect it, I had no choice but to let him know it was your fault I didn't have the silver buckle." She watched my face carefully.

He hates me for that? Or for loving Lois? This dame is full of crap. There's something else and she either doesn't know what that might be or she's withholding information.

"So he's a collector of war relics too, and you had his cash? Must've been some serious money."

"I had a substantial down payment, which I needed to spend before the transaction could be concluded."

"What about the money you got from Stella?" I asked. "That was pretty substantial too."

"It was already committed to pay off old markers."

"You're a gambler as well?"

"My asshole brother was the gambler, remember him? The body in your office?" Her eyes narrowed, lips flattened and paled with anger, disgust and something more like regret maybe.

"You mean your brother Greg? He's hard to forget."

"Right, that asshole. Now what are you going to do with me?" she asked and frowned cautiously. "You taking me back home?"

"No. I can't do that now, can I, but I'll think of something."

The best option, I thought, *is to take her to the cabin Dunbar rented for a month upstate.* I went back, straightened up the frozen beef, grabbed my blanket, and locked up Lou's place.

"We're leaving," I said and lifted her before she could protest. "Give me any trouble and you'll ride in the trunk."

Her face displayed her contempt. As I watched her, I felt quite certain that she was more complicit in Palmer's activities than she admitted and in ways I would need to unravel soon.

I'll get to the heart of all that later. I put her on the rear seat, dumped the blanket in the trunk, and climbed behind the wheel.

Chapter Thirteen

We reached Brooklyn before sunrise. Fortunately, Katlyn remained quiet and subdued during the ride. I parked in the driveway between the house and the garage.

Stella snored lightly as I entered the bedroom. *Glad you didn't miss me, doll,* I thought wryly and smiled at her.

She woke with a start as I shook her shoulder lightly. When she opened her eyes and recognized me, she jumped out of bed and threw her arms around me.

"I don't know whether to kiss or to punch you," she said softly.

I solved it for her and pressed my lips tight against hers.

When she pulled back a moment later to catch her breath, I said, "We won't be setting up the Lionel train set today. We have to leave right now."

"Why? What happened?" she asked, sounding alert and wary and maybe frightened.

I told her what I'd tried to do and ended up doing, without all the sordid details, and watched her eyes widen.

She nodded when I finished, but looked worried. "I knew she'd be nothing but trouble, Marlowe. I'll go pack us some clothing."

"Thanks, I'll put together food and drinks for the trip." I lit a cigarette and enjoyed the first inhale.

Fifteen minutes later, after collecting Gabby, his food, and his leash, we drove the Shore Parkway and then entered the Brooklyn Battery Tunnel.

Once beyond city limits, Stella turned and examined Katlyn. "We'll need something for her to wear."

"She's dressed good enough for me," I retorted and sounded as uncaring as I felt.

Stella put her hand on my forearm and squeezed lightly. "I understand how you feel about her. I do too. After all, she shot me, attempted to kill me. But if you get pulled over by the police, how do you explain the way she looks?"

"She was a drunk we picked up and decided to give her a lift home," I said quickly and thought, *She's possibly an accomplice to a goddamn killer and she will scream bloody murder to any cop who stops me.*

"Um, she is tied up, Marlowe."

I wanted to argue that Katlyn knew Lois and her killer, set up Paul and me for target practice, and was somehow deeply involved with Palmer, but also knew that Stella had a valid point and that I should not ignore her opinions.

"All we have are men's clothing, right?" I asked and glanced at her.

"That'll have to do," she said. "Pull off onto the first quiet side street you come to. Then you can watch her while I get her dressed."

"You stupid bitch," Katlyn cursed. "Don't try to touch me or I'll claw your whoring eyes out."

"She is tied up good, isn't she?" Stella asked worriedly.

"You can count on that, but you'll need to untie her to change her clothing." I attempted a grin as if I wanted her to believe dressing Katlyn might be easy, but it fell flat.

Katlyn had already provided the knowledge that she was more than a run-of-the-mill pain in the ass. With a nod, I indicated the brown paper bag on the floor by Stella's feet. "Use what's in there. It'll knock her out for a while."

She lifted the sack and peered inside, pulled the glass bottle out, and read the label. Her lips moved silently, and she glanced at me twice before speaking.

"What store did you buy this from, Marlowe?" She frowned as our eyes met. Her forefinger clicked the brown glass.

"I used a five-finger discount at a doctor's office on the Upper Eastside."

"Think he might miss it when he opens his office tomorrow morning?" She rubbed the label.

"Think I might really give a damn if he does?" I winked and my grin felt more relaxed. "I left no fingerprints or trace of my visit behind."

She laughed dryly and shook her head, but I thought she seemed displeased with my response.

"You gotta do what you gotta do sometimes if you're going to get the job finished," I said and knew it came out sounding like an excuse.

When I turned off the highway onto a lonely side street with only two houses on it—both at the far end—Stella pulled on the rubber gloves, opened the bottle, and soaked a strip of gauze. She got out and climbed onto the rear seat.

Katlyn looked ready to fight for escape, bite Stella if necessary to accomplish the goal. She even snarled like a cornered rat.

I lifted my .45 from the holster and jacked a round into the chamber. There had been a bullet in it. That round popped out and landed in the middle of Katlyn's lap like a sucker's bet. Illumination from the overhead light sparked the brass casing, and Katlyn's gaze fell to examine it, and then back up to stare into the end of the big Colt's barrel.

After that, she did not move or look away until the drug dropped her into unconsciousness.

"That was nicely dramatic." Stella handed me the bullet after checking the bottom as if unsure if the .45 was live or expended.

"That's the way some people like it best, helps them understand meaning and conclusion," I said and pocketed the bullet.

She untied Katlyn and held up the blue jeans and a red flannel button-down shirt that she would use. I turned away before she removed the sunflower-covered cotton nightgown.

"Leave her with bare feet," I said and got out.

While she made Katlyn look presentable, I walked Gabby down the street and back, pausing often for him to smell objects I did not want to know about. He finally lifted a hind leg by the side of an empty trash can as if he needed his relief to make enough noise to warn off other animals regarding his ferocious presence. And there were no available sofas in the area.

Then he scratched at the ground as if digging a hole and gave a short bark of happy satisfaction. He was educating me about how dogs and some people have much in common—posturing, that is.

When I returned to the car, I looked at Katlyn.

"Tie her up please," I said to Stella, took the soiled nightgown, and locked it in the wheel well in the trunk along with the chloroform, gloves, and gauze.

Following that, we made good time. Our captive remained unconscious until after I parked in front of the cabin. The country quiet felt like a relief from trying to evade a killer in the canyons of the city.

Together, Stella and I hauled Katlyn inside and put her on the bed in the bedroom Dunbar used during his brief stay and then tied her arms to the bedpost with the cloth belts I used on her earlier. I dropped her purse on the table by the sofa.

Too bad we don't have the book that Paul read, I thought. *Twiggs might learn something about living and dying from its author.*

After closing the bedroom door, Stella took my hand and led me outside. We let Gabby run and bark at the birds.

"What's on your mind, doll?" I asked and tried to read her expression. We strolled to the edge of the lake, stopping about fifty feet from where Dunbar dropped bleeding in the water.

"How about kidnapping, burglary, and assault?" she asked but did not look my way. "What were you thinking?"

"Who do you think Katlyn might want to report that to? The shooter? If she goes to the cops, I'll tell them what I know from what she told me. Katlyn knew an awful lot about this guy Palmer to have made any of it up. She's too smart to try something like turning me in when she knows what I've learned about her activities."

Stella seemed to mull that over and then shrugged as if her deductions came up inconclusive.

"She could lie to the cops. Tell them she didn't tell you anything about Palmer."

"She could, but I don't think she is quite clever enough, and she is a bad liar. You can read it in her eyes. Any cop worth his salt would see it. Besides, she has a rap sheet after what she did to you and her relationship to her brother."

She nodded, stayed silent a minute. "We can't leave her here alone," she said at last.

"No, we can't do that. I guess you'll have to stay with her. You could keep her tied to something so she can't break free and hurt you while you're sleeping." My suggestion did not sound workable even as I spoke the words.

"If anything happens to me or to her, Marlowe, I won't have a car to use to go for help if you have it in mind to return to the city." With both hands, she scrubbed her face, rubbed her eyes, and then ran her fingers through her hair.

"No, and I don't know what to do about that yet." I grasped one of her hands and we walked along the lakefront.

We located a dry log and sat, stared at the water a minute as if an answer to the problem might appear from the mirage-like shimmer on the mirrored surface. Then, I knew how to solve this one.

"There's a train station in town. You can drive me there in the morning, and I'll take the train back to the city." Gabby appeared, took a scratch behind his ears from me, and darted back into the woods while barking at whatever elusive animal he scented and chased.

"Are you sure?" She looked relieved.

I nodded and glanced at the horizon. Clouds rode it, catching the early pinks and oranges of sunset. Birdsong made our surroundings a bit surreal compared to how I'd lived over the past few weeks. There was a different type of life around the lake. Life that knew a freedom I never did or would. I could not say that I missed it either.

"There's no working phone in the cabin. How will I know when you'll be returning to get us?" she asked a moment later and picked at her shirtsleeve nervously.

"One way or the other, I'll get word to you, or take the train back and bum a ride out here." I knew she was afraid and put my arm around her shoulders. Inviting me into her life must have felt like discovering that the Cole Brothers Circus elephant ran loose in her home hunted by a pride of hungry lionesses or insane clowns. I knew I was a piece of work and felt bad for her, but I did warn her ahead of time. Sometimes justice for me is worth almost any price as long as I don't cross the line that is the law. I knew I'd come close in the past, had now with Katlyn, but I felt strongly that she was the key to not only Lois' murder but to Palmer.

She twisted side to side, as if she needed to work out a serious cramp. "You think the gunman might return here soon?" She glanced at me, but managed to keep her face nearly expressionless as if she did not want me to read her feelings. I did not need to. She radiated fear, and an emotion with a deeper manifestation: loneliness.

"I think it's highly unlikely. He knows we left here and returned to the city if the guy I knocked out in the parking garage reported back to him. However, he does not know where we stayed once we arrived in town, and can't know now whether we're still anywhere in the city or if we left again. I'll also bet he thinks he understands me well enough to be aware that I'd not return to a place where he could easily sneak up on me and put a bullet in my head while I slept. So no, he doesn't know we're back at the cabin."

"Okay, that sounds about the way I was thinking. And of course you'll be extra careful when you get home?"

I opened my mouth to respond and felt the words dry out on the back of my tongue as a loud crash and scream ripped through the pseudo calm Stella and I conjured.

"Katlyn." Stella jumped up and ran to the cabin before I could stop her.

Chapter Fourteen

Stella and Gabby beat me inside by a good ten seconds. I found Stella staring at Katlyn with both hands pressed hard against her mouth as if she needed to scream but nothing would come out. Her eyes were wide and filled with horror.

Gabby whined and ran out of the bedroom with his tail between his legs.

Katlyn Twiggs lay half out of bed, half on the floor and looked nearly dead. When she fell, she tangled her arms with the headboard. Both of her shoulders appeared grotesquely dislocated, as if she thought she could use the bedpost to snap the belts and slipped, twisted, and somehow dropped off the side of the bed.

That must've hurt like hell, I thought grimly.

Clearly, the escape attempt was not one of her better decisions, if any had ever been good since her collusion with her brother Gregory when he decided to do a double-cross with men who took no prisoners and had no problem killing him to prove their point of noninterference in their affairs.

Gabby reappeared briefly, tail drooped between his legs. After a quick sniff of Twiggs' feet, he darted into the living room as if he knew what would happen next and wanted no part of it. I felt certain that I would find him hiding behind the sofa and for a moment yearned to join him in a place where I would not be discovered.

Mercifully for us Katlyn passed out. Her breathing came in jerky, shallow sobs of pain.

I used the opportunity to free her hands and to reset the shoulder joints. The left one made a hideous wet snapping sound. Stella moaned and collapsed on the floor in a faint, folding up like a marionette that had its central strings cut.

Frowning, I placed Katlyn on the bed, tied her hands and feet to the bedposts. Then I carried Stella into the living room and placed her on the sofa. I cracked open the fifth of bourbon Dunbar brought with him just in case he got bored with my company. I'd found the bottle of booze in the nightstand alongside his bed. I was surprised and pleased to find the seal intact.

One good strong sniff brought Stella around. Her eyelids fluttered and lifted slowly. I fetched an on-the-rocks glass, filled it half full of ice from the old-time oak icebox adjacent to the kitchen sink, poured bourbon into it, and held out the stiff drink.

"Try a swig of this," I said and laughed with relief as she coughed after a long swallow.

"My God, Marlowe, are you trying to choke me to death or get me drunk enough to take advantage of me while I'm defenseless?" she asked hoarsely and coughed into her fist. Her attempted humor perhaps was poorly timed, but the relief I felt was a blessing. *If any damn thing about this might be one.*

I found it too difficult to stop laughing. I felt as if I'd lost my mind. Every thought was funny, and then Stella joined me until tears streamed down her cheeks too.

The dog seemed to enjoy the hilarity. His tail rapidly beat the floor while he sat at my feet watching us.

Still chuckling, I used a clean handkerchief to wipe Stella's face. Then I patted the top of the dog's head.

"Sorry," I said. "That shouldn't have been so damn funny."

I nearly started in again and bit the inside of my cheek. Then I felt calmer than I had for days, and more in control too.

That got me thinking seriously about the string of crimes I'd committed to get information out of Twiggs. For a minute, I felt stricken with guilt and knew I'd more than likely get busted for it, wondered how I might explain my actions to Paul. Then I decided that Katlyn's admissions and the information she told me regarding Palmer would smooth it over satisfactorily. Didn't help me feel less guilty, but even then I couldn't think there'd been an alternative.

In addition, she was an accomplice and a material witness. Hell, I couldn't forget her attempt on my life and Stella's too. For some reason I kept pushing that aside as if because she was a woman such a thing could never happen.

But it did, pal.

Dunbar might not be thrilled with my performance, but if the facts I gathered through our conversation brought a killer to justice, a killer who also shot a cop and an innocent bystander, he and the courts should accept my actions as necessity, I hoped.

"I'll light a fire," I said after finishing with difficult thinking, and hoped I would succeed with the fire. I'd never dealt with a situation such as the one Palmer and Twiggs dragged me into. It was uncharted waters and I truly felt a bit fearful.

"I'll fix us something to eat," she said, sounding calmer now that she had a mundane and predictable task to perform.

I used my Zippo to ignite newspaper under a stack of dried oak faggots, a name I have never understood the roots of.

"We only have canned stew and water," Stella called from the kitchen.

"That'll have to do for now." Thinking back, I recalled loading food in the car before leaving Irwin's house. "There are supplies in the trunk. I'll get them once I'm done in here."

To my surprise the kindling caught, and a moment later flames licked the sides of the dried split oak logs.

When I returned with an armful of groceries from the car, I heard Katlyn shout, "Hey! Where the hell are you? I need a goddamn bathroom, and my arms and shoulders hurt like hell. What did you do to me this time, you assholes?"

Not as much as I'd like to do, I thought and wrestled with the urge to grind my teeth.

Stella met me at the kitchen doorway, watched silently as I put the supplies on the table, and gave me a helpless shrug when our eyes met. Her face told me she wished Katlyn would have stayed unconscious for the night and she would like to be somewhere else too, no longer tangled in the aftermath of Lois' death.

Hell, doll, you volunteered. But I felt sorry she had.

"If you can help her, I'll let her see the .45. She seems to respect that," I said quietly.

Stella bit her lower lip as if to hold back contradictory dialogue I might disagree with and nodded offhandedly.

When she stepped into the bedroom, Katlyn grimaced with obvious exaggeration as if the pain from her shoulders or bladder might be more than she could endure.

Spare me the dramatics, I thought. *Pee if you need to but get it over with.*

"I'm going to make you pay for this, bitch," she said with venom in her words. She glanced daggers at me and added, "You too, Black. You think you can get away with kidnapping and threatening to hurt me? You have no idea who you are dealing with. I'll call the cops the minute I can and turn you in."

Please skip the bullshit, I thought. Using my thumb, I slowly flipped off the safety and held the gun where she could see it.

"Regardless of what you imagine about your own conduct, when it comes to your dealings with Bobby Palmer or what you knew about Lois, reported to Palmer about Paul and me fishing, just your being aware that he killed her and not reporting the crime to the police immediately means you aided and abetted a murderer, Katlyn," I said using a dead monotone. "In New York State, that's the same as if you aimed the gun and pulled the trigger yourself. If you don't get a ride in the electric chair, you'll get twenty-five to life. And let's not forget shooting Stella and taking a shot at me. I dug out the bullet to give to the cops. The rifling from the barrel will prove it was from your gun."

She continued to glare, but remained quiet while she seemed to sort through the implication of my short lecture. Then she allowed

Stella to tie her hands after she was off the bed and on her feet.

As the women reached the bathroom, I put my foot where it would block the door from closing.

"Don't watch me, you lousy bastard," she cried, sounding defeated, and allowed Stella to lower her jeans.

I looked away before the waistband was opened or any private exposure could transpire until I heard the toilet flush, and glanced back in time to witness Katlyn swing her arms up and over Stella's head as Stella faced me, straightening after she pulled up and buttoned Katlyn's denim trousers.

Immediately, she had Stella in a chokehold and made her objective plain by yanking back and brutally enough to make Stella's eyes bulge.

"Don't come near me, Black, or she dies while you watch." She pulled harder, knuckles whitening. I knew she would kill Stella if she continued applying pressure. "I'll snap the bitch's neck and I can do it too!" she screamed.

It was not difficult to believe her.

Stella gasped, choked, and slowly turned deep crimson. Her arms flailed helplessly as she attempted to reach Katlyn's hands or arms, and found she could not. Her eyes were focused on me, expressing a terror that ripped into my heart.

With heart pounding, I deliberately, so Twiggs might see exactly what I did, raised the Colt, aimed, and pulled the trigger. In the small room, the blast was loud enough to make my ears ring. I could smell the cordite. Stella cringed, but could not move.

Katlyn physically cowered and clenched her eyes tight, making her face appear compressed. The .45 slug burrowed a nice irregular thumb-sized hole in the wall six inches away from the left side of her head. Its heat must have singed her ear.

Before she reacted further or recovered enough to resume her assault, I took two steps and slammed the barrel against the base of Katlyn's skull. The blow felt an awful lot better than it should have.

She collapsed against Stella. I struggled and wrestled desperately to separate them. Stella was alive, coughing and gasping when I finally freed her from Twiggs' chokehold. My heart was pounding.

Without another thought, I let Katlyn drop to the floor with a boneless thud and, carefully, gently checked Stella's neck.

"Looks like you'll have a few nasty bruises," I said, "but nothing feels broken or damaged."

"Thank you, Marlowe." Her voice sounded hoarse as she rubbed her neck, gingerly prodding the muscles. "It seems like you keep saving my life." She tried a smile and failed. "Maybe it's habit forming."

I put my palm flat against her cheek, unable to come up with a good response, and let her read the emotions and apology in my eyes. *You should have stayed the hell away from me, damn it.*

She leaned the weight of her head against my hand as if to demonstrate her trust, which I was sure I did not deserve.

I kissed the top of her head before I dragged our prisoner to the bedroom and placed her on the mattress, where I tied her down again.

When we returned to the kitchen, I said, "If you'd stay away from trouble for a while, I wouldn't have to keep rescuing you." *Meaning stayed away from me.*

Stella smiled, seemed to find what I said humorous enough under the circumstances, and then prepared franks and beans in a frying pan with hands that still shook from her ordeal. Occasionally she reached up and rubbed her throat.

After we started eating, I examined her carefully. Her neck had swelled. "We do have a serious problem with Katlyn, don't we?"

Nodding, Stella drank a large swallow of bourbon. "I don't think I can handle her alone. She wants me dead too."

"No, you can't do it. However, I could shoot her in the knees," I said with dry humor and heard a trace of deadly intent in my voice that widened Stella's eyes.

After slowly running my hand across my chin and feeling a day's stubble, I leaned back and crossed my arms over my chest. "I'm kidding around of course."

"I know," she said. "But it got me thinking in ways I'm not too proud of."

"Me too. This business will either kill you outright, eat you alive, one piece at a time, or make you so hard inside no one'll ever get past the barriers you erect to stay sane and alive."

And keep the people you care about alive too, I thought but did not say it aloud.

"Clearly, I made a mistake bringing her up here, but at the time, I couldn't think what else to do. Guess I could have turned her over to the cops, but the way I got her confession made that impossible. She would've denied everything, and I'd be in jail for kidnapping, and Palmer would remain free."

"I know," she said. "I think you did the right thing, but now it's gotten very complicated."

She scraped back her chair and stood, carried our plates and flatware to the sink, filled it with cold water and added soap.

I thought perhaps my words had her thinking hard about her decision to become a private cop, and felt sure that she would change her mind long before we located, apprehended, or killed Bobby Palmer.

Listening to her working as she set up a large pot to heat dishwater, I went over, leaned a hip on the counter alongside the sink, and massaged her neck and shoulders.

"Tell you what," I started, "I'll go visit Dunbar at the hospital tomorrow and see if he's up to leaving his confinement and staying with you for the type of convalescence that might make him feel better or at least more useful. I know he hates lying around with nothing to do."

She nodded, moaned under my ministrations, dried her hands, and then faced me. Her arms went around my shoulders, and in twenty seconds, we were on the floor in front of the sofa. After thirty minutes of passion that felt a lot closer to raw emotion than love, sweat made our bodies glow in the firelight.

I lit two cigarettes and gave her one, then went out and poured heated water on the dishes in the plugged sink.

After that, I fetched a wool blanket, returned, and let her rest her head on my chest while my heart slowed and I covered us with the blanket. We listened to fire crackling the logs, watched the flames dance the thickening shadows, and for a brief moment I experienced what I knew would not or could not last, or be a permanent part of my life. For the first time since Lois died, I again knew how it felt to be happy with a woman I could easily spend my life with. However, that would not be in my future. Lois was my final attempt with that part of normalcy.

"Tell me, Marlowe." Stella spoke quietly, sounding like she'd awakened from a pleasant dream.

"Tell you what, doll?" I stroked the hair off her brow with two fingers.

"How can someone as young as you be involved in the kind of work you do and be so focused and determined?"

Her question took me by surprise. "I'm not a cop anymore," I answered evasively, knowing what she meant.

"I didn't mean it that way." She turned her head and kissed my chest.

She did not distract me. "I started young. I enlisted in forty-three, right before my fifteenth birthday. I lied to get in so I could fight to save our country. Guess I looked older, or they felt a desperate need for recruits."

"You stay in for two years?"

"Something along those lines. I finished my reserve obligation last year."

"That makes you about twenty-three, twenty-four now?"

"Yeah sure, that's close enough. At least according to my birth certificate that's my age." I hadn't meant to expose that raw nerve, and knew she would exploit the opening to a piece of my character that I rarely allowed anyone to investigate.

"What do you mean by that?" she asked, sounding innocent enough.

I glanced down, expected to see the top of her head, but her eyes returned my gaze with expectancy. She had beautiful eyes.

"Before I went to basic training, I was your typical kid. I liked girls, and cars, played stickball in the street and skated in the winter, and spent long summer days at the beach. After returning stateside in late forty-five, I felt like an old man all tired out and used up.

"Some days I couldn't recall how I once lived, what I once enjoyed. Then I started learning about how many of my closest friends had died or been severely injured during the war. That's when I turned away from the past completely. I concluded right then that I'd never look back again.

"There's nothing there except memories of my old man's grave disappointment that I hadn't amounted to much of anything as far as he was concerned. Never mind that I did my duty, took a bullet in France, held my buddy's hand as the last of his life wheezed from the large shrapnel wound torn through the left side of his chest." I caught myself losing control, but did not want to stop as if just this one time it might be safe to share my emotions with her. Besides, she did not try to encourage or interrupt me with more questions.

"After I found a place to live in Brooklyn, Paul Dunbar convinced me to join the cops. I walked a beat, watched hookers get manhandled by pimps and beaten by Johns, occasionally killed in the process. I saw drunks and drug users fall face first into gutters while everyone looked away as if those guys, many of them veterans, might be less than the rest of us and did not deserve the common decency that came with birth in our great nation. And then there was the parade of crooks, killers, and other slime balls marching through the courts. If they could afford the best attorneys, they either got reduced sentences or walked free without a day of punishment.

"What pissed me off the most was when a Negro guy I knew was a veteran got beaten by two cops downtown for mouthing off at them, and the cops' superiors looked the other way.

"I told Dunbar off when he defended them without knowing the facts and resigned the following morning; decided I could and would do better as a private cop. Yeah, all of that did make me cold, determined, and focused."

Again, I stopped myself. I wanted to tell her about how many men from my unit we left behind buried in Europe. How many of them were blown to bits, so we never found enough to ship home, how many of them lost limbs and would remain crippled forever, or the poor bastards who lost their minds after one too many bullets or mortar rounds, artillery shells blasting holes in the earth several feet away.

We left the real heroes buried behind us, and brought home the wounded and the walking dead, and I became determined to honor their memories in my own way by handing out justice to the bastards who wanted to tear pieces from the society that those boys died to protect and preserve. However, it seemed I could never do that when I wore the blue uniform.

Finally I said, "Hell, if you weren't there you can't understand. I talk to a few guys at the VFW hall, but most of them want to forget too, or get too drunk to remember instead."

"I lived through the war in Europe, Marlowe, remember that. We got trapped in Germany." Her voice came out muffled against my chest and I could feel her tears on my flesh.

"I remember very well," I said too harshly. Her father trapped his own family behind enemy lines under the hobnailed authoritarian rule of lunatics. The greedy bastard put money before family and love of country.

Now he was on his way to Israel for a new type of justice for those who participated in or supported mass murder, genocide. He'd get prison time, not death by hanging, but in the end he might be sorry that the Israelis allowed him to have what he helped to deny millions of Jews, the opportunity to live a long life. Her father would be released a ruined and broken man.

I thought Stella might insist on hearing more and braced myself to tell her that I'd already shared more than I intended.

But I was wrong. Stella fell asleep with her ear where she could hear my heartbeat, and I wept inside for the friends I'd lost, those left behind in the forests of Germany. And too for the horrendous loss of Lois, her love and her friendship, whether she was a hooker or not.

She'd become a real pal, something I'd found rare in a relationship with any woman before her and knew I might never find again. And for the loss of the child I'd never know, love, and watch grow into an adult. Becoming a father would be elusive too, if not left out of my life permanently.

I felt unsure how that last thought made me feel, but refused to let it sway my decision about marital involvement with Stella or any other women.

When I drifted off, I realized that Katlyn had not awakened, and then thought nothing more until morning sun lit the room.

Chapter Fifteen

After helping Stella with Katlyn, having breakfast that we cooked together and fed part of to Twiggs, I went out to the car.

Gabby ran to the end of the lake as I drove off at mid-morning. Stella stood nervously in the doorway, and I worked hard at ignoring the expression that furrowed her brow. By the way she fingered the edge of the dishtowel clutched in her right hand, the intensity of her fear at being alone with Katlyn for as long as the two hours I expected to be away was evident.

Hell, I couldn't blame her. Katlyn had now attempted to kill Stella twice without remorse. If I'd not been in the cabin the second time, I would be planning to bury Stella instead of driving to get Paul. Worse still, her death would be on my head. Regardless of what Stella said about her involvement, I was the one who dragged Twiggs back into her life.

Yet I knew in my gut that Katlyn had failed to disclose a murder to protect the killer. And who but she could know what other violent crimes marred her past. When it came to breaking the law, it seemed some women proved themselves as capable as any man, past or present.

Paul Dunbar sat in bed reading Sun Tzu's *The Art of War*. The door to his room stood open, so he'd failed to hear me when I entered, or he could have decided that I might be another nurse with a hypodermic he should ignore until I dragged a metal chair over and sat next to his bed.

He glanced up and actually seemed pleased to discover me seated alongside him.

"In case you're wondering, Betty's fine. I really don't think she misses you too much though, pal. She gave me a lot of attention like she was thinking seriously about having a new man in her life," I said with a grin. "She kept flipping her tail in my direction. So I'm real sorry that I've got to tell you this, but I'm thinking it over real sincerely."

"I'm not worried about you, Marlowe. I saw you with Gabby. You're too much of a dog person for Betty to get serious about you. She can sense things like that, you know." He grinned too. "Thanks for checking on her."

"How old is that book?" I asked with a nod.

"This copy's new, but the original was written about twenty-four hundred years ago."

"You think what you're reading could still be relevant millennia after the fact?" I asked to keep the small talk progressing and us away from the tensions that stressed our friendship over the past three or four years. Not to mention telling him about Twiggs.

He stared thoughtfully and closed the book on his finger to mark his page. "I think Sun Tzu would've given Ike and Mac both a run for their money."

"That's saying a lot in his favor." I looked around the spartan room. There was too much shiny chrome and white ceramic and bland green paint for my taste.

He watched and said, "Boring damn place, isn't it?"

"I'll take your word for it because I can't think of any reason I might want to find out otherwise." I stared out the window at the distant mountains. "View's all right if you like that kind of thing, but nothing moves. It's like looking at a window in a Rockwell painting. Me, I'll take a line of skyscrapers and traffic any day of the week."

He chuckled, appeared to be on the mend, and also seemed to feel more relaxed. Dunbar looked a few years younger too.

"You look better," I commented and waved a hand to indicate his face.

"Same for you, Marlowe. Thanks for dragging me up here to the hospital." His eyes expressed his gratitude too. "You know you probably saved my life this time."

"Wouldn't do for me to leave you in the lake, Paul. Most likely that would've killed the fish we couldn't catch. All of them. Besides, you're right, I'm not a cat person."

Then he cut to the chase, but not without a lazy smile to let me know he had not overreacted to my usual dry humor.

"Glad you feel that way and I'm sure Betty will too. Now tell me you found the son of a bitch who shot me and he's behind bars or…"

"No, not dead or locked up, but I'm sure I know his name now and what he looks like. I'll have his ass in a sling in a few days." My voice hardened. "I also know he killed Lois too."

"Guess we were wrong on that one. Sorry, Marlowe." Dunbar glanced away, lifted his book, inserted a bookmark, stared at the cover, and asked, "Who is he?" Quietly, he placed his book on the nightstand.

"Name's Robert 'Bobby' Palmer." I filled him in on the events of the last several days, including a watered-down version of getting Katlyn to the cabin, watched expressions ply his features, and knew he felt sorry to have missed the action but felt satisfied with the outcome. He did not seem upset with my kidnapping activities either.

Then I told him, "Palmer shot Stella too and killed Lois, but I think he's only out to kill the others to get to me according to what Katlyn Twiggs said. I don't know why the hell he'd do that except that I know he did kill Lois, maybe learned after the fact that she was my fiancée, and more than likely knew I'd come after him."

When I finished, he slowly shook his head and said, "Katlyn Twiggs, never did trust her. Not sure I'd believe a word she said. I never heard of a Bobby Palmer, but Sherman Horst should be able to give you enough background from Palmer's time in service if he's real."

"I'm planning to give him a call as soon as I get back to town. As far as Miss Twiggs is concerned, I tend to agree with you, but she might lead me directly to Palmer."

"You don't think returning to the city is turning yourself into a walking bull's-eye, do you?"

"You know a better way to pull this bastard out of hiding?" I stood and fished out my Camels, but did not light one.

"You'd best watch your ass, Marlowe. This guy Palmer sounds like a real pro. Maybe I should call the precinct and tell them about him."

As he said it, I got an eerie sensation that I knew Palmer, that I'd encountered him somewhere in the past. However, I could not think of more details to explain how or when I might've met him or heard about him. I did not spend a hell of a lot of time with the Marines during the war, and didn't set foot in the Pacific Theatre. We had our own sharpshooters, a few of the best as far as I was concerned.

"Hold off awhile and give me the opportunity to find him first. If I do then I'll let your boys know where he is and they can go in and lock him up."

After I'm done with him, they might need to scrape the bastard up off the floor.

"I'll give you a maximum of five days, and that's pushing it with Steiner, if he learns about Palmer. In the meantime is there anything I can do to help?" Dunbar asked, as if he wanted to fill in the quiet stretch of his convalescence.

"Depends on whether you're ready to leave this comfortable reading room or not." I surveyed his room again as if needing to evaluate it before drawing a conclusion. It still smelled like antiseptics. My nose wrinkled.

He grunted what might have been a chuckle. "I'm more than ready to leave here. Don't get me wrong, Marlowe, I mean, I like reading and all that, but I miss doing something constructive like solving crimes and kicking some ass occasionally."

"I hoped you'd feel that way. Here's what I need," I said and laid out my plan.

Paul listened carefully, nodded frequently, and when I stopped talking said, "Has it occurred to you that this guy Palmer, if he's for real, is a sharpshooter, a sniper with a hundred and fifty-two wartime kills, and he keeps missing you? Remember that he didn't kill me or Stella when he had us in his sights."

It had occurred to me, but I frowned thoughtfully and said, "What're you getting at? He's intentionally trying to miss me and hit whoever is unfortunate enough to be with me at the time but not kill them either?"

"Seems more than likely to me." Dunbar nodded knowingly and waited, watched me expectantly as if he'd said, *Does he have your attention?*

"He's taking out friends and associates first as punishment, you think? To hurt me?"

"Either that, or we'd all recognize Palmer if we saw him, and he wants to let us know we're high on his list." Dunbar swung his feet off the bed and stuffed them into his white hospital slippers. "If that's the case, he must have something to cover up that's a lot bigger than a single murder. That is if we can prove anything of what you told me. As I said before, Twiggs is not what you might call a reliable or even stable witness. No judge in the city would count on her testimony without corroborating evidence after the way she covered up for her deadbeat brother."

I nodded agreement, thinking that a jury might convict on enough circumstantial evidence, but I kept that thought to myself. Besides, if Palmer had the connections Twiggs claimed he had, then he might be able to buy his way out of trouble.

"So you think that maybe we've all seen his face and it's distinguishable enough that we might identify him in a lineup." I stood and placed the chair back by the window.

"It's worth keeping in mind, Marlowe."

"What about Lois?" I glanced outside, saw blue sky and high clouds that looked like paintbrush strokes.

"Lois either knew him too, or he killed her to get your attention and bring you to him, or he really did think she was a hooker and he has some kind of serious problem with women who prostitute for sustenance." With his robe on, Paul went to the door, opened it, and looked down the hall.

"The bastard has more than my full attention, I'll tell you." I refused to defend Lois again as I observed him. "Think the nurses are waiting to catch you trying to sneak out?"

"They're all at their station, but, oh never mind, one of them looked up." He waved her over. "Let me get signed out and I'll follow you to the cabin," he said before the nurse reached him.

"Think you can drive, or do you want to leave your car here and come back later?"

"Yeah, I can drive." He hesitated, opened a closet and removed his suitcase, placed it on the bed, and selected clean clothing to wear. He seemed to be moving with a lot of care, which made sense. I knew he was dealing with pain.

"I want this bastard caught as badly as you do, Marlowe. Find him and force a confession so we don't have to rely on Twiggs' testimony. I doubt her words will convict him, especially if she claims that she was physically coerced by you to force her cooperation."

I did not express how good it made me feel to hear his words, or how much I liked the idea of our putting aside our differences and working together. Paul Dunbar was the best damn cop I knew. A son of a bitch at times, but focused, dedicated, and committed to finding the truth.

Yet he was unwilling to step one foot beyond the boundaries of the law to put the proverbial nail in the coffin of injustice.

Me? As I said, I used a sledgehammer when I needed to. However, my tactics worked well only outside of a courtroom. Katlyn was an unscrupulous and untrustworthy woman. Moreover, I knew Paul was right about her testimony's value to a judge and jury.

The hospital staff delayed him for half an hour, but we arrived back at the cabin before the two hours I promised Stella had passed.

Chapter Sixteen

She met me at the door with a knowing look that told me she checked the time before greeting us. Her smile and hug felt warm and welcome. Her eyes showed me her wariness and fear.

When she glanced over at Paul, I could see concern shift her features. She shook his hand, held it in hers a moment, and asked, "How are you feeling, Detective Dunbar?"

"I suggest you call me Paul, Stella. I'm on the mend, and thank you for caring enough to ask." He smiled.

"Your coloring looks good," she went on without addressing him otherwise.

Dunbar glanced down at his hand after releasing hers and frowned as if he thought he needed to confirm her opinion.

Always a cop, I thought and shook my head with a wry grin.

"To tell you the truth," he said, "I've been a lot better, but I'm glad Marlowe was around to save my ass, if you'll excuse my French. Now, I'm ready for some action." His grin grew lopsided and I swear I saw color in his cheeks as if he'd blushed because of his use of profanity in front of a lady.

If you could only hear Stella when she's angry, I thought, but said nothing to spoil the moment. It was not often that I saw Dunbar paint himself into a corner. I wanted to enjoy the experience, savor the moment as my father used to say.

Stella's mouth moved as she struggled to bite back her infectious grin, and she nodded without comment other than, "You know I speak French too."

I chuckled when Paul did not seem to understand her comment at first and then he laughed lightly.

After clearing her throat with the side of her fist pressed to her mouth, she went on. "Oh, and Katlyn will provide you with plenty of action, not to mention her French. You can count on her." When she said Twiggs' name, she glanced quickly at the closed bedroom door behind her as if concerned that Katlyn might fly out with hands twisted like demon claws and try to kill her again or gouge out her eyes this time.

"Then she'll appreciate this," he said and lifted out his gold badge.

Relief moved down Stella's face. Her brow smoothed out, eyes widened, and she grinned with true enthusiasm.

"I am so very glad you're here, Paul," she said. "I put a kettle on for tea. Marlowe informed me that you prefer tea instead of coffee."

"Tea would be terrific," he said, following her into the kitchen.

I shut the front door after greeting Gabby, who insisted on jumping up to try to lick my face. I scratched behind his floppy ears, gave him a quick pat on the head, and then went to the kitchen for a cup of coffee.

The New York Central's River Division train to the city left Newburgh, the closest stationhouse, at 11:37. The old brick and concrete station looked classy with large arched windows and an ornate overhang above the main entrance. The scene behind the station and across the Hudson River was a breathtaking view of the mountains with the river running between them as if, like Moses parting the Red Sea, it sliced itself a path as the water hurried southward to join the Atlantic Ocean. The mountains appeared carpeted by a dark blue-green forest that seemed to move as one when the wind blew like giant lungs.

I walked into the richly wood-paneled waiting room at 11:00 and watched Stella drive off to rejoin Paul.

They had two cars, but I wanted to get back into the city without Palmer learning about my return, move around freely once I arrived without using a vehicle that Palmer or one of his cohorts might recognize. I knew I still felt paranoid, but I chalked it up more to caution than fear.

I paid the Albany to New York full fare, four dollars and twenty-eight cents, so I could enjoy the dining car.

When the train rolled in, the massive steam locomotive impressed me. It had six main wheels as tall as me, with four smaller ones to the front and four more to the rear of the drive wheels. Steam seemed to billow from everywhere, hissing the air.

"What do they call a machine like that?" I asked the guy manning the ticket counter while pointing at the window behind him.

He glanced over his shoulder and grinned. "That beauty is the J-1 Hudson number 5270. She's pulling three Pullman coaches and a dining car. And let me tell you, my friend, that is one nice riding train."

"I'll give you my impressions of it when I return." I tipped my hat and boarded the front Pullman.

After locating an empty window seat about halfway down the second car, I sat, pushed back my snap-brim, and thought about my conversation with Dunbar.

If the three of us knew Palmer, recognized him on sight, then that should narrow down my choices from several million to, say, one hundred or less.

Dunbar and I knew many of the same people, but when you add Stella to the equation, she became a wild card. She could not have possibly known more than a handful of men and women Dunbar and I knew if that many.

The conductor shouted, "All aboard." He signaled the engineer with a wave before closing the door, and the sound of steam powering those huge wheels blotted out everything else.

Except a new passenger who walked into the Pullman with steps of determination, as if she searched for someone special.

I watched the tall redhead in heels with long legs and striking green eyes that seemed lit with blazing energy I was not certain I wanted directed at me when she paused in her inspection of the car and glanced my way. Her examination reminded me of a marauder searching out vulnerable yet strangely elusive prey.

She wore a nice navy blue dress suit with brass buttons, matching hat, and shoes with three-inch heels, and a shoulder bag the same color. I could see the seams of her flawless silk stockings straight up the back of her shapely rounded calves when she turned to look at the door behind her as if she'd forgotten something, or waited for her companion.

After a moment, she continued down the aisle and hesitated alongside the row of seats ahead of me. Again, her gaze met mine, but she did not express any kind of emotion I could understand or read easily. I got the feeling she knew me, decided I was again being paranoid, and glanced out the window to examine moving scenery.

However, I did not pay attention to anything but the shuffling noises she made when she settled into the seat directly before me after cramming her plaid overnight bag in the rack above her. I could smell her flowery perfume.

After a minute, she removed her hat, which exposed orange-gold hair with highlights that sparkled like living sunshine.

With an intentional shrug, I pulled a magazine from the seatback pocket, turned it over, and found I held a slightly dog-eared copy of *The Atlantic* magazine from July 1950. That was the same month I discovered Katlyn's brother Gregory dead in my office.

I hated coincidence, and usually rejected the idea of the occurrence offhanded, but felt inclined to accept this as one despite the fact that it might be what Stella would think of as an omen, and then shook that off as foolhardy too.

After several pages of ads, I stopped at The Report on the World. I read an article about Joe McCarthy, the blunderbuss in congress, and decided I still believed he was just plain sleazy. I did not like politicians much, would not give you a dime for most of them, and that one looked too slick for his own good and mine.

DEATH LEAVES A SHADOW

The train rolled along at a steady pace by the time I headed for the dining car. Once I found an empty table, I sat, lifted the menu, and watched as someone took the seat straight across from me. The redhead.

It's not unheard of to share a table in a dining car, but usually common courtesy leads a person to ask before sitting without invitation. However, she was gorgeous, and intriguing.

Who am I to complain, I thought and relaxed. In my opinion, I'm far from the most attractive guy around. I've been in a few serious fights, shot a couple times, and never tried to hide the scars. Not that I could if I knew how.

She picked up another menu and acted as if she sat alone, or as if we were there together and I'd had a memory lapse.

I ordered from a breakfast menu and decided a buck and a quarter was good enough for scrambled eggs with thin fried potatoes.

After the porter took our orders, I looked my uninvited guest square in her eyes, felt something stir in my chest.

"I'm Marlowe Black," I said cordially.

"I know who you are," she said in a rich, sexy contralto. Her green eyes, like moist shamrocks, glittered under the light from the small windows alongside us.

"How could you possibly know me?" I asked, not at that point caring that she hadn't told me her name. But a feeling of caution wormed through my gut.

"I work for a law firm on the floor above yours in the Flatiron Building."

Son of a gun. "You're a lawyer, miss?" I tried my luck, but sounded skeptical.

"Pamela Gentrey and, no, I'm not. I'm a secretary."

A well-paid one too, I thought. "A legal secretary makes a lot of money?"

"Enough to get by comfortably."

"If you don't mind my asking, why are you on the train?"

She shrugged with obvious indifference. "Returning to the city. I went to Albany for records we didn't have time to wait for and stopped overnight to visit my mother in Newburgh like I usually do when I ride up this way."

Seemed logical enough to me. Mail delivery in town could be impossibly slow.

"I don't recall ever seeing you in the building," I said. *What the hell, talk is cheap and it's an easy way to pass the hours.*

"You always act preoccupied, like a man in a hurry who doesn't have much time for casual moments when I saw you last."

"You mean like small talk?" I asked.

She caught on and smiled, dazzled me with an expression beautiful enough to skip my heart for a beat or two.

Who the hell are you really? I wanted to ask. *And what the hell do you want from me?* Instead, I watched the porter return with our orders.

She ate with finishing school refinement. I ate like an ex-GI still hurrying to cram it down and get out of the way of the next guy in the chow line.

After finishing, I shrouded my plate with a white linen napkin embroidered with the New York Central logo, and shook out a Camel.

"You mind?" I asked and held up the pack.

She dabbed at her lips with a clean corner of her napkin, leaving behind a lipstick stain, smiled in a way that told me she liked my asking, and said, "No, I'll have one though if you don't mind."

I flipped open the Zippo, lit both, watched her over the flame, appreciated the flame's reflection in her round, lively eyes, and then poured us fresh coffee.

"What's it like working as a private detective?" she asked, studying me with a polite but serious frown that pinched the flesh above her pert, uplifted nose.

"A lot like combat. Some days there's nothing doing, and others the action never ends. Especially with the type of cases I normally accept."

She tilted her head, smiled, and said, "Right, like the man discovered in your office back in July after the fourth and then too that shooting in the hall outside your office a couple of weeks ago. A woman got shot, right?"

"You seem to know a lot about me," I said and wondered why. Sure, we shared the same building, but the Flatiron Building is huge with lots of offices. I had a feeling she'd been keeping tabs on me, which led me to wonder more about the implications of the possibility of her spying.

She simplified things. "The attorney I work for needs a man like you once in a while."

I opened my mouth to announce that I don't do legwork for lawyers like spying on spouses or tracking down insurance scammers, but hell, lawyers had client money to spread around, and on occasion, I did have a difficult time finding work and paying the rent.

"What type of work would he want me to do?"

"He only practices criminal law. The work would not prove boring, and he will pay whatever your rate is plus expenses. Also, he pays a sizable bonus if an assignment is finished early."

Rolling in dough, I thought. *That's my kind of guy.*

"What's his name?" I drained my cup, ground out my cigarette butt, and stood.

She accepted my proffered assistance, clasped my hand, and rose to her feet gracefully. She stood about an inch or so under me. I guessed her heels added three inches, so that made her about five foot three and slender.

"Thank you." Her grip felt dry and strong. The whiff I got of her perfume again. It reminded me of Evening in Paris, a scent my mother often wore when she and my father went dancing.

I nodded and released her hand, followed her back to the Pullman, and we sat together.

"My employer is Del Bartholomew. Have you ever heard of him?"

I came close to whistling in surprise. Del, short for Delbert Bartholomew, practiced criminal law by often representing members of the mob. He was not quite a consigliore precisely, but came close enough for me to give him the title. Vinnie Castillo spoke of him as if Del could qualify to become a minor Roman god, or a Roman Catholic saint.

"You feel safe working around those people?"

"You mean the mob boys?" She flashed a dazzling smile that lit her face as if she felt seriously amused by what she thought of as the naiveté of my concern.

"Of course I do and why shouldn't I? They seek out Mr. B for help with their legal affairs. Occasionally one or two will flirt with me, bring flowers or candy, but they know me. They're not about to muck up a relationship as important as the one they have with my boss."

'Cause he always gets the bastards off or gets them reduced time if not, or time served, I thought disdainfully.

"I'm not positive I could sleep nights if I worked to help save men like them," I answered honestly.

"We have other clients too," she said, still grinning, which made me feel too righteous for a private cop with a reputation for knocking heads together to get at the truth.

"Tell you what, give me a call when you need my help, or stop by my office and we'll discuss details," I told her to lessen the effect of my previous statement. It would never do to have men like Vinnie start believing I might be righteous, a deadly sign of weakness to be sure.

"I will," she said. "Maybe one day soon we can get together for lunch and talk about some non-work-related matters."

"Sounds great, or dinner maybe," I replied and knew she'd gotten to me.

"Tell me about your name." She crossed her legs, smoothed her skirt carefully over her knees, and turned in her seat to face me.

"Marlowe?" I asked and when she nodded continued. "Dad was an Elizabethan scholar, taught at City College. I guess he thought by naming me after his favorite author, I'd make something of my life the way he did with his life, like getting a PhD. Truth be told the name kept me fighting to prove my virility while growing up." I shrugged. "Guess that made something of me all right, a brawler, and a good soldier."

She laughed, started talking about her own life and parents, Irish immigrants who came over penniless and prospered due to persistence, long hours, and honest hard labor. She was an only child and loved her parents with a passion I found difficult to comprehend, not that I did not feel that way about mine, but…

She said she struggled as a child with what she called the curly red hair curse of "oh, isn't she cute" pinched cheeks, and people who either thought touching her hair or rubbing her head might give them luck or bless them with something Irish folks knew that they struggled to possess and understand like kissing the Blarney Stone.

Or she dealt with the superstitious who thought redheads might be demons or witches, and the occasional orthodox Roman Catholic who would cross herself and hurry away as if to wash the sin of contact from her mind in a confessional.

God alone knows where those braindead individuals hailed from, but they all should be rounded up and exiled to a small island in the South Atlantic where they can chew each other's fingers until death do them part. I felt stunned listening to her. Ignorance is not only bliss; it is also revolting stagnation.

The train stopped in Weehawken, where we boarded a different train into the city. I did not get the opportunity to look it over, but knew it was not coal-fired steam. They'd gotten banned from running through the city a lot of years in the past.

"We shouldn't be seen together once we reach the station," I told Pamela, trying to speak casually.

"Why? You married and your wife is waiting for you on the platform?" Again, she grinned that wicked smile she displayed for me earlier.

"Nothing like that, doll. I'm having a bit of trouble with a guy and don't want to drag you into the middle of it. He's not exactly what you might call your friendly next-door neighbor type."

She studied me a moment as if puzzled, and finally nodded as though somehow she'd thought it through and understood the implication of my words. "All right, but we can sit together for now."

"Yes, of course we can and we should," I said and found us seats in the rear of the car.

Pamela chatted about city life, Broadway shows she'd seen lately, people she knew, and made me feel like an outsider. Hell, I went to Giants ballgames in the summer, hockey in winter, and in between hung around with friends from the war, and a few I had known since childhood in the local tavern.

In comparison to her, I sounded like the proverbial stick-in-the-mud and oddly enough felt relieved when the train finally rolled into the station and stopped.

"You go ahead," I said, watched the beautiful sway of her hips when she walked off, and wondered if she'd added the movement for my benefit. *Wishful thinking, pal.*

Five minutes later, I disembarked and entered the middle of the first crowd I approached. I did not see Miss Gentrey.

It felt good to be back in the city as if I'd been gone for months, but somewhere out there Bobby Palmer watched and waited. I hoped my luck would hold and his would run out first.

By the time I reached the street, I worked my way into a moving crowd of men, so despite my casual attire, with my snap-brim on I looked like an ordinary guy in a sea of fedoras.

DEATH LEAVES A SHADOW

I waved down a Checker cab and dropped into the rear seat as the cabbie pulled into traffic.

He left me on West 21st Street, a block from my office building. A quick look around led me to feel confident enough to head straight for the building's delivery entrance at the back. The door stood propped partially opened with a small stack of empty wooden crates. I stepped inside and to be on the safe side drew my Colt. Except for a second stack of unopened crates, the small foyer appeared empty.

I wanted to feel good or at least more confident when I reached the shelter of the alcove, but only felt more vulnerable and exposed.

Taking the steps two at the time, I reached my office, unlocked the door, went inside quickly, closed and relocked the door.

Without pausing to do more than a cursory check, I waited for an operator and then gave her Sherman Horst's phone number.

Sherm worked as our company clerk in Europe during the war. Now he worked in records storage, still a clerk, in the Army wing at the Pentagon Building. He was also a dedicated Senators fan. Poor sap. His team plunged helplessly to the bottom of the standings.

After he picked up and said, "Sherman Horst," I said without an introduction, "I need information on a Marine sharpshooter, a sniper named Robert 'Bobby' Palmer. Claimed he had a hundred and fifty-two kills. He fought in the Pacific."

"Marlowe, if I didn't know better, I'd say you sound a bit harried. Everything okay?"

It's hard to lie to an old friend. I gave him an abbreviated rundown of recent events instead and heard him whistle one long soft note.

"I'll get right on it. I've heard of this guy Palmer. He's one hell of a shooter. Give me about ten minutes or so. You at your office?"

"Yes I am, and thanks, Sherm." I hung up and went to the window, did not stand in front of it, but off to one side.

I stood there looking out and down until the phone rang ten or fifteen minutes later.

After snatching it off the cradle, I said, "Yeah," and got a nasty surprise.

"Glad I was finally able to get in touch with you, asshole."

"What do you want, Palmer," I said, guessing it was him, and heard him draw a breath as if surprised.

"Nice fast detective work, but it won't save your ass this time."

"Guess we'll see about that, Bobby." I hung up before he could respond. His voice sounded vaguely familiar, but I could not readily picture him in a particular event or place.

Five minutes went by and the phone rang again. This time I heard Sherman.

"Marlowe, Palmer's had a couple scrapes with the law up in Connecticut. Seems he jumped bail and disappeared over a shooting in Bridgeport down by the docks. However, his wife has an address in Manhattan over in Stuy Town. Seventy-six dollars a month in rent for a first-floor apartment according to an attached note. Can you believe that?"

"That's the old Gashouse District up by the East Village. I went to church up there once when I was a kid. Visiting an old aunt for a weekend."

"Hmmm." He sounded uninterested and gave me Mrs. Palmer's address.

"Thanks, Sherm. I owe you."

"Not this time. Sounds to me like this guy Palmer needs to be caught and punished in a bad way."

We chatted a minute or two about baseball and hung up. By the time I reached the hallway after locking the door, I heard feet hard on the steps like someone angry and in a big hurry. They sounded heavy, like the pounding steps I heard moments before Stella was shot.

Shit, not again. I ducked and moved across the hall to get out of the line of fire. *This bastard is too damn good at finding me.*

A single gunshot echoed as plaster fragments rained on my head from the ceiling where I saw the bullet lodge.

I did not want to have another gunfight in my office building, did not want any more innocent blood on my hands, and ran for the fire escape.

Chapter Seventeen

Less than a minute later, I reached the street and kept running. Then I heard him fire twice more and knew that the son of a bitch did not care how many bystanders he killed while trying to stop me.

Bobby Palmer ranked as one of the top five sharpshooters in the Marines during the war, and I knew he did not mind now if he took out the people around me before he decided it was my turn. Obviously, there was more to his plan than Paul or I considered, or he was just plain crazy.

Of course, there were always the bums who heard about my successes and decided they needed to prove themselves to be better than me, so they challenged with threats not terribly dissimilar to what Palmer did. That happened to a couple of cops I knew, and both times the challengers went down permanently.

At that moment, I didn't have time to contemplate the implications of my assumptions. If Palmer continued to shoot from behind me, he would take out pedestrians or a cabbie and doubtless enjoy the carnage he'd created and my inability to stop him from doing it before he would disappear again.

Without hesitation, I turned the corner, ran along East 20th Street, and headed directly to Stuyvesant Town and Peter Cooper Village.

The gunshots stopped abruptly as if he needed to reload. I ducked into a corner deli by Gramercy Park and grabbed a copy of *The Daily News*, held it up, and watched outside as discreetly as possible. No one ran past the storefront. I did not recognize any of the average-appearing Joes who strolled in, and none fit Twiggs' description of Palmer. Of course, I had to take into consideration the possibility that Twiggs lied about him and/or his appearance.

My breathing slowed. I bought a great-smelling hot coffee and a buttered hard roll and sat on a bentwood chair at a small round café-style wooden table with a red-and-white checked tablecloth. The table stood to the left side of the door. I wanted to give Palmer a few more minutes to locate and finally confront me, but did not believe he would show. He liked the element of surprise too much.

He never entered the deli, but honestly, I didn't feel relieved.

Part of his lousy fucking game. I wanted more than ever to find and stop him.

After crumpling up the white waxed paper the roll came in, I tossed it in the waste can by the door, finished my coffee, and left.

Outside the air felt cooler, the sun hung high and shone bright. A line of small white clouds like smudges dotted the horizon between buildings. Slowly, I looked around like a lost tourist and got approached by a bum seeking a handout.

"Got a dime, buddy?" he asked woefully. His poorly groomed light brown greasy hair looked like he'd hacked it off with a pocketknife. He smelled like a week-old sack of fish. However, his brown eyes looked clear, filled with intelligence not fogged over like a drunk. He grinned feebly and displayed a good set of slightly misaligned teeth. He needed a shave.

"What happened to you that got you living on the street, pal?" I asked curiously.

"Government money ran out 'fore I found myself a job and still haven't found anything that pays real money."

"You a veteran too?"

He fished in his pants pocket and came out with a Wounded Duck pin, showed it to me, and nodded. "Europe with the Ninth Division."

"You're a grunt?"

He nodded and grinned crookedly as if to acknowledge the obvious.

"Me too," I said, gave him an abbreviated history and a dollar.

"Good luck," I added and walked into StuyTown, located the building I needed behind a manicured waist-high hedgerow, and knocked on the front door with the number Sherm gave me for Mrs. Palmer's apartment.

I half expected she would not be home, but a few seconds later, I heard the lock turn, open, and then the door swung wide.

I removed my hat and held it in my left hand. "Mrs. Palmer, I'm Marlowe Black. I'm trying to locate your husband. Do you happen to know where I might be able to find him right now?"

"You an old friend or are you a cop?"

She was not what you might call beautiful, but she wasn't bad either, on the plain side with a slightly bent nose and a wide mouth. She wore red lipstick and rouge to highlight her high cheekbones. Her wide-set eyes looked gray, her hair a color that my mother once called dirty blonde. She was also a bit overweight and wore a baggy, flowered housedress that hung to mid-calf with a wide ribbon belt, which made her look okay to me.

I saw something in her eyes that told me she was clever, smart enough that she'd easily read through any smoke I threw up attempting to obscure my purpose for standing outside her front door.

"Neither. I became a city cop after the war, but went private." I fished out a newly printed business card and handed it to her.

"Marlowe Black. Nice-sounding name. So what did he do this time?"

"Bobby? I need to question him about some legal trouble he might be involved with."

"Can you be more specific please, Mr. Black?" She handed back my card and smiled without enthusiasm or humor, eyes hiding whatever emotion she harbored over Palmer's behavior or his current whereabouts.

"Someone took a couple shots at me, and a witness described a man who we identified as Bobby Palmer."

Now her smile turned into a grin filled with a derisive kind of mirth. "You're alive, walking and talking, Mr. Black. Either the man shooting wasn't Bobby, or you're the luckiest man living in the city of New York."

I could not help smiling and nodded my agreement.

"Lucky, and I want to find him before my luck runs out." My voice held a note of cold warning.

Her eyes narrowed briefly, long enough to make me wonder about her integrity or possible participation in Palmer's recent activities. Too quickly, the look faded and she turned her head as if she meant to call someone from another room. She reached back, lifted a torn envelope from a well-polished dark walnut table with a white marble top that stood against the wall. It bore a finely embroidered white linen runner. The table was a style my father would have identified as late Victorian. He liked his antiques.

My hand moved toward the .45 under my left arm and stopped when she again looked at my face.

"Bobby walked out on me several months ago. He's got himself some little blonde bimbo now, but he sends me money when he can." She handed me the empty envelope. I saw a return address and I knew I had him.

"Thank you, Mrs. Palmer." I took the envelope, folded it in half, and quickly stuck it in my inner jacket pocket before she could change her mind. I reached out my hand. She accepted and shook it. Her palm felt dry, soft, and warm.

As I walked down the street and turned the first corner I approached, I pulled the envelope out and read the address.

The bastard lived in Brooklyn a couple of blocks behind where Lois resided across the street from me.

The cab fare was worth the time saved, and I felt excited when we rolled to a stop at the corner of Palmer's street. I paid the cabby a large tip and jumped out.

If I found Palmer at home, I knew one of us might not live to enjoy another sunset, but I had a hunch he remained in Manhattan searching for me.

I walked around the block and found an alley that came up behind his three-story brick apartment building. Stepping over and around accumulated trash, old bald tires, a broken wooden kitchen chair with three legs and peeling green paint, I chased off a pair of dogs that looked too mangy to stay alive. I could smell the rotted trash they dug through looking for food.

Palmer's apartment was on the ground floor. Directly below his place was a basement with an outside entrance. I decided it might be the best way to get into his building without detection. A locked padlock hung in the hasp. I searched the trash in the alley until I located an old bent and rusted tire iron. After a minute of my prying, the screws in the wood frame popped free like fragmentation.

With a grunt from me and a screech from a rusty hinge, I raised the door and climbed down the concrete block steps, brushing aside several unoccupied spider webs. The chamber below smelled moldy, and too like familiar perfume. That made me hesitate a moment.

Then I located a long pull chain dangling from an overhead light, gave it a tug, and felt pleased when a hundred-watt bulb illuminated the space around me. And then I felt something else, something like dread when I examined the walls.

On three of the walls, photos and newspaper clippings of murder victims, prostitutes according to the headlines, hung in organized rows. I counted twenty-five. The oldest dated back to late '45; the newest was the clipping for Lois. Alongside the news article—the only one not claiming the victim had been a prostitute—about Lois' death, he had taped a black-and-white photo of her that he must have taken moments before she died.

She sat naked in the chair with her hands folded neatly on her lap holding a small black pistol like the one Dunbar handed me the day he came by my office to tell me the news about her death. The connection might have been tenuous, but it felt like an unwelcome snake uncoiling in my head that locked onto and twisted through my feelings for her.

DEATH LEAVES A SHADOW

Her beautiful flesh showed no signs of a struggle. Blood ran from the corner of her mouth, but I saw no visible bruising. I wondered what he had told her to effect her submission. However, Lois' eyes looked wide with the horror she must have felt by his presence as she stared at the person behind the camera. Her eyes told me that she knew her attacker, or the photographer, and hadn't anticipated the behavior he exhibited.

I felt every ounce of rage I had ever owned building in my chest. My breathing hissed rapidly, and hot tears ran down both cheeks. I ignored everything but what I stared at. The bastard must have dressed her before he shot her since the cops who found her stated she looked as if she'd recently arrived home from work. I felt convinced he raped her, but I could not tell from the photo.

When I looked at the other clippings, I saw that each one had a black-and-white photo taped to it.

Below each picture, there was a small brown paper bag nailed to the wallboard with a tarpaper nail. I knew I needed to open the sack under Lois' photo, but could not move my hands.

Somewhere in the middle of Europe on a frigid December night in 1944, when I finally concluded that the God I knew as a child had somehow disappeared into the mist that grew from the smoke lifting off thousands of gun barrels, I experienced true fear. If my God abandoned me, I decided then, what is there for me to depend on for survival?

The next day, the fighting resumed. The two guys hunkered down behind a felled tree about twenty yards from where I'd sought refuge were blasted into a spray of bone and flesh fragments that showered me with death's unrelenting truth.

Deep inside my chest, a spark ignited and roared into a blaze that drove me to my feet. I watched my fingers as I fired and reloaded without once seeking shelter. When the firefight died, I remained untouched, except for the gruesome remains drying on my clothing and flesh.

The answer I sought was born in fear and the desperation of survival. I could and would count on the single being that must always pull me safely from any difficulty. Me.

Fear evaporated, and maybe a small part of my soul rekindled into belief in a power in the universe that could create and destroy without reason, and at that time and since, that belief was enough. Why look for more when the obvious stares brazenly at your face?

With a yank and the sound of torn paper to violate the stillness created in my hesitation, I removed the sack from the nail and with only slight vacillation opened it and peered inside.

I lifted the bag, felt its weight on my palm, and closed my fingers on its contents, felt something soft and something hard. Immediately, bright yellow caught my attention.

I heard a sharp intake of breath as I lifted out a woman's matching underpants and bra, both yellow and lacy. The set was a gift from me to Lois on her last birthday. We both laughed at the idea of me walking into Macy's and boldly purchasing lingerie for my lady friend. We talked about how many guys might do the same for their girls and decided not too many. But hell, I loved Lois and she looked super wearing the gift when she put it on and modeled it an hour later.

With a cold dread spreading quickly from my heart through my chest, I placed the underwear on the marred surface of a used workbench and lifted out the remaining article. He had neatly wrapped it in waxed paper with folded ends like a gift, and sealed the package closed with masking tape. *Son of a bitch.*

I did not need to unwrap it to know that what I held on my palm was Lois' right ear. The burn of bile filled my mouth, but I'd've rotted in hell before I vomited. I swallowed hard until all I tasted was the nastiness of stomach acid, and a vile awareness that Palmer held her severed ear in his hand while the flesh was still warm, the blood dripping to pool and coagulate on his palm.

I didn't know I still cried, did not think about anything else, but clasped the Colt with my hand, the safety off, and wanted to kill Palmer right then, one shot between his eyes. Better yet, I'd start with a knee and work my way over and up until only one round remained. The last would be the best.

Noise from someone approaching, pushing aside trash, brought me back to my surroundings. I yanked on the chain and extinguished the light so the only illumination came through the opened doors. The tip of the .45's barrel remained visible in the rays of yellow sunlight that ran jagged lizards down the steps.

A couple of kids, young boys not yet in their teens, stuck their heads into the stairwell. When they saw my gun, or maybe the look on my face, which told them I wanted someone to shoot in the worst possible way, their eyes widened almost comically if the circumstances had been different. They turned and ran like hell through the trash-strewn yard yelling to each other to move faster and don't fall.

I replaced everything in the paper bag and set it on the floor under Lois' picture on what I then thought of as the wall of death.

Five minutes later, I closed the outside basement doors, arranged the lock and hasp so they appeared untouched, and then walked down the block to the deli Lois and I used before and after we got serious about each other. I dialed the cops and reported my findings, the address. My breath came hard as if I'd run from Manhattan to Brooklyn to use the pay phone.

I hung up before they could ask the normal questions any cop wanted, and reflexively checked for a refund in the slot at the base of the phone like a frantic act of lucidity while I moved trance-like through my life's stage show of the absurd and the insane.

What the hell is happening with this world? I thought, rubbing my thumb over the scar from where I dug a bloody moon into my palm while talking with Paul when he first told me about Lois.

How does it come down to us allowing people like Palmer free access to the innocent?

I shuddered, felt soiled, itchy as if something happened under my flesh and now I knew I'd need to peel it off and replace it to feel whole again.

After waiting until the first prowl car screamed down the street, I purchased a cold bottle of Ballantine Ale, stepped outside, and downed the brew without coming up for air.

I needed to learn if Palmer raped Lois before he killed her and then sliced off her ear the way some Marines had done in the Pacific as a way to show the enemy what to expect when they captured them, and as a way to prove the kill to other Marines.

Why in God's name does Bobby Palmer hate me so much? I lifted my hand to throw the bottle, but instead set it down carefully.

I did not know why anyone hated, and truthfully no longer gave a damn about Palmer's reasoning. The time had come around for the deliverance of justice my way. Palmer had made a single fatal mistake. The bastard left me alive.

I realized that, as it turned out, Katlyn Twiggs had told the truth apparently. *Maybe there is hope for her, and maybe not. Only time and her decisions will unravel her future.*

Chapter Eighteen

After Brooklyn, the city morgue was my first stop. According to his secretary, I would be interrupting Pat Solok in the middle of an autopsy on a lower Eastside robbery victim from the previous night. Arms folded, I nodded with feigned patience as an acknowledgment of her dilemma and then promptly ignored the rest of her attempted persuasion. I strode past her desk without a glance back at her as she called for me to stop.

Pat looked up sharply when I shoved open the door with both hands. When he saw me, his eyes flashed something that might have been apprehension, which I interpreted as unwelcome surprise.

"You look like shit, Marlowe. What the hell've you been doing?" He scrubbed blood off his gloves using what once was a white terry cloth hand towel. Then he peeled off the thick rubber gloves with a snap as he walked to the exit. I followed him out.

Once standing outside of the building, he stripped off his protective garments and said quietly, "I need a goddamn smoke. Care to join me?"

I had yet to speak a word, and learned that all I was capable of doing was to nod and walk with him back to the loading dock at the rear of the building, where he tossed his bloodstained outerwear in a wire-framed canvas hamper awaiting pickup by whatever laundry company had the contract with the city.

The air smelled like rain, but I felt nothing. He offered me a Marlboro, lit it for me when we both saw that my hands shook bad enough that I could not open my lighter's cover.

"Jesus, Marlowe," he said softly. "I've known you for years and don't ever recall seeing you this bad, so spill it, friend."

I bit down hard enough to bite through the filter, spit it off the loading dock, and watched as it splashed in a puddle of oil left over from a leaky crankcase.

After a long pause during which my mind wandered to the sound of Lois' laughter and back to the black-and-white photograph of her naked, seated holding the handgun used to kill her, I cleared my throat and glanced at one of my oldest friends.

"Why didn't you tell me about her right ear, Pat?" My voice sounded harsh with grief and I knew it expressed more than what I'd experienced in Palmer's cellar.

"Jesus Christ." Pat's mouth flattened with the realization and acceptance of the knowledge I now had that he'd not thought to share with me on my previous visit to view Lois' body.

"How'd you find out about her ear?" he asked, which was his way of telling me he thought he understood and accepted my insinuation but still needed to hear my explanation.

After several long drags on the cigarette, I described to him what I'd found as graphically as police pulp fiction, with a voice free of inflection.

His faced paled as he fought against the revulsion that must have churned through his gut. He put one hand against the brick wall behind him as if needing to brace himself. Then Pat nodded without stopping like he'd lost muscular control of his neck, and finally crossed himself twice, looked skyward, and mumbled something I did not hear, or did not care to hear.

People who prayed for escape from the societal horrors that happened to some of us on what seemed like a daily tribulation troubled me enough that I turned away from them and religion. I felt sure that they wouldn't do anything to change or solve the problems as long as they believed they personally knew a God who might do it for them if only…

To hell with all of that. Either we take responsibility for our lives and behavior or we become the same as those who hurt us or try to destroy innocent lives.

"Oh my God, Christ, Marlowe," he muttered, sounding as if he wanted to weep instead of speak. "Her ear was missing, but the bullet exploded through the right side of her skull. I thought her ear had... well, been disintegrated," he finished, stared at his hands, seemed surprised to witness them shaking, and glanced up with questions in his eyes that I could never answer if I'd wanted to try.

Hell, Pat, I can't answer them for myself, I thought, filled with profound dread that felt like acid burning a hole in my brain.

"What kind of lousy bastard would do something so horrible to a woman as nice as Lois?" Now he sounded about ready to scream, or worse.

His words and unspoken emotion stirred nothing inside me, but I stepped closer, put my hand on his shoulder, and, when he looked at me, watched his eyes. "Thanks for trying to protect me, but now tell me if he raped her too."

Pat, red-eyed, did not look away, as he said solemnly, "I'm sorry, Marlowe. I only performed a preliminary workup. The apparent cause of death seemed obvious enough and I saw no need to do more. Now I wish I'd looked further. The boys might've investigated her death differently if I'd found evidence of rape." He sounded like someone had told him a loved one died unexpectedly and the death was something he knew he might have prevented, if only he'd acted sooner.

At least that explained to me why he hadn't said anything about Lois' unborn child and the fact that Palmer killed two people, not one. I wondered about that, but failed to question him since I felt overwhelmed with anguish at the time.

I squeezed his shoulder, turned, and jumped off the loading dock without speaking again. I heard Pat calling my name and ignored him.

A quick phone call to Phil Ball and I learned that the cops who searched Palmer's apartment found it empty of personal items. Palmer was gone, two steps ahead of me again. *But not for much longer. I'm gonna find you and kill you with extreme pleasure.*

An hour later, I sat on the train riding to Newburgh. All I had for a connection to Palmer was Katlyn Twiggs. I knew that somehow, I needed to make her an offer that she might find difficult to walk away from if she thought about refusing me. Of course, I did not intend to let her walk away from what she did regardless of the circumstances—no matter how incidental her activities with Palmer proved to be. I meant to send her to prison for years if not life.

I couldn't think, didn't want to know where my mind traveled, or if the primeval part of it demanded that I walk arm in arm with Mephistopheles and Beelzebub as old friends do when journeying to act out a plot to alter another person's destiny, or help them fulfill the one they'd desired and created but not yet attained.

Rarely, but occasionally, true justice demanded that I grasped some intangible clue or piece of evidence by stepping beyond the boundaries of the law. When that occurred, justice also demanded that I, as the man determining its scope, be damn sure of what I planned to commit before taking the first irrevocable step. It always felt complicated, but that was the foundation of what I considered to be my personal beliefs.

In my mind, Katlyn deserved the electric chair for hiding the truth and therefore aiding Palmer, which I thought made her as guilty as the man who pulled the trigger.

However, the justice I intended would not kill her unless she provoked the act with violence of her own, or was indeed sentenced in court so she would receive the jolt of voltage needed to punctuate her life gravely.

Unexpectedly, the train stopped and I found myself at the station in Newburgh. I waved over a taxi and paid the driver to take me as far as the road leading to Lake Orange and a future neither I nor Katlyn could have imagined.

The sun sat right above the horizon, which surprised me. I had not thought about time since discovering Palmer's trophy wall of death. Hell, I had not thought of much since I yanked the pull chain on the ceiling light in Palmer's basement and finally opened the small brown paper bag.

Now, as I walked the dirt road past the lake, heard and watched a flock of Canadian geese as they skipped to a landing on sunset-orange water, I felt something move and then shift inside me.

I tried to understand what went wrong in Palmer's head.

A sniper witnessed each shot fired from the moment of its inception until it exploded inside the intended target. They could never look away fast enough to avoid the results of their craft. Most snipers I knew always tried for a clean head shot and never discussed their successes or failures or, for that matter, what they saw when the bullet arrived to meet its target.

Nothing too clean there, I thought, and found my humor flat and useless. At the time, the failure went unnoticed as I struggled and fought to keep the image of the paper bag's contents from forming a vivid picture behind my eyes, where its indelibility would haunt me forever, stoking the rage that I knew simmered like an out-of-control inferno waiting for the single flicker of the spark for its intention.

The cabin came into view with light in the windows, shadows moving behind curtains. My palms itched and I vigorously scrubbed them on the seams of my trousers as if I tried to peel off something filthy.

Gabby ran out from behind the cabin, barking and wagging like he'd discovered a long-dead friend who had returned to the living. His front paws hit my chest as he bounced high to greet me and knocked me flat on my ass.

I did not have time to scold him before he stood on my chest and his tongue slobbered across my face. His stubby tail moved fast enough to rock his haunches. Finally, I rubbed behind his ears and felt the block of cold anger thaw inside me, felt a slight release of pressure like a steam valve popping.

Damn dog, I thought, not wanting to feel, not wanting to accept that life moved on whether or not one person was brutally ripped from the planet's population. Hell, life did not even stutter, as if Lois' years meant nothing to anyone but me. For the rest of humanity, her life was a missed heartbeat that would not slow down progress or time.

When Gabby decided he'd concluded his greeting, he turned and trotted to the cabin's front door, which now stood wide open.

Stella, backlit by light from inside, waited without moving, possibly trying to judge my emotions from a safe distance.

"You didn't let me know you'd be returning today," she said in a careful, calm voice that almost hid the concern I read on her face.

"You don't have a phone up here, doll." I stood, dusted off, and walked to her, stopped when I could see her features more clearly, the frown of concern that cut across her brow.

"What happened to you, Marlowe?" She sliced through the bullshit I wanted to pile up so she would not know what I'd experienced. Her hand lifted, fingers brushed my cheek with more tenderness than I felt I deserved right then or maybe ever.

After a deep inhale, I held it for thirty seconds. "I found Palmer's..." *What could I call it?* I thought. "He kept fucking trophies," I mumbled rapidly.

"Don't tell me he had something of Lois'?" Her eyes widened and then narrowed as she glanced toward the lake.

I looked too, studied the geese now gilded orange by the setting sun.

"He kept several items." I reached to move her aside, but my hand stopped, hovered an inch away from her face as if I might pass her the vision of what I'd held in my hand earlier if not careful.

Stella clasped my wrist, pressed her warm, soft cheek firmly against my palm, and I felt her shiver as if she read my thoughts, saw the images I then tried to hide from myself. Tears filmed her eyes, and she leaned and kissed me with unexpected gentleness, accepted the rough kiss I ground into her mouth.

Then I heard Paul call, "Marlowe, that you? How did you make out?" He sounded like a concerned friend wondering what kept me outside so long, although I thought he knew the answer.

Stella took my hand and led me inside, where I found a fire roaring in the fireplace. Paul Dunbar sat comfortably in an old overstuffed green armchair with his feet encased in black leather slippers resting on a matching battered hassock with a book resting open on his lap. He studied me as I neared him and nodded knowingly.

"That bad?" he asked.

I nodded. "Let's take a walk."

Stella tugged my hand, gazed into my battered eyes, and said, "I'll fix your supper." She let my hand drop and went into the kitchen.

Dunbar removed his slippers, pulled on his shoes, and followed me outside.

"Tell me about it, old friend," he said and I did tell him every damn detail of what I saw, what I touched, what I smelled, but not what I felt. The hellishly tangled emotions were impossible to express with words.

"I can't let you hurt Katlyn Twiggs," he said quietly after I finished. "She's a material witness, and the prosecutor will need her testimony to put this bastard Palmer away despite what I or you might think of her ability as a witness."

"You know me well, Paul. But I don't want to hurt her, and won't unless she turns on me and I need to..."

"And then you can claim self-defense. Don't do it this time, Marlowe. You'll never get away with it, and I can't imagine you living with yourself once you have had enough time to understand your own motives afterwards. For Christ's sake, she's a woman. Palmer probably coerced or forced her to help him. Some women like to be slapped around, makes them feel necessary or important."

"My plan is to use her as bait to draw Palmer out where I can find him." I lit a cigarette and offered one to Paul. He took it and lit it off mine. "I'm sure she knows how to get in touch with him. And, I'll need your help."

He nodded as if he knew where I was going. "I'll offer her a deal, but it will be total bullshit."

"Good, she doesn't deserve more." We stopped walking at the edge of the lake. The orange glow faded. "I need her willing to return to the city and not wanting to run off or to hide from me when I leave her alone."

"Let me think on it until we get back to the cabin." Paul snuffed out his cigarette with his heel—ground it deep into the damp earth.

I flipped mine into the lake and watched as the sparks sizzled and drowned. Neither of us spoke about the last time we stood at the lakeshore.

Dunbar was all cop, but then I expected nothing less. The past dropped where it belonged in his life, and he could and would keep his personal history suppressed so he might work his job without the interference of doubt or hesitation. If a cop failed to accomplish that much self-control, he needed to get into a different line of work the way I did, or maybe the way I failed to. Driving a newspaper delivery truck might prove the easiest route to retirement. I doubted I'd live that long and did not really care.

Bad enough getting old without feeling unnecessary too, I thought.

My past hung around like storm clouds and demanded I tend to it like a gardener managing tangles of prickly vines that twisted and throttled his ripened tomato plants. In me, the past necessitated my call for validity, but sometimes the law prevented its satisfactory conclusion. My style of justice filled the bill to perfection, but would not this time.

Dunbar was correct. Twiggs, despite her corruptness and violent past, was a woman, and I'd already pushed the boundaries of decency to convince her to tell me what I then knew about Palmer. Katlyn would not have talked at any other place where I might have hidden her, if finding somewhere else in the city to talk to her was at all possible.

Trying to trace a person in New York was like searching for a particular face by standing on the top of the Chrysler Building and looking down to the streets with binoculars. When they chose to, New Yorkers disappeared with little effort.

"I'll work with whatever you come up with, Paul," I said and turned to walk back to the cabin.

Dunbar's hand dropped on my upper arm and stopped me.

"Don't go near Twiggs tonight." He looked at me and I knew there was something else too.

"What, Paul?"

He released my arm. "Stella has it for you in a bad way."

I opened my mouth, but only a resigned sigh slipped out. "Don't know what to do about that," I admitted.

"Give her a chance. She's a great gal despite the mess her father dragged her into." He nodded at the cabin. "Let's go. She's most likely got your dinner ready by now."

"I don't think her loving me is a good idea," I said and walked alongside him.

"Didn't think you would, but she does and it's a serious thing, not infatuation. So be gentle with her. She understands your loss, but she could never understand the depth of your feelings for Lois or the way you think about her death. Right now, Marlowe, you're like a fully armed Sherman tank rolling down Madison Avenue."

"That obvious?" I asked and watched him nod. "Both his basement and finding the trophies…nasty fucking business."

I hadn't informed him of my unborn child, did not know why, and decided I'd keep it to myself for a while longer to sort it out in my head.

"And you had to take it out of the bag to examine his handiwork," he said without judgment or expression.

"You know how it is."

"I do. I'd've done the same damn thing in your place." He reached and opened the door.

Odors of cooking wafted out and surprised me with the fact that I felt starved and wanted to eat.

Dinner consisted of a hamburger with a slice of fresh onion, boiled potatoes with melted butter, and fresh green beans. I used ketchup on the burger, which leaked through the bread, but tasted great.

Stella sat with me, but did not talk. She must've understood my need to think and decided she'd respect it, wait me out until I felt human enough to breathe and act in a way that would prove less offensive than I'd felt when I approached the cabin an hour earlier.

Paul went into the bedroom where Katlyn remained imprisoned. I heard them talking. She shouted, "No, not for that asshole Black. He kidnapped me."

Paul said something in return, but spoke too low for me to hear his words. Just as well. The sound of her voice raised the hair on the back of my neck, made my skin crawl. Somewhere in my mind that woman already died. Katlyn was, as my old man once said with an ironic smile when discussing the corn he planted, living on borrowed time.

And you get what you fucking have coming to you, I thought viciously. An army buddy once told it was called karma. Treat someone bad, someday the same would happen to you.

After wiping my mouth with an old yellow cloth napkin, I smiled weakly at Stella.

"That tasted terrific. Thanks." I reached for her hand. It felt warm because I was cold, but not from the weather.

She kissed my palm. We stood and embraced, which lasted about fifteen seconds before Dunbar interrupted us.

He cleared his throat as if he'd gotten a bone stuck in it. "You two got a minute for some serious talk?" he asked without revealing that he caught us in an embrace meant to lead to other goals.

I nodded, stepped back from Stella, and turned to face him. "She ready to cooperate?"

"I think she is. I made a deal to get her twenty-five to life instead of death should she be convicted as an accomplice to murder." He looked contemplative, as if he wanted to say more but the words he needed did not assemble into a sentence that might express the thought succinctly. "Although she mayn't get convicted for more than an act of coerced complicity if she hires the right attorney." He shrugged.

"I'll talk to her outside." I did not give him time to respond and went out to wait under the light of a half moon and scudding clouds. The stars looked like explosions of promised possibility.

The door opened and closed behind me. Footsteps approached and I listened to Katlyn's breathing. She sounded like she ran a mile.

After a long minute or two, she cleared her throat. "What do you want me to do, Black?"

Be civil, I thought with dry sarcasm, and said, "Return to the city and get back to your normal routine. Then I want you to call Palmer and set up a time to meet."

"I told you no one calls Bobby; he calls you or kills you, whichever he decides is better for him at the moment."

Glancing over my shoulder, I tried to smile but failed. It felt like a snarl.

"When you talk to him, Katlyn," I said, ignoring her statement to tell her that I knew she failed to be honest, "you tell Bobby that you know where to find me. After that, it's my turn. Do this right and I'll stand up for you in court."

"Why in God's name would you do that?" She sounded skeptical, and should have. Yet at the same time, she sounded like part of her wanted to believe me, which was enough for me to manipulate her.

"That should be obvious even to you, Katlyn. He killed my girl, and now I want a piece of him."

She shuffled as she walked. I looked down and saw that her ankles and her hands were tied.

Katlyn raised her arms as though she thought I had not noticed her predicament. When I did not move to untie her, she dropped her arms in resignation.

"Detective Dunbar put the rope on. He's the law. Only he can remove it." I walked around her, watched her turn in a circle to keep an eye on me. "How the hell did a woman like you end up in such a mess? You only go for dangerous men?"

Her face contorted as if she was shocked or insulted, and then she laughed a sound like a snort or a bark. "Yeah, Black. That's it. Why? You want to have your way with me? You're a dangerous man, Black, maybe me standing here all trussed up is giving you an erection."

She laughed then and the sound relit my anger seriously enough to give me an urge to slap her. I jammed my hands in my pockets and fingered loose change.

"If I could have my way with you, Katlyn, I'd find a way to get you locked up for life. And that's it," I replied without thought and regretted it, but did not refute the statement. "I'm using you to get to Palmer. Other than that, your life has no value to me. Dunbar made you a deal and I'll stand behind it, but only because I want Palmer, not because I think you deserve my help. Moreover, when and if they release you from prison, I will be standing outside the front gate to greet you. Sooner or later, you'll step into a mess you can't escape, and I'll be there when you do."

She looked stricken. Perhaps for the first time in her life she knew her fate, and also saw she could do nothing to alter its course.

Momentarily, I felt like shit, but then just as quickly I did not give a damn. "We'll be leaving in time to catch the first train back to the city."

I grasped her upper arm. She tried to pull away, but stopped and raised her eyes to meet my stare. "What's to stop me from telling Bobby what's going on and letting him help me after he kills you,

Black?" she said with venom.

"Paul Dunbar." I led her into the cabin, into the bedroom she used, and closed the door after leaving her inside.

The fire still blazed, but standing directly before the hearth was insufficient to warm me. Again, I rubbed my hand on the seams of my blue jeans, but that was not enough to get the feel of her off my flesh. After washing up, I changed into clean clothes.

Stella waited by the fireplace, came over when I approached, and stood behind me, put her arms around my chest, and held me like I was more important to her than any other man alive could be.

I wanted to suggest that she make a more appropriate selection, that I might be the man who would live to bury her. However, I drew a deep breath, held in the air, exhaled slowly, put my hands on hers, and closed my eyes. I felt as if I'd experienced more than one lifetime's horrors.

Death is the ultimate test of faith. I wondered why I remembered my CO, my commanding officer at that moment. Captain James Todd Wright had led with his presence. At the start of the war, he was an enlisted man from Savannah, Georgia. With time, diligence, and due to extreme bravery, he quickly earned the rank of staff sergeant. After a string of catastrophic battles along the path through Europe to Germany, he became a field-commissioned lieutenant. By mid '44, he was our company commander.

By then, I'd already fought with him for over a year and remained a friend despite the fact that I refused to climb into an officer's uniform. I gained the rank of platoon sergeant, felt grateful I lived long enough to have that honor, and never desired higher accolade. I would have been fine dying with three stripes sewn to my sleeves.

As the Battle of the Bulge ground our company into memories and remains we would never identify, Wright must have sensed the cloaked demon that caressed his neck as it accepted him.

We hunkered down in a bomb crater, running low on ammunition and hope. He turned to me during a lull and after we both lit cigarettes said, "You know, Marlowe, my pastor back home once stated in a Palm Sunday sermon that death is the ultimate test of faith. I think by now I'm ready for that test; how about you, my friend? Together, we've watched a lot of good men die."

"My faith ran dry a few months ago, sir," I said without revealing the surprise I felt, and cupped the ember of my cigarette to pull in a long drag of smoke without illuminating our location.

He laughed lightly. "That's what I appreciate most about you, Marlowe. You never bullshit anyone for any reason. Hope you never change. I'm going to fetch the ammo I see laying over there. We're both getting low." He pointed at a fallen GI and moved five feet to the right. His head crested the edge of the crater, and a German sharpshooter drilled a neat hole through the center of his forehead.

The fire snapped and a log rolled to the edge of the hearth. I moved Stella's hands and used the brass tongs to place it back in the center of the flames.

I've never answered the inquiry "Why him and not me?" because if I asked it for Captain Wright, then I'd have to ask it for every guy I knew who fought and died and all those I wasn't acquainted with too. Hell, those heroes deserved respect for their sacrifices, nothing less, like second-guessing circumstances and fate.

Perhaps part of the ultimate test of faith is accepting that I lived when others died because I'd not yet accomplished the tasks set for me by the Creator, but those who died young had finished. On the other hand, maybe I was plain lucky. Either way, second-guessing achieved nothing more than added grief.

The faith that remained inside me after the war counseled me that there had to be a reason for living, but I may never recognize it. If life came to each of us without constructive purpose, then chaos replaced sanity, and war would prove to be the consequence of providence, not the ill-thought-out decisions of lunatics and men hungry for personal gain. Although the two may be one and the same. Guess I'll never really know.

I stood after closing the fireplace screen to keep in sparks, took Stella's hand, and led her into the bedroom we'd been using. Paul slept on the foldout sofa with two blankets over him, or at least he pretended to sleep.

I found comfort and relief in Stella's embrace and, after her loving, found I could sleep at least fitfully.

Loud thunder shook the cabin around 3 a.m. I rolled from the bed, threw on my pants, and found Paul standing at the open front door.

Silver tongues of lightning etched the blue-black sky above the lake, struck a tree, skidded off, and sizzled into the water's surface. The breeze that blew in our faces smelled like new earth and a summer's potential in some profound ways abandoned by the living.

My emotional heart felt hard, cold, and I yearned to sense a type of passion I realized would elude me for the rest of my years: Love. No, I did not feel bitter or even resentful about that loss, but determined that I wouldn't succumb to that emotion's temptation in an uncertain and dangerous future as demonstrated by my history.

And no, I'd not be delivering newspapers at 4 a.m. to alter the self-established direction of my life.

I shot men when not to do so meant being shot, and would fire again when necessity or fate required that I convey outcome to any person trying to kill another or me. Because of that single truth, I would not invite another woman to fall victim to my chosen destiny, my life preferences.

Chapter Nineteen

Not waiting for sunrise, I woke Katlyn and with Stella's assistance got her cleaned up and dressed so she looked presentable for the return to the city. Stella gave her the extra pair of flat-sole shoes she'd brought to the cabin, and handed Twiggs a five-dollar bill to cover cab fare and food.

I watched and said nothing regarding the exchange as Twiggs stuffed the cash in her purse. Then I spent several minutes persuading Stella to remain in the relative safety of the cabin, and assured her that when I finished in town, I'd return to her.

After a hot breakfast of eggs, bacon, toast, and two cups of black coffee, Paul drove us to the Newburgh train station.

He shook my hand as the train rolled in and said, "Good luck, Marlowe. If you need anything, leave a message at this number. I'll check in every day starting tomorrow. Don't waste too much time finding Palmer."

He handed me a small business card that, ironically, belonged to the lawyer upstairs, the attorney who employed the gorgeous redhead Pamela Gentrey, Delbert Bartholomew.

I did not inquire why he chose that particular attorney, nor did I mention the interesting coincidence, positive that time and events would expose both if I could be patient enough and lived long enough, and I accepted his offer.

On the reverse side of the card, I saw Katlyn's home phone number written in Dunbar's handwriting but did not say anything as he raised an eyebrow in warning. Paul had been busy thinking and planning while I'd been away searching for a killer.

He passed an identical business card to Katlyn too, but without handwriting on the reverse.

"You might need this," he said knowingly.

When he turned in my direction again, I said, "Thanks, Paul, I'll call if I need you," and followed Katlyn onto the train and sat in the seat behind her.

She was free to escape, and I to capture her and haul her ass back to the freezer if necessary to obtain her absolute cooperation.

However, Katlyn did not move except to occasionally glance longingly out the window and to pass her ticket to the conductor when he stopped and requested it.

He gave her the once-over, I suppose curious about why she wore men's clothing, but said naught other than "Thank you, ma'am" with a brief nod.

Katlyn disregarded him as if he did not exist. I raised my unpunched ticket as distraction in case he decided to prod her, as men are prone to do with a woman who gives the impression of being lost and unaccompanied as Katlyn did just then.

He notched my ticket and slid the stub in the metal receptacle at the top edge of the seatback behind me, outside slot, and said, "Thank you, sir."

"You're welcome," I returned, removed my hat, and dropped it on the seat next to me. I did not find a magazine in the seat pocket, so I leaned back, closed my eyes, and waited for the ride and my quest to end finally.

After the second train stopped in Grand Central, Katlyn stood and faced me. "You'll either be dead the next time I see you, Black, or I'll be dead before then. Bobby's not very forgiving."

"Don't get your hopes up too high either way, Katlyn. I mean to make certain you land in prison and I don't think Palmer wants to kill you. If he did you'd likely be gone by now."

I followed her off the train and stopped walking so I could see her in case she ran. I was not sure why she'd flee, but too much had happened since she entered my life a year ago, most of which, regarding her, I did not want to re-experience.

She blended into the first crowd she approached, and I wondered if she would do her part.

I could not go anywhere familiar, so decided to visit Irwin Cohen and use his basement for a temporary office.

He had it filled with a miniature world built around a gigantic collection of American Flyer two-rail model trains that he ran during his off hours. He became a Lilliputian figure who could exist only in a shrinker's land of toy trains, steam locomotives, and the call of the imaginary conductor as he announced succeeding stops.

Every Christmas, Irwin opened his basement to any family or kid who might want to be awed by the layout's intricate details once he added snow to the structures and ground and placed tiny gifts on flatcars. And him a Jew. How do you like them apples?

He owned the midtown building from which he worked and rented offices to several upstanding citizens who operated anything from an insurance business to a dentist on the fifth floor. Seemed like adding insult to injury, but what the hell, if you're in enough pain, climbing five flights to gain relief might be a suitable distraction in a perverse kind of way.

I rang his buzzer while standing in the small foyer after checking for a tail and found I was alone, which meant Katlyn did not run to the nearest phone to report to Palmer that I had returned to the city. Maybe she planned to obey Dunbar after all. I still harbored serious doubts. She gave off an impression of intelligence. I found her too damn proud; a woman who thought of herself as a clever operator able to get away with acts of indecency toward others. Although I still felt lousy for the way I treated her to get her to squeal on Palmer.

Irwin responded to the buzzer with a sharp "Yeah?"

"Hi, buddy," I said. "I need to get into your basement. Can you buzz me in and meet me downstairs?"

I listened for a click, a loud buzz, heard both, and entered the security of his building. The basement stairs ran down on the left side of the building at the bottom end of several flights of fire stairs down from the roof.

When I flipped up the light switch mounted on the wall alongside the lower access to the basement, a train whistle blew. I smiled.

A powerful-looking black Atlantic steam locomotive with the number 300AC stamped in silver on the sides of the cabin below the windows chugged past where I stood puffing smoke like a genuine engine. It pulled two long, heavyweight dark green Pullman cars. The last one had an observation deck where a young-looking couple stood on the platform as if they waved good-bye to family they thought they might never see again. The smile that creased my face was a pleasant surprise, and I anticipated the small train's return.

Before the engine came around a second time, Irwin appeared as if by magic. He had a private elevator from his second-floor office to the basement.

"You're looking better than the last time I saw you, but I get the distinct feeling you haven't completed your—what should I call it? Case?"

"Good enough for now, Irwin, and no, I haven't, but the pieces have started falling into place. I anticipate that I'll be finished in another day or two and hoped to use your basement as an office until then."

He smiled with that knowing look he gets when he reads between the lines, dissects, and understands motives most people would never catch onto without his type of intuition.

"There's a small apartment in the back with a kitchen, bath, and separate phone line. You don't need a telephone operator with that line. I had it set up for special occasions like this one."

"You're a true friend, Irwin." I patted his shoulder and walked to the rear of the cellar.

The passenger train chugged by, and he stopped to look for a moment.

"Need to clean and lube her," he said, and then glanced over at me. "Have to do maintenance like the boys do on the real ones." He sounded serious. I smiled and nodded.

When we reached a closed door, he lifted a key from the small change pocket in the gray vest he wore and passed it to me.

"You expected someone to come and use the apartment?" I asked and nodded at the door.

"No, but you know how I am, I get these feelings once in a while…"

"And act on them without waiting when most people would pass up a possible opportunity," I added.

"And that, my friend, is one-half of luck," he said with a satisfied grin.

"What's the other half?" I suspected the answer.

"Preparation." He lifted his hand in an abbreviated salute and then pointed to the apartment's door.

I opened it, flipped on a wall switch, and confronted a neat, cozy, furnished room.

"I've got a client coming in at two." He pulled the gold link chain and fob that held his gold pocket watch with a steam locomotive engraved intricately on the back, and snapped open the lid. "Ten minutes. You need anything, Marlowe, call upstairs. Otherwise, use the basement door at the top of the steps exiting from the apartment's kitchen. Comes out on the alley."

I shook his hand. "Thanks again, Irwin."

"Hey, I take care of my own, friend." He turned and left. A minute later, the basement lights went off and the train stopped chugging. The silence became too much to bear. After I closed the apartment door, I located a radio and tuned in to the familiar companionship of WNYC.

I kicked off my shoes and dropped on the green sofa. I dialed the phone number Katlyn gave to Paul.

She picked up and answered after two rings.

"I'm ready, Katlyn. After you talk to Palmer, call the attorney's number Paul gave you. I'll check every day at ten and five until I get your message, but don't wait too long. You don't have too much time left." I hung up, did not want to hear any more of her bullshit. The sound of her voice made my skin crawl.

Silence replaced everything but my thoughts. The city, the town where some generations of my family had been born and raised, did not feel comfortable. I did not like the realization and could not decide if the problem grew out of the events I'd gone through over the previous few weeks, or something deeper. The more I thought about it, the worse the dilemma became until I could not stand another minute of sitting alone in the semi-darkness.

I pulled my shoes on, grabbed my hat, and left. Neon beer signs lit the high windows of the bar at the corner. Cheering voices of drinkers rooting for the New York Yankees filled the joint. It wasn't easy for a Giants fan, but hell, I needed a stiff one. I entered, bought a shot of scotch and a beer chaser on tap.

After the second round, I caught myself cheering when one of the bombers drove a ball over the left centerfield wall, and the night passed in a haze of drowned remembrances and choked regrets.

Chapter Twenty

I don't enjoy hangovers. Regardless of how much I preferred to take pleasure in drowning my sorrow, I forced myself off the barstool and out of the tavern before I drank more than enough to bring one on the next morning.

Halfway down the alley behind Irwin's building, at the entrance to the basement, I spotted a pair of tall, masculine shadows that moved like vultures waiting patiently for an unsuspecting victim.

Quietly, I lifted the Colt from the holster and carefully flipped off the safety with my thumb before entering the alley. The odds were real good that Twiggs double-crossed me and Palmer sent two more goons to deliver a final greeting. I did not think about how they might've located me, but knew that Palmer was damn good at what he did.

I kept my back to the wall. Subsequently, illumination from streetlights failed to reach me, and then I moved toward them cautiously.

When I could visually define their silhouettes, I saw that they faced the street at the alley's opposite end.

After slipping off my shoes to avoid scuffing the pavement, I crept close enough to place the gun barrel against the back of the skull nearest me.

"Breathe hard and you're a dead man, pal," I said in a half whisper.

He gasped surprise and started to turn to look at me. I pressed the barrel hard against his skull, directly behind his ear, and told him, "Honest to God, don't trouble yourself by looking. We're both aware of who you're here to find. Now how about you enlighten me as to who the fuck sent you and why he did."

His partner stepped from behind him so I could see his features in the weak light that trickled the length of the alley from behind me.

"Paul Dunbar said we should check up on you," he said and flashed a detective's shield.

Swell, I thought, *and I came close to shooting first.*

"How the hell'd you know where to look?" I asked.

"Paul thought you might be visiting your old army buddy Irwin Cohen since not too many people know of the relationship. You can't stay at home due to the fact that some creep is out to gun you down should he find you without your suspecting that he's there."

"Paul is a smart guy," I said with a weak grin, not sure how he learned about Irwin and me.

Cohen and I met after we were assigned to boot camp. We teamed up and trained together for six weeks. Irwin wanted to go to the front line and fight the Germans, but the U.S. Army determined that they could best utilize his talents elsewhere. His German Jewish World War One refugees turned immigrant parents taught him to speak read and write everyday Low German. I did not see him again until after VE Day and was delighted he survived as he was for me. We swapped stories over several beers in a local downtown gin mill.

"He's that, all right," the cop said encouragingly.

"How about your names before I lower this," I said and nodded at the .45.

"Tommy English," the detective said and put his badge in his jacket pocket. "My partner is Daniel D. Davis."

"DDD?" I asked and released the pressure of the barrel against his head. "What's the middle D stand for?"

"David." He reached back and scrubbed his fingers through his scalp where I had pressed the gun barrel. "Dunbar told us you wouldn't take any chances. Guess we should've been looking both ways."

"I got lucky," I said magnanimously. "The nearest tavern is a block north from the other end." I stepped back, dropped the Colt in the holster, and retrieved my shoes. "I'd invite you inside, but it's late and I have an early appointment."

English watched me like he thought I might turn and race like hell down the alley, which made me know I stood with cops. Otherwise, one of them would have shot me by then.

"Paul also said to tell you that you're not to go killing anyone without unassailable provocation that will pass a hanging judge's muster."

I grinned at a statement so typical of Dunbar's humor. "Did he spell out exactly what he meant by unassailable and a hanging judge? Or do you think he intended to leave that to my discretion?"

"He said you'd know what he meant, wise guy, and also said that Stella agreed." He shrugged as if that made very little sense to him. "He said it seems the dame wants you to be around after you've cleaned up the shit you'll be grinding under your heel." He grinned that time at the images his words drew for him.

"Like Paul, the woman has a way with words, but she isn't thinking straight," I informed him without realizing that the alcohol I drank influenced my thinking and caused me to express personal sentiment to strangers, "if she believes there's any reason to have relationship expectations with me living my kind of future." Which I did not think would be long or something any sensible woman might enjoy sharing.

"Yeah, I can understand that. We went to your girl's funeral. You lose someone close the way you did her, and everything inside sours worse than curdled milk," Davis said.

"Thanks for the support back then. It means a lot to me. I owe you both. Now, I should get inside. Tell Paul I appreciate his watching my back like he did during the war."

"Will do," English said and I watched them until they turned the corner at the east end of the alley.

It's difficult to reckon with a man of Paul Dunbar's character. After I quit the force in disgust due to the justice system's reluctance to punish those who can buy their way free, Paul treated me like something he'd toss out with the trash, as if my act condemned his personal beliefs and code of honor as well as my own tarnished versions of the same.

Hell, I left the Army and moved from OD green fatigues to the dark blue of a New York beat cop thinking I could continue to make as much difference as I'd made fighting Nazis. In several cases, I had, but a couple of times a high-priced lawyer gave a criminal who should have been easily convicted a ticket to walk away from the crime he committed.

To me, witnessing such activities made being a cop seem like a useless pastime. I could not imagine myself remaining in uniform when by removing it I could apply enough pressure to the right people and be sure that equal justice would indeed get served.

I reentered the basement apartment and saw that a bit of illumination bled in through sidewalk-level windows to light up everything I needed to finish the day with a wry touch of normalcy. Although for me, normal had become as slippery as live electric eels in a bucket of cold saltwater.

When my head hit the pillow, I went out until 5 a.m., and the sound of a delivery van rumbling up the street and the rattle of milk bottles woke me.

I could not help but wonder if Katlyn would contact Palmer before the new day turned into night. I hoped she would call him and not force me to imprison her again. Dragging her into the meat locker awoke feelings I did not want to sort through, and therefore I didn't feel ready to haul myself through a second session with her.

However, my life and liberty ranked higher than Katlyn's self-determination ever would. I planned to do my utmost to honor my commitment to Paul and keep her alive to stand trial after she squealed on Bobby Palmer while under oath.

Of course, I was not convinced that in the end she would turn on him. She seemed more concerned about not getting him angry than about keeping me from ending the charade of her life with a few long years in prison for her role in Lois' murder.

As the sun forced red-orange light through a cloudbank to glow and glint off the myriad panes of window glass on the buildings outside, I left my temporary home and walked to a small corner diner I'd passed the previous night.

The early morning crowd ate without conversation, thankfully. I sat at the counter and ordered scrambled eggs, toast, bacon, and a pot of coffee. The coffee tasted memorable, the food adequate but too greasy. The guy on the stool alongside me read the *Times*. He rustled the pages by shaking them each time he turned to the next page and then folded the paper to read while sipping coffee and eating a Danish. I read over his shoulder and bided my time.

At 9 a.m., I left and went to a small shop near the theatre district next door to the Cuban Casino on the corner of West Forty-Fifth and Eighth Avenue.

I'd passed the store several times before and thought on each occasion I should stop in and see what the proprietor sold that I could use.

Since they handled nothing but costumes and other accessories for part-time actors and actresses, I hadn't taken the thought too seriously. Now, I needed help so I could move freely around town.

A small bell chattered when I opened the door, but no one appeared from the back. Then I walked into rows of costumes and knew I'd made the correct decision.

I picked out a new-looking prewar brown striped suit with wide padded shoulders and matching trousers. The shoes I selected were brown-and-white spats with a high sheen. The tie was wide and blood red; shirt white as bleach.

When I reached the counter a short woman, about fifty years old, stepped from behind a long blue beaded curtain that seemed to separate the rear of the store from the front. She stood a couple inches shorter than I did, with long, wavy brown hair streaked with silver, and she kept errant curls off her face with gold barrettes.

Her features looked pleasant, with enough lines and wrinkles to give her the appearance of an intelligent woman who enjoyed sharing her humor with others. Her wide-set hazel eyes examined what I held and she nodded.

"Good morning, sir. I can see you're a man with expensive tastes," she said with a hundred-dollar smile. "I didn't know there was a play in town that called for a 1930s look."

"I'm going to a costume ball over in Jersey," I lied with unexpected ease. "I also need a way to disguise my face, but don't want a mask or makeup. Do you have any suggestions?"

Her smile widened. "Absolutely, you wait right there, sir." She went behind the curtain, where I heard her rattling something metallic. When she returned, she held a large metal box about two feet by one and six inches deep. She placed it on the counter and lifted the lid. Inside, I saw what looked like a bunch of small furry caterpillars, but was instead facial hair.

After a moment's consideration, she selected a mustache and trim Van Dyke beard and said, "You'll need to remove your hat, sir."

I did and she held the two pieces close to my hair, nodded, and said, "Let's see how this will look." She came around the counter and held them to my face, seemed pleased, put them on the counter, lifted a small jar, and dabbed on facial glue. A minute later, I looked at a stranger's face in the hand mirror she held up.

"How about a pair of eyeglasses?" I asked.

"Excellent idea," she said and went back behind the curtain, returned with gold-rimmed spectacles with plain glass lenses, and handed them to me.

I put them on and no longer saw any of my old self in the mirror.

"How much do I owe you?" I asked, feeling satisfied.

"Fifty dollars even should cover it all," she said. "That is, if you're planning on keeping it."

"I am," I said. "I like the way it makes me look." I paid and left wearing my disguise with the suit, shirt, tie, and a jar of glue in a large brown bag.

Back inside the basement apartment, I showered and dressed in my new duds, then returned to the street feeling confident that Palmer could bump into me and would not know with whom he'd collided until I pressed the end of the .45 in his ear.

I didn't know right then if I would pull the trigger and finish him off, but there was nothing more on God's corrupted Earth that I wanted then but for the bastard to die slowly and painfully.

Murder was vile enough, but the possibility that he raped her too somehow seemed more than perverse.

What type of gutter trash perverted son of a bitch brutalizes a woman that way and then lives with himself afterward?

Not paying attention to where I walked, I bumped hard into a woman with two shopping bags, watched helplessly as she lost her grip on one and the contents spilled over the top of the damaged bag. Quickly, I took the bag, straightened it up as best I could, and then picked up the items that hit the sidewalk: three pairs of silk stockings and a dark blue jar of cold cream, which fortunately remained unbroken.

"I'm sorry," I said and looked at her face. She appeared to be about my age with striking blue eyes and a pageboy haircut that framed her heart-shaped face with the color of platinum silk. She wore pink lipstick and matching nail polish. "I hope I didn't ruin anything."

"I don't believe so," she said in a sweet voice. "Thank you for picking everything up."

"You're welcome," I said, tipped my hat, and watched her walk off.

The day warmed up and I wondered if my disguise would prove to be worth the effort as sweat ran down my chest and back. Without hesitation, I went straight to the Flatiron Building and entered. When I passed several people I have seen in the building numerous times before, none gave me a second look.

Once inside my office, I sat behind the desk and called the number off the card Paul gave me before I left the lakeside cabin.

I instantly recognized the voice that announced what office I dialed.

"You should've told me you knew Paul Dunbar," I said without introduction.

"Hi, Marlowe. I hoped I'd be hearing from you soon." She ignored my proclamation with a chuckle. "Paul is an old friend of Mr. B. He does detective work for us on his days off."

"And you need me too?" I asked, and then realized that it had been through Paul that she knew enough about me to recognize me and feel comfortable enough to approach me and even sit uninvited to share breakfast on the train down from Newburgh.

"For the days when he's working or for the odd case he can't investigate due to a conflict of interest."

"Must happen a lot, knowing Paul's code of ethics the way I do."

Pamela Gentrey laughed, and I liked the sound as much as I had on the train. It was easy for me to picture her intense green eyes as they expressed her amusement.

"He's strict about which cases he's willing to work on."

"That's why he's a New York police detective and I'm a private cop."

"So what can I do for you, Marlowe? Call for a lunch date?"

"Not today, doll, but when I'm finished with the job I'm working, I'll ring you back."

"You can count on that as a date, buddy," she said and sounded inviting and interested.

"The other reason I phoned is that Paul told me to call this number to learn if you've heard from a woman named Katlyn Twiggs."

"Oh yes. Now there is a name one doesn't soon forget." Pamela spoke with caution as if she wasn't alone and did not want whoever stood alongside her to overhear the conversation.

"Did she call your office?"

"About ten minutes ago as a matter of fact. She left you a message."

"So you were getting prepared to give me a call," I said.

"I was, but I'm also serious about lunch and maybe dinner too."

"Me too, doll. Can you tell me the message?"

"You in your office right now?"

"Downstairs," I told her. "Are you coming here to deliver it in person?"

"I need to get out of the office and run a few errands. See you in a couple of minutes." She hung up.

I pushed the hat off my brow, wiped sweat with a handkerchief, and glanced out the window. The building's super had replaced the broken window glass.

The clouds I'd seen earlier gathered and threatened to turn humidity into long overdue rain.

After a few minutes of staring into the gray sky, I heard light, unhurried footsteps in the hallway approaching the office. I stood and opened the door and confronted Pamela. She wore a form-fitting red cotton dress with matching shoes, lipstick, and nail polish.

"Oh, I'm so sorry," she said. "I came looking for Mr. Marlowe Black. Does he happen to be in right now or has he stepped out for a minute? He was expecting me." She held out her hand.

I accepted the invitation and shook it, smiled, and said, "He's expecting you too, doll."

"Marlowe? Is that really you? How strange you look." She leaned to look at my eyes and nodded. "Very nice. May I come in?"

"Please do." I moved aside, watched her walk into the center of the room, and then shut the door.

"Why the get-up? This have anything to do with the case you told me about on the train?"

"Yes, it does." I pointed to the guest chair and, after she sat, went behind the desk and sat too.

"I think I like the way you looked on the train better than this." She waved a hand at my face.

"Trust me, so do I." I took off my hat and dropped it on the desk, hung my new jacket on the chair back.

Pamela snapped open a small red glittery purse with lots of pearls, lifted out a folded sheet of paper, and passed it to me. "She is a most unpleasant woman, your Miss Twiggs."

"She's that and more than you might imagine." I took the note but did not unfold it.

"Aren't you going to read it? I already know what she said." She grinned and nodded at the paper I held. "After all, I'm the person who wrote down her message."

"True," I said with a chuckle and scanned the message. Palmer knew I was in town, but not where. Katlyn planned to meet with him at seven tonight at the Artists and Writers Restaurant on West Fortieth about a third of a block west of Seventh Avenue. The nearest landmark for me would be the New York Herald Tribune Building.

I felt pleased and relieved he had not selected Bryant Park. That would have been a setup for sure.

I glanced at Pamela and saw her intent look of interest.

"How about joining me for a late dinner tonight?" I asked casually.

"Do you think it might be dangerous, what with Miss Twiggs involved and all?" she asked, but didn't sound too concerned, only curious about the work I did. She could not know Katlyn the way I knew her.

"Exciting maybe, but dangerous? I don't think so. Katlyn and her companion shouldn't recognize me in my new disguise." I passed a hand in front of my face.

"What time do you want to pick me up?" she asked, eyes alight with interest.

"You live here in town?"

"Yes. I have a second-floor walk-up over a deli off Bleecker Street, on Perry."

I passed her a pad and pencil. "Why don't you jot down the address so I don't get lost."

After she finished, I read it, tore off the page, folded it, and stuck it in my pocket.

We did small talk, which I performed better I thought than either of us expected. When she left, I tried to decide what to do with the remainder of the day and concluded that Paul's cat Betty might be in need of food, water, and a clean pan of sand.

The subway was crowded, but with my disguise, I didn't worry about it and relaxed for the ride.

Betty lay stretched out on the front windowsill when I approached. One long Siamese leg dangled off, so when I jammed the key in the lock, she had to stand before she could jump down and hide.

For whatever reason cats do anything, she decided to return to the windowsill and stood on it where she might examine my activities. Maybe she liked my disguise better than the original. She arched her back and quivered the tip of her tail and then settled down in the cloud-faded sunlight. Her intelligent, blue-eyed, penetrating gaze narrowed but stayed on me as I moved through the apartment. Her ears stayed up and alert but moved like radar.

I overfilled her food bowl, washed out her water bowl, and filled it too. The tray of sand smelled and looked downright nasty. The stench of ammonia overpowered the room. I dumped it outside, found a hose and washed the pan, used a rag to dry it, refilled it, and put it back inside.

Betty watched it all through slit eyes as I reentered the front room.

"Paul is fine," I said, sounding like a fool who thought that a cat might understand the words.

However, I swear, she perked up, lifted her head, and made a low sound in her throat that was not quite a purr precisely, but more like a hum of pleasure.

Damn clever animal and I'm stuck with a dog that hides from trouble.

I locked up and went back to the subway to reach the nearest branch of my bank, where I got a wad of cash to get me through the next several days.

By then, it was noon and I felt bored. After returning to my basement apartment, I went out and turned on the American Flyer toy trains, watched the small steam engine pull its load for as long as I could stand it, shut everything off, and left.

I decided what I needed to do was to scout around the neighborhood where Palmer and Twiggs planned to go for dinner. I shrugged off the jacket and hung it over my shoulder so I looked like an ordinary businessman out for a walk or off to an appointment and strolled north.

The afternoon slipped by slowly. After walking through the theatre district, I went to the public library and researched snipers; men who lie in wait for hours without moving enough for a passing animal to spot them. A few used camouflage and a few did not, but all had several traits in common. A sniper must be determined, patient, and as quiet as a lioness stalking gazelle, and they, unlike the lion, rarely missed when they finally pulled the trigger.

The best shooters worked with single-shot, bolt-action weapons with mounted scopes they did not always need to use to take aim. Instead, they spent days on a firing range perfecting their skill. Their shot groups looked tight and accurate, which is a feat that's difficult to match.

By the time I left, I had one remaining question, the same that nagged at me for days. Why didn't Bobby Palmer shoot to kill both Stella and Paul? I came up with only one conceivable reason. Paul was correct. Palmer wanted them to live but wanted me to suffer, worry about his motives and his next move.

It was as if we played chess after denying me both knights and bishops. The odds ran heavily in his favor. However, odds are odds and nothing more than that.

Other than a friendly wager for a cold beer and five dollars with Phil Ball over the results of a ballgame, I never gambled and wasn't about to start then.

I hired a Checker cab and picked up Pamela at ten after six. She was not quite ready. I paid the cabbie and went into the deli beneath her apartment while she finished with her hair despite the fact that I thought she looked terrific when I first knocked on her door.

She joined me as I drained a bottle of Coke on the front stoop. Pamela wore an off-the-shoulders blue dress made from a silk-like material. It dipped in front to display enough shadowed cleavage to draw the interest of any man she passed, and low enough in the back to get me wondering what she wore underneath. The dress gripped her waist tightly and then flared out to the middle of her calves. She unquestionably had my complete attention.

After returning the bottle for the nickel refund, I used a pay phone and called the cab company.

Finally, we entered the restaurant at five till seven, got a table near the door, and ordered drinks and roast beef dinners. Pamela looked and smelled gorgeous and had every guy in the place watching every move she made.

She wore a light amount of makeup that highlighted her cheekbones and intriguing eyes. Her hair sparkled like polished gold with a lot of red highlights. If I had not faced the door, she would've distracted me enough that I'd've missed Katlyn Twiggs when she entered, accompanied by a man who looked tough, clever, cagy, and eerily familiar.

Twiggs wore a nice light green evening dress. The pale material shimmered as she moved and accented the body beneath. She wore heels and stockings that exhibited her lower legs while she walked with Satan's steering hand on her elbow.

Bobby Palmer ignored her babble about the restaurant's decor and carefully glanced once around the room. I knew beyond doubt that I witnessed an experienced killer. His gaze, though not stopping, managed to examine with care each and every face, including mine. If he recognized me, the man had ice water in his veins. He did not show any reaction other than placing his hand on the middle of Katlyn's lower back as he guided her to the table the maître d' led them to across the room from where we sat.

Pamela continued talking, nervously, too loud for the occasion, and watched them walk through the dining area after she noticed my attention wandered from her as my gaze moved to study the couple.

When they passed beyond where I could see them, I turned back to her and smiled. She hadn't turned around to observe where they went, and grinned knowingly at me.

"That was tense," she said very seriously.

"Only for you, doll. Do you think Miss Twiggs might've recognized your voice?" I asked to tell her I thought she might have spoken too loudly.

"She didn't appear to look at anything other than where she placed her feet. I believe she's scared half to death right now."

"Justifiably. Palmer is a rapist and a killer. She must feel like Lucifer's frigid breath is running down the back of her delicate neck."

Pamela blanched. The color ran from her face and a serious blush of anger replaced it quickly.

"Sorry," I said before she expressed outrage in that same loud voice as before. "I thought you knew about him."

"How in God's name would I know something like that if you didn't tell me, Marlowe?" She leaned halfway across the table so she did not need to speak above a harsh whisper.

I leaned closer to her, close enough that I could smell her perfume; see the faint lines between the corners of her mouth and nose. Her eyes widened as if she thought I might try to kiss her, or tell her an important fact that would change the direction of her life.

Unable to decide which might be the correct reaction, I then smiled when I thought that at the moment the two could be interchangeable in her mind, or at least in mine.

"You don't need to whisper. They can't hear you now," I said quietly and grinned. "You're one serious lady."

"I'm not sure how you mean that, Marlowe. Am I a serious lady, or a lady who is serious?"

"Is this one of those trick questions women like to spring on us poor unsuspecting saps?"

She chuckled and leaned back in her chair as a waiter approached with our dinners. I had him bring fresh drinks, and watched Pamela as she delicately cut her meat, speared a piece with her fork, dipped it in brown gravy, and slipped it between her lips. I felt transfixed, but the aromas lifting from my plate swept away the feeling with palatable invitation.

Someone played piano, the evening passed like a date, and I relaxed after my third scotch. Then I saw Palmer stand, wait for Twiggs. He placed his hand on her elbow and steered her so she walked directly alongside our table.

Brusquely, he bumped into Pamela's arm as she lifted her glass of wine. Then, Palmer lifted his hand, seemed to move casually, and using two fingers twisted Pamela's wrist slightly as if to help her, which dumped wine over the exposed top of her chest, down inside the front of her dress, and on her lap too.

She gasped and jumped, but was unable to get to her feet since Palmer hovered directly over her. She put her glass on the table and reached for the top of her dress.

I suspected his contrived movement was intentional as if he'd spotted a woman he wanted to victimize and decided he needed a closer inspection. I did not think he recognized me since he had not once looked in my direction for my reaction. He was an overconfident hunter who kept his focus on his prey, knew exactly what to do, and how to deal with male competition should he be confronted by it.

However, the night turned and went wrong from that moment on. When Pamela yelped and tried to leap to her feet, I stood to interfere and collided with Katlyn. She looked at me and must've recognized me by my eyes. She gasped loud enough for Palmer to hear her, and she grabbed my arm as if to hold me back.

Palmer kept busy apologizing to Pamela while he quickly wiped at her chest with a napkin without touching her too offensively, which I thought to be perfectly ironic knowing how he enjoyed fondling women abusively. Oh, his fingers brushed the top of her breasts.

I thought he was finished and turned to face Katlyn, free myself from her before Palmer caught on. I heard Pamela say something about stopping, glanced back, and saw Palmer push down her dress enough to expose most of her breasts. I knew he meant to shove it down until her chest was completely exposed.

He nearly succeeded, leaving Pamela fumbling to keep herself covered as the wine soaked through the material below.

Katlyn must've known Palmer's routine. Her role, it seemed, was to keep the guy occupied while Palmer accomplished his humiliation. I couldn't figure how they would get their victim away from her companion, but knew I was witnessing an act as repulsive as any I'd seen yet.

Then he placed one hand on her back and seemed to be working loose the zipper. He grinned, which told me he succeeded, and Pamela's dress seemed to sag. If she hadn't had a two-handed grip on it, or had been standing, I knew it would be down to her waist by then. As it was, I saw one side to the bottom of her ribs. He was undressing her successfully inside of a few seconds since he'd dumped her wine.

I nearly slapped Katlyn away, no longer caring if Palmer knew I was Pamela's date. He had to be stopped.

You arrogant son of a bitch, I thought, jammed my hand under my jacket, shoved Katlyn aside finally, and started to move toward him. I wanted to shoot him, but decided kicking the crap out of him would do if I could keep poor Pamela from being entangled further than she'd already become by then.

Pamela jumped and glanced over her shoulder. Judging by Palmer's arm, I knew he had reached down inside the back of her dress.

I lifted the .45, but instead of shooting him, I called loudly and waved over a waiter.

"Need some help over here!"

"No we don't!" Twiggs yelled, which got Palmer's full attention. He stopped moving and stared at me. I knew he immediately understood what happened the instant his eyes shifted, as if his target moved just enough to one side to throw off his aim. He lifted his right hand. It was big, well-muscled, and had manicured nails. He used it to make a gun, pointed it at my face, and dropped his thumb like a hammer.

"Bang," he said softly.

"Fuck off, Palmer," I returned. "Get your fucking hands off her now." I waved the .45 at his face.

Then I heard someone scream, "He's got a gun!" Most of the people in the restaurant raced to the door as if they were afraid I might shoot them all.

Without a word to Twiggs, Palmer shoved her aside and stormed from the restaurant, moving through the frightened crowd effortlessly. Katlyn fell into my chair as if her legs would no longer hold her weight.

"I'm dead now thanks to you," she whispered with dreary resignation that under other circumstances would have torn into my heart.

"I recognized your voice," she told Pamela, "but hoped you weren't with *him*." She nodded at me. "Bobby insisted we stop by to say hello. I didn't know he'd assault you, but now I'm really screwed badly."

"He wanted to molest me, you miserable little bitch of a woman!" Pamela hissed as she reached back and pulled up the zipper, adjusting her dress as she did.

Stunned by what I'd witnessed, I said nothing for a long minute, and then said finally, "I'll take you to Grand Central in the morning, Katlyn. You can catch the next train out of town and head back to the cabin. Paul Dunbar will protect you once you arrive at Lake Orange." The words twisted something deep inside me, but I'd made that damn promise to a cop. There was no turning away from responsibility, no way I could justify allowing Palmer to hurt or kill her.

She looked relieved and said, "But after he's done with you, he'll find me sooner or later and kill me then."

The waiter brought wet towels for Pamela and took them after she finished cleaning up. Her dress was soaked through.

As I saw it, I knew I let her down too, not doing something to stop Palmer sooner. Yet he moved too fast, and Palmer was slick enough to disguise his efforts as helping after an accident. I doubt I would've managed to prevent much, except maybe make things worse for Pamela.

She was very angry. I could see in her eyes that most of her rage came from the confrontation, and that she may have believed it had been her fault somehow.

"Sorry you went through that," I said, walked around the table. I draped my jacket over her bare shoulders to afford her some privacy. "I couldn't move fast enough to stop him, and damn Katlyn, she was helping him by blocking my movements."

"I know. You looked like you wanted to shoot him." She smiled weakly, and I thought I read relief on her face. She took my hand and I had the headwaiter phone for a cab.

Outside, I looked for Palmer and did not see him, wasn't surprised he was gone, but felt glad when a Checker cab rolled to a stop at the curb.

It took nearly an hour to get Katlyn Twiggs safely into her Bowery apartment after I made certain that no one tailed us there by paying the cabbie to take a circuitous route downtown.

"I know a nice little bar down near where I'm staying," I said to Pamela once we secured Twiggs for the night. "Care to join me for a nightcap? I owe you that and more."

"After I've changed into something dry. I need to soak this dress or it will be ruined."

I glanced down, saw what I expected, and looked at her face. She colored and turned her head away from me, which made me feel like a heel for looking.

By ten we sat at the bar listening to jazz from the radio instead of another Yankee game. They had the television off; the blank screen was a pleasant relief.

After she finished a second glass of cheap white wine I bought her, Pamela hit me with a conversational brick. "I know that man."

"Which one?" I watched her in the bar mirror and waved for the bartender to refill her glass.

"The man who accompanied Miss Twiggs to dinner." She lifted the glass and gazed into the pale liquid.

"Then he did intentionally run into you the way Twiggs suggested he did." *Son of a bitch wasn't trying to stop the drink from spilling when he took her wrist. He was dumping it on her!* But I already knew that much.

She nodded tensely, started talking as if unable to hold back any longer. "Robert Palmer. He tried to hire Mr. Bartholomew early last year about something that happened up in Connecticut, I think. He kept returning every day, was very annoying and persistent. He liked to rub my shoulders with his fingers over the front, and stared at my, um, chest while he talked as if I did not have a face. I found his behavior to be very frightening, threatening, and knew he wanted to do much more to me than give me a casual touch on the shoulder when he walked past my desk.

"I was not really surprised that you told me he's a rapist. I might've become one of his victims tonight if not for you. The way he was leering at me, ogling my chest while he sopped up the spilled wine. Twice, he tried to force his hand under the front of my dress." She shivered and shook her head, talking as if to stop meant forcing herself to relive it all in her mind. "Once he opened the zipper…he almost managed to reach in enough, oh, God. He would've destroyed me completely if I hadn't been able to hold my dress up, and then what would I have done? My back was exposed. He was so close to strip—"

She shuddered, drained her wineglass, and continued as if unable to stop herself. "Marlowe, if Twiggs hadn't gasped when she did, which made him hesitate, he'd have succeeded, oh God… He's very strong and was very close to overpowering me, and another second or two—"

I touched the back of her hand, wanted to redirect her talk, but did not want to stop her entirely. Pamela needed to release the fear, get rid of the feeling of being something less than human to Palmer.

"I think I might've passed out if he did that to me." Her face turned a dark crimson as she drained her glass and held it up for a refill.

"I think I would've stopped him before he succeeded," I said, knowing I wanted to, but for a moment hesitated, wondering if I might've made it worse. *But worse than what? He was goddamn close.*

And that's how he would've claimed his prize. Assisted you out to the street as if he was helping a woman home who drank too much. Put his suit coat around you to hide what he did. And then, he would've taken you wherever, raped and killed you, I thought with disgust and anguish. Her being in the situation was my fault entirely. My not being able to stop him sooner, plain wrong. Clearly Palmer and Katlyn had done it all before, possibly many times.

It seemed Pamela felt determined to talk until she said all of what was on her mind.

"Finally, Mr. B had me call the police the last time Palmer stormed into the office." She frowned. "Oh my, did I almost say what I think I almost said?"

"You said nothing offensive, doll. So Del didn't want to represent him?"

"Del had me do research on him and that's when I discovered that Mr. Palmer already had an attorney."

What the hell is going on here?

"What did Del do during the war?" I asked.

"He was involved with intelligence, attached to the MPs. I think that's what he said once." She twirled her glass between her palms without spilling a drop of wine. She had long, slender fingers, which made me think of Lois.

"Palmer is hiding something." I promptly thought of the wall of death and added, mentally, *something besides that*. "But what? Maybe crimes he committed during the war and something else since then too. According to his military records, Palmer was a sharpshooter in the Pacific, an excellent sniper."

She took a sip and set the glass down. "You think he knew Del during the war and came by to meet with him t…" She stopped abruptly; her eyes widened and filled with deep visible concern. "To hire or force Del to represent him? Or to set him up and kill him."

"That might make sense if he's trying to kill off people who knew about his past. Your boss may have knowledge about whatever Palmer did that got him in trouble in Connecticut, and now Palmer wants to hide it from local authorities." Again, I thought of the twenty-five women he'd killed in New York and knew he'd killed a few in Connecticut too and most likely while overseas.

What set him off to kill the first one? I wondered. Maybe a Dear John letter during the war, or was he raping and killing civilians while on leave for his twisted sport of divide and conquer? Was Delbert involved with investigating Palmer while he wore a uniform and quit once Palmer got discharged?

That all made a lot of sense to me.

"You need a ride home." I finished my beer and turned the stool to face my guest.

"I can take a cab." In the mirror, I saw Pamela smile nervously as if she wanted to extend an invitation but felt shy suddenly.

"My car is parked outside city limits right now and Palmer might recognize it, so a cab it is. I'll keep you company." I stood and watched her face.

"I don't mind going alone." Her smile brightened significantly.

The game is afoot, I thought and wondered where it would lead us if

I played along. I rubbed my nose and finally nodded.

"I'd feel better if you let me accompany you home, Pamela. Besides, I invited you to join me for what turned into a nasty disaster of a dinner."

"The night might have a way of turning itself around and into something a lot more pleasant before it has to end." Pamela moved, slid off the stool, and ended up less than a foot away from me. I could smell the wine on her breath, her perfume, and feel her body heat.

"There's always that chance," I said, thought of Stella, winced inwardly, and decided enough was enough, but didn't say anything about my feelings to Pamela. I did want to get her home safely. So I played the role of seductive gentleman and held out my arm. Her hand slipped possessively around my elbow as if we'd been walking together for years.

I paid the bartender and asked him to phone for a cab, told him to give the taxi dispatcher my name to be on the safe side.

The air outside felt balmy for late summer. What I could see of the sky looked filled with constellations of faint stars dimmed by the city lights around us. I thought I could smell a hint of rain, but I could not see the horizon, could not know if clouds gathered and darkened out over the ocean.

More than ten minutes passed before the cab rolled to a stop at the curb. I opened the door and assisted Pamela, could not help but notice her long, shapely legs as she swung them inside the cab and her skirt rode far above her knees.

I paused and enjoyed the show while she slid across the seat, revealing even more silk stocking as she twisted to move in completely. I felt positive that she knew I watched her and wanted me to speculate on what might happen later after we reached her place. That was not difficult to hypothesize.

Then unexpectedly the cab raced from the curb. The driver floored the gas pedal. The tires squealed and spun up a cloud of black smoke and fumes. The back door slammed as he roared around the corner, cutting off Pamela's scream of fear.

Shocked by what transpired while I stood helplessly watching, I waited seconds too long to react.

Running with the Colt in hand, I reached the corner in time to witness the fading taillights two blocks down the road. I knew Pamela was in life-threatening trouble, and there was only one thing I could think to do that might give me half of a chance to keep her alive—visit Katlyn Twiggs and convince her to tell me where Bobby Palmer would take her.

Chapter Twenty-One

Clearly, Palmer followed us when we left the restaurant, went to Pamela's apartment, and then to the bar afterward.

Too late, I knew then the way Bobby Palmer moved through town, located and selected his victims without suspicion, drove them to the place or places where he raped and killed them, and then delivered their remains to the unconsecrated earth of his choosing. Somewhere, the bodies of twenty-four women lay buried and forgotten for now if not forever.

Palmer could've driven and parked anywhere at any time of day or night and no one would have suspected him of criminal activity. No one ever looked twice at a cab unless attempting to hail it for a ride, but now I could give Paul Dunbar additional information to help him solve a string of murders if I failed in stopping Palmer.

Two minutes later, the cab I called rolled to a stop in front of where I waited.

I rapped on the driver's window and nodded when he turned to look. He was a dark-skinned man who appeared more startled than I felt after the first cab drove off without me.

"I need a ride to the Bowery," I said as if unsure whether he'd go there that late at night. Some cabbies would've refused the fare.

"Well then, you'll need to tuck your ass in the back, man, unless you'd be thinking of running alongside my car. Either way, the fare will work out to be about the same." He had a strong Jamaican accent. His smile started slow as he tapped the meter, and nodded at the expression stitched across my face.

Funny guy, I thought, but could not suppress a tired and crooked grin.

"Think I'll ride if it's all the same to you." I sat on the torn and frayed upholstery and closed the door, which creaked and snapped from one too many accidents. I watched him raise the flag on the meter before he pulled away from the curb.

We chatted about baseball. He followed the Giants too, and we passed the time in light traffic until reaching the street where Katlyn lived.

"Thanks," I said as I opened the door and overpaid him enough that he could've called it a night right then.

"You want change?" he asked expectantly, with a tinge of regret.

"Keep it," I said. "You're a good sport. It's been a pleasure riding with you and I need you to wait for me. If you do, I'll double what I gave you. My wife is inside making out with a bum she met through her part-time secretary job. I'm going to bring her back home if I have to carry her over my shoulder. All of that be okay with you?" I used a strong Brooklyn accent like the one my uncle Jim had.

He studied my face a second or two and nodded. "Don't be doing anything stupid, man. I don't wanna be getting between you and the cops. But what the hell, this could be fun. I'll be here waiting for you." He shut off the engine, killed the lights, and glanced at me in the rearview mirror when I swung my legs out. He smiled as if he knew I might provide serious entertainment to take the edge off an otherwise dull night.

I used the long blade on my pocketknife and jimmied open the front door. Moments later, I stood outside the Twiggs' apartment, raised my hand, and thought, *Swell, pal, knock on the damn door as if there's a snowball's chance in hell they plan on welcoming you inside.*

Before I broke in, I walked down the hallway in both directions, did not hear a sound from any of the other apartments, returned to the Twiggs', and pressed my ear to the door panel. Inside sounded as quiet as out with a distant sound of snoring like the last time I dropped in unannounced.

Again using my knife, I wedged the blade between the door and the jamb, twisted, pried, and popped open the door. It made a sound like a floorboard snap, loud in the stillness of night, but not enough to disturb the sleepers inside the back bedroom. Two of them snored like drunken sailors after their first night of shore leave. After folding the blade into the handle, I dropped the knife in my pocket.

I walked softly to Katlyn's room, hesitated when a floorboard creaked, found her bedroom door ajar, lifted the Colt from under my arm, thumbed off the safety, and used the barrel to press her door open.

She jumped off her bed and moved in my direction, opening her mouth as if she wanted to scream but fear choked off the sound. I thought she believed I was Bobby Palmer there to cut her throat, since the room was dark enough to screen out my features. I wanted to tell her to relax, but worried that if I spoke, the sound might wake her parents.

Her right fist clutched a long, wicked-looking butcher knife in a way that told me she knew how to use it to cut and maim, and was prepared to drive it down into my chest. She was not going to give me an option to alter her decision, and then the time for trying passed.

She charged me. I turned to the side and stepped away. She ran past, spun around, and met the fist I swung to meet her retaliation. We connected hard enough to skin three knuckles, but the blow landed square on her jaw and she went down at my feet. The knife dropped with a thud, stuck in the floor alongside my left foot and quivering like a tuning fork.

Strangely, I admired her show of courage and felt bad for what I would need to do despite her bravery.

I caught her before her head hit the floor, listened to the sleepers, felt satisfied we hadn't disturbed them, jammed the .45 into its holster, and tucked the knife under the mattress. After a quick search, I located some cloth belts and pocketed them for later use if needed.

Katlyn felt lighter than the last time as I swung her over my shoulder. Her bare feet hit my knee and bounced against my thigh as I slowly walked down the stairs and onto the street. The street's winos lay passed out in the alleys and missed the action.

The cab sat by the curb where he'd parked. The driver, when he saw me approaching, reached back and popped open the rear door. Then he started the engine and turned on the headlights.

"That didn't take you long, man," he said with a knowing look of appraisal, obviously enjoying himself. "You got yourself a fine-looking honey there, man," he said. "Ain't no wonder it's so hard to keep her at home."

I dumped her in the back, shoved her across, and climbed in. "Yeah, and I caught them in the act. He had his hands where they didn't belong, and when he wakes up he'll have time to seriously reconsider his choices."

"Remind me not to mess with your girl, man." The cabbie chuckled.

"You're all right in my book, friend. You know that?" I patted him on his shoulder.

His chuckle became a deep, rich laugh, and when he drove, I directed him to Lou Wilson's butcher shop on Third, paid him as I said I'd do, and bade him good night after dragging Katlyn from the cab.

Five minutes later, she again lay propped up against a stack of frozen beef in cold storage. She did not really deserve it, but I had nowhere else to take her.

She came to and really screamed when she saw me; understood where she sat and, I felt, knew the time came for whatever result she chose as the next step on the new path her life took because of her reckless decision to join, work with, and perhaps care for Bobby Palmer.

I shook her hard enough to snap her head sideways.

"Be quiet and listen for a minute," I yelled as loud as she screamed. "I didn't want to bring you here, but you tried to knife me and if we stayed there, we would've woken up half of the neighbors."

And hell, I don't have any other place where I can interrogate with this type of privacy.

"You're here because I need your help. Do you understand me? I don't want to hurt you again."

When her fear reduced to sobs, and she nodded that she understood, I told her about Pamela's abduction and studied her eyes. She did not react visibly.

"Just tell me where the hell I can find Palmer so I can stop him before he rapes and kills her too."

Her eyes moved as she looked around, examined my face, and then focused on her hands. She lifted them as if surprised she was not tied up and then she recited an address in the Bronx. She did not look up at me and I doubted her truthfulness.

"If you're lying to me, Katlyn, I'll be back to turn down the thermostat and this time lock the door."

"You're leaving me alone here with this?" she cried and looked at her surroundings.

I waved an arm to indicate the butchered remains. "Could be your kind of company, Miss Twiggs. If you lied you should get accustomed to it," I said and regretted the words as they slipped out. "Look, if something goes wrong for me, Lou the owner will be around about six. Tell him I dropped you off and he'll set you free and get you a ride home. Don't screw up with him either. He knows all about what you did to Lois." I lied convincingly.

"You don't know that I only took the pic…" she started and stopped abruptly. "Okay, you win, Black," she said hurriedly as if because of her fear, she spoke out of turn to distract me, but I did not have time to learn more. "I give up. Do whatever you have to and I'll go along with it."

"Yes, I do win, don't I," I agreed and left to find Palmer while mulling over what she almost said. *She took the pic? The black-and-white photos?* My blood ran cold at the idea she witnessed and photographed Lois' rape and death.

The last time I drove through the Bronx, I dumped a kidnapper's body in the gutter behind Woodlawn Cemetery. He had snatched Stella as a way to get to me, swiped my car, and forced me at gunpoint to drive to a rendezvous with his collaborators, whose plan included killing us. Then they'd planned to leave our bodies to rot unceremoniously among forgotten tombstones.

Unfortunately for that schlep, his gun went off when I slammed on the brakes. The shot shattered the top of his head into fragments that littered the upholstery. Okay, so timing was critical. I needed to wait until he held the weapon at the right angle and then I jammed the brake pedal with both feet.

For me, the Bronx is not a place I'd want to call home for obvious reasons, and the southern districts, where the address was, were starting to look seriously rundown, or run over.

Poverty settled in pockets like birds of a feather and eroded the community into abandoned buildings, broken windows, and shuttered storefronts.

Without access to my Olds, I was unsure how I could reach Palmer's place, grab Miss Gentrey, and escape quickly enough for him to find it difficult to detain me. Of course that precluded the assumption that he would not be dead by then, or me.

You'd think I'd learn, I thought. *Every time I get involved with a good-looking woman, I get in a fix I have to fight my way out of, or she ends up dead.*

But what can you do? When you roll the dice there is no chance in hell you can know the outcome until the bones stop after bouncing off the wall.

The thought cleared my mind enough to get me thinking I'd ask Irwin for a loaner. The man had enough cars to fill a used car lot out in Jamaica, Queens.

I walked a few blocks until I could hail a cab, returned to Irwin's building, and found him in the basement running his trains even though it was the middle of the night.

"Marlowe," he called out when he saw me. "I thought you might be gone for good."

"Not yet, but I'm working on it."

"Don't rush. I've got no problem with your being here, and I like the way you handled those cops a couple of nights ago."

"You don't miss a thing." I could not freeze the humorless grin before it formed.

"No, now what can I do for you?"

I told him about my dilemma, and he dug in his pocket, pulled out a key, and tossed it my way. After grabbing it mid-flight, I looked at it and saw an ignition key embossed with Chevrolet.

"The car is parked out front. Try to avoid getting a ticket," he said and turned back to his trains.

"Thanks, my friend, I owe you another one." I did not want to find out if he'd anticipated my need for transportation too.

"Forget owing me anything, Marlowe. Take care of the problem you have and live to tell me about how you did it, and I'll consider the debt paid in full."

I did the only thing I could do. I shook his hand and without saying another word left to take a short trip north where I might find the type of bleak darkness that made a moonless late October midnight seem inviting.

The Chevy sedan started without a hitch, and two pumps of the gas pedal. Thankfully, unlike Stella's new Chevy, this Bel Air had a three-speed stick shift on the column.

Twenty minutes after I left Manhattan, I parked a block from the address in Morrisania that Twiggs provided and checked the load in my Colt, jacked a round into the chamber, and flipped off the safety.

The air was cooling and again felt like rain hung on the horizon. A steady, muggy breeze blew in from the southeast carrying the aroma of cooked beef, but I was beyond caring about distractions.

The house where Palmer stayed proved to be a turn-of-the-century two-story wood structure with a broad and battered porch wrapped across the front. The building looked like the type of cottage once sold through the Sears Roebuck's catalogs.

The azalea shrubs that someone planted as ornamental bushes had overgrown into a tangle of branches sheltering assortments of household and windblown trash. The steps leading to the porch looked worn thin in the center, cracked, unpainted, and ready for a nice hot fire.

I walked around the back of the building, spotted a concrete stairway leading down to a door that I decided would open into a basement. The steps would not creak, and someone had swept them clear of debris and dirt.

Carefully, I went down and when I reached the door found four small panes of glass with a thick film of scum that told me the windows hadn't been cleaned in at least a quarter of a century.

The doorknob was one of those old glass knobs used on inside doors in expensive late nineteenth-century homes. In the keyhole, I saw an old-time skeleton key, which proved seriously too convenient for me. I squatted, slid the key out, peered into the hole, and spotted a large burning candle about fifteen feet inside the basement. Behind the candle, I saw a chair facing the door.

Pamela sat on the chair with a gag in her mouth and her hands bound behind her. The rigid chair back pinned her in place. Palmer had secured her ankles to the legs of the chair. He had removed her dress, but she still wore a white slip that covered most of her legs from the knees up.

Palmer hadn't used ropes. He had tied her with what appeared to be silk scarves, which told me why Lois hadn't showed the bruising associated with being held in place with ropes. Palmer knew how to cover all of his bases.

I saw Pamela's eyes closed. Her head leaned forward so her chin rested on her chest. From what I could tell, she still had both ears. I could not see Bobby Palmer, nor did I see any kind of movement.

Then I felt something hard and cold pressed firmly against the back of my neck and caught myself before I reacted with a shout of surprise at the frigid chill of unanticipated death now gnawing the length of my spine.

"I have Katlyn Twiggs stashed in a butcher's meat locker downtown," I said and felt pleased at how calm I sounded considering how hard and fast my heart pounded in my chest. "Something goes wrong here and the cops get her."

"You think I give a damn about that stupid bitch or the cops? They aren't clever enough to find me or to solve a simple case of assault," Palmer stated arrogantly.

His voice sounded different in person, clearer, more distinct, and I knew where I recognized him from.

"I found you. Besides that, the cops know your name. You need her, Palmer. You need her free."

"What the hell do I need that whore for?" he asked. "She sent you here, didn't she?"

"Yes, but I left her with no options except to tell me where to find you or freeze to death."

"That shouldn't be much of a problem for a bitch with a heart as frigid as hers." He lifted the gun from my neck. "Turn around slowly, and don't be stupid."

I did and faced the hit man who tried to get Stella almost a year ago. At the time, I stopped him by firing a round into his chest, which left him on the floor with a sucking wound and about three minutes to reveal who hired him to kill Stella. If he failed to obey, I'd've let him bleed out before I left. When he told me the name of his employer, a woman named Twiggs, I called the cops and they sent an ambulance, which obviously saved his life. *Too bad.*

A glance at his bandaged left arm told me he was also the guy I shot after he took down Stella in the hallway outside my office.

"Glad I saved your worthless ass the first time we met," I said.

"Damn shame about your friend Melody though. She caught me off guard."

"That makes two of us, Black. Too bad I cannot repay the favor. As far as Melody's death goes, she should have done what I told her, collected the evidence I'd left by mistake. According to Katlyn, she read in the report that your ignorant cop friends did not find my house keys. Then Melody should have gotten the hell away from there before anyone caught up with her. It turned out to be her bad luck an asshole like you entered the apartment the moment you did. That's kind of weird timing, Black."

I refused to react and watched his face. It remained impassive, the emotional void I expected a sniper's face to show as he lined up his target with his finger lightly pressing the trigger.

"Katlyn will be in someone else's hands when the sun comes up. He'll take her to the police where she'll sell you out to keep from doing hard time. That's why you need her free, Palmer," I reiterated to emphasize its importance and hoped he would agree with my assessment.

Slowly, I lifted out a pack of Camels, shook out two, and offered him one. To my surprise, he accepted and took a light off my Zippo.

"I'll swap you Twiggs for the dame you've got inside. No tricks and no cops."

He inhaled long, illuminating the stone and concrete stairwell with orange light, studied me as if he wanted to memorize my features, and nodded slowly.

"Bring her here before six this morning, and I'll trade you a redhead for a blonde." He spoke as if dealing in ordinary commodities he might trade or sell at a downtown market.

The bold bastard held out his hand, but what the hell, if you're going to roll the dice with Lucifer, I say go the distance, and I knew Dunbar wanted him alive too. I shook his hand. It felt cool, dry, and hard, not quite human.

"I'll be back inside of an hour. Don't do anything more to Pamela. I'll convince her to forget she ever saw you."

"If anyone can do that, it would be you, Black. One hour." He turned his back to me and walked up the stairs into the shadows beyond the top of the stairwell.

I wanted to put a slug in the center of his back, knew I could before he'd react to stop me, but a deal with the devil is still a deal, and I knew that might turn into a decision I would come to regret.

Besides, I wanted him alive to stand trial with Katlyn for Lois and my unborn child's deaths. And Paul wanted him alive so he could be coerced to tell the cops where he buried twenty-four dead women.

Therefore, I waited until I finished my smoke and went back to the Chevy without looking around. Hell, the man was a sniper who had let me live up until then. If he wanted to take me out, he would do it whenever and wherever it pleased him.

Now, I would attempt to reshuffle the deck and deal him a new hand with one wildcard held out: my rage.

Chapter Twenty-Two

While I drove again I started thinking about the other twenty-four women Palmer had killed and understood that if they were all hookers, then it was likely that no one had reported their disappearance. Bobby Palmer knew his business, but also knew where he'd buried them. They, too, deserved proper burial. Their families, regardless of how they thought of the women, needed that at least too.

The drive to Lou's butcher shop went faster than I expected. The Chevy ran nice enough that I briefly rethought my desire to own an Oldsmobile, but I liked the lines of my Olds better. Looks have to count for something.

The alley alongside the butcher shop remained wrapped in shadows. The overcast sky looked lifeless, and the street lighting faded halfway down the alley. I found the back door still locked, and I used the key Lou gave me.

When I pushed open the locker door, Katlyn looked dead. I felt something molten yet cold run from the center of my chest out to my fingers and down to my toes. Her legs, arms, hands, and feet glowed blue under the dim illumination. My heart skipped.

I promised Dunbar I would do everything in my power to keep her around at least long enough to testify against Palmer, and no matter how I felt about her and her behavior, I did not kill without provocation and never wanted to kill a woman.

She was an accomplice to murder, maybe an unwilling one, and deserved the law's punishment, which was what I'd get if she died while in my custody.

"You can't be dead," I said softly and walked to her. I pressed the pads of my fingers against the artery in her neck, felt a steady pulse, and breathed a sigh of relief.

Her hands felt like icicles. I hoped she didn't have frostbite. Her skin looked dead white.

Moving fast, I slung her over my shoulder, again thought about how much lighter she felt since the first time I carried her, and went outside the building.

After I sat her against the butcher shop's brick wall, I went back inside, rearranged the carcasses, and closed the big freezer door. I listened to hear the blower come on, and went out into the damp air, locked the outside door on my way.

Katlyn remained where I'd left her, eyes closed, head resting on her shoulder. I squatted before her, took her hands, and felt a stab of relief with the realization that they'd warmed up. I rubbed them vigorously and then carried her to the car, put her in the backseat, used the cloth belts I found at her apartment, and tied her wrists and ankles together. Based on my experience with her, I knew that I needed to bind her. Katlyn might wake up, put her hands over my head, and attempt to choke me to death with the cloth belt that held her wrists together whether I might be driving or parked.

I checked the bindings and used my belt to tie the cloth belt around her wrists to the belt around her ankles.

She did not make a sound until I drove along the FDR Drive.

"What the… Where am I? Black? You driving?" Her voice sounded scratchy, like a dame who'd been smoking for fifty years.

"I'm driving. We're going to meet your friend Bobby Palmer."

"He'll kill me." She gasped a sound of terror.

"That might be what I'd consider to be a problem of your own creation. However, I doubt he'll hurt you since me and Detective Paul Dunbar will know that I left you with him."

"Why are you doing this to me?" She sounded like she hadn't heard a word I'd said.

"If you think back to what I told you a few hours ago, you know the reason. He snatched my friend off the street with me watching. I'm trading you for her."

"I didn't have nothing to do with that, Black."

"Right, you and Bobby are pen pals only. You must've known what he might do if we met the two of you in the restaurant. And you damn sure knew what he planned to do to Pamela if he had gotten her alone after his after-dinner performance."

"What'd you do, hogtie me like a pig?" Her voice got stronger. I heard her struggling.

"Didn't want to have to worry about you choking me like you did Stella."

"You're starting to get to know me pretty good. Maybe we should team up and take over the town." She laughed, but I heard no humor in the sound.

"Right," I said. "And maybe stepping in cow shit will remind me of fresh-cut roses and bring me good luck as it oozes between my toes."

I steered the Chevy across the Triborough Bridge into the Bronx and hoped Katlyn would shut up.

She mumbled something, but I ignored her and rolled to a stop a half block from the house where Palmer held Gentrey.

"We're here," I said a bit redundantly, opened the car door, and stepped onto the road. I went to the back door, popped it open, and looked at her face.

"I need assurance of your cooperation, or I'll knock you out and carry you inside."

"You're the boss for now, Black. Tell me what to do."

I pulled her to the edge of the seat and released my belt, ran it through the loops to keep my trousers up, untied her ankles, and helped her from the car. Her hands felt warm and her heart raced enough that I could feel it in her wrists.

I guided her around the house, down the concrete and stone basement steps by her bound wrists, and stopped. I looked back for a minute, knowing that Palmer could pull a smooth double cross and take us both down within five seconds after aiming the first shot.

Nothing happened, which got me thinking maybe he believed in keeping his word.

Fat chance, I thought, *fucking bastard's insane*, and twisted the glass door knob, had a flash of the Mad Hatter run through my mind, and worried more when the door swung silently open on recently oiled hinges.

Five tall white candles ringed Pamela, highlighting her with flickering yellow light. The bastard had stripped off her slip, exposing more of her beauty than any decent man wanted to under most circumstances. The small gold cross she wore on a thin chain around her neck sparked light from the nearest flame.

I diverted my eyes, felt a thick wedge of pain in my throat as the photo of Lois came to mind. Pamela still wore her underwear, but nothing more, and I hoped he hadn't raped her while I retrieved Katlyn.

Goddamn fucking damn it, my fault again, I thought and then roughly shoved the emotion aside. *This is no time for emotional self-flagellation.*

I pushed Katlyn ahead of me to keep myself between her and the door.

"How do you like the way your girlfriend looks tied up and ready for some fun?" Palmer said sickly from the shadows across the cellar. "Looks like you got Katlyn all tied up and ready too," he added as if he thought we might be performing the same rituals, which turned my stomach with its parallels and similarities. In a way, it made us too alike, which caused self-doubt at a time when such might hurt Pamela and me badly. I shook it off with a promise to think through what I'd done to Twiggs once I freed Miss Gentrey.

"This like the ritual or something that you used with the other twenty-five women you killed?" I said and fought the desperate need to fire into the shadows until he fell dead at my feet.

"They were all paid whores. Who'd miss them?"

"Not Lois," I said. "I miss her."

"Her too, Black," he said flatly. "Maybe she changed for you, but I knew her from before. Hell, I saved you from the embarrassment."

You sick fucking son of a bitch, I thought, but his words stung me bad. *Should just shoot the shithead where he stands and be done with him.*

Then my heart jumped in my chest as I heard the sound of a hammer drawn back into firing position.

"Easy does it, Palmer. It might surprise you to learn that I informed the local cops about where I'd be and how long before I expected to reach a pay phone to call and report that Miss Gentrey is safe and with me."

"Don't think I'm a fool, Black. You are not that stupid. You involving the police is like me nose-diving off the Empire State Building and expecting a soft landing like that dame back in the thirties landing on the roof of a car." He snickered what I guessed to be his version of a chuckle.

"After I told them where to find your wall of death, you think every cop in town, and the federal boys too, aren't interested in your activities past and present?"

Palmer stepped from the shadows, holding the gun, a long-barrel .44, down by his side. He lifted it and aimed at Pamela.

"I don't give a damn about cops, and you didn't answer my original question, Black."

"I forgot the question when you cocked the hammer." I intentionally sounded disinterested despite my accelerated pulse and the beads of sweat that exploded across my brow and ran down my back.

"I asked you how you liked the way your little girlfriend looks all tied up in her underwear and ready for some serious fun. She's got terrific gams, doesn't she? Not too skinny and not too heavy. Like she's a dancer or something, you know? I love to look at beautiful women when they're sitting like this waiting for me to enjoy them." He waved his free hand in her direction.

To me the man sounded like a highly dangerous killer balanced on the knife-edge of something deeper and crueler than insanity. Whatever happened to him during the war and the years after had ripped open places in his mind that exposed the fire and fangs all of us visit church to avoid. It's when we learn that such evil might reside in our own minds and souls that the meaning of worship takes on a new life, and puts a gravely different definition on the purpose of our existence as I'd just discovered for myself.

My old man, the college professor, also had a degree in philosophy. He once declared that humans possessed the true embodiment of good and evil. The two forces lay like the scales of justice, balanced until we added, or allowed someone else to add, to one side or the other. Enough in either direction would tip a man into a state of abnormality in modern society.

Bobby Palmer's scale teetered over and broke.

I took a few seconds and carefully examined Pamela, tried to tell her with my eyes that she would be fine once I could figure out a way to get through to Palmer, but she only glanced up with a look of absolute terror locked onto her features. Her flesh looked bleached and shiny with sweat. Carefully, I stepped closer to her.

"No talking to the girls, Black."

After a quick glance over my shoulder, I nodded.

"Wouldn't know what to say to her at this point." Instead of whispering to her like I'd intended, I placed my left hand under her chin and gently lifted until she stared at me. I mouthed, "I'll take care of him. Hang on."

She blinked and I knew she understood, but the knowledge did not extinguish the fear that seemed to eat at her mind.

"You're right, Palmer, she has great-looking legs." Then I turned back to him.

"We can see a lot more too," he said. "My favorite photographer could take us pictures." He glanced at Katlyn while he walked directly to Pamela, stopped alongside me, and pointed the .44 at her head. His words finished what Katlyn started to say earlier, and her complicity grew deeper.

How many did she photograph? All twenty-five?

"That's not necessary." My heart skipped. "What do you think she's going to do, pal, jump from the chair and kick you in the balls with her bare feet?"

Katlyn laughed, and quickly cleared her throat when Palmer turned his head like the predator he was and glared in her direction.

"You betrayed me once already, little bitch. Don't think I'll forget that any time soon," he told her and slapped her hard enough to stagger her.

Obviously, he thought he was in complete control, but I needed to intervene to slow him down before he did use his gun on one of us. I walked across the room with my back to him.

"The view is better from here," I said and smiled when he looked at me. "Seriously, come over and take a gander at the way the candlelight shimmers on her skin. It's kind of romantic." I sounded serious, twisted, and nearly gagged on my words. I knew then that I'd allowed events to spiral out of my control if they'd ever been mine to direct in the first place. I should not have worried about seeing him at trial, about locating the bodies of the other dead women, or how Dunbar would have reacted.

I should have drilled a .45 through the center of his back an hour earlier when I had an easy shot. Now, three of us were close to joining the missing twenty-four, and I thought Palmer knew the exact moment he'd planned to kill us.

He came to where I stood, stopped, and waved Katlyn away from Pamela. She moved behind but between Palmer and me.

"What do you think? Can I shoot through her bra straps from here? Two shots and then we'll see what she's hiding underneath it. I got me a nice healthy handful at the restaurant, real firm and tight." He laughed, but it sounded like a hysterical giggle. "I know what you're

DEATH LEAVES A SHADOW

thinking, Black. He can't do it without drawing blood. I can, but so what if I don't? Tonight is her special night."

Before I could act in response and stop him, he lifted the .44, aimed, and fired two quick rounds in succession that clipped the straps over Pamela's shoulders. Only a highly experienced sniper could have pulled that off without killing her.

The white material burst in a shower of fine particles, and the noise rattled around the concrete and stone cellar. Pamela cringed miserably and screamed. I saw small beads of red droplets slowly run down her chest and knew he'd gotten the first taste. I needed to make sure the first blood he drew would be the last.

"I like to put the killing round in the center of the ear when I shoot from a distance. Works like a bull's-eye," he said seriously. "Usually, I fire a small caliber so the bullet rattles around inside of the skull, tearing everything up."

Palmer raised his .44 again as if thinking that if I let him fire it twice, I would be okay with his firing it a third time. The exchange was off.

Quickly, I stepped back and shoved Katlyn into him before he shot again. As my hand went under my jacket and clutched the butt of my Colt, he hurriedly pushed Katlyn away, reacting like a machine geared into action without a stop button.

He drilled a single bullet into the hollow of Katlyn's throat from a distance of less than three feet. Her neck exploded in a shower of blood and tissue.

Katlyn's eyes registered surprise and betrayal when they flicked in my direction, then widened as I raised the Colt without time for an accurate aim and fired three rounds at Palmer. Katlyn slipped to the floor.

I hoped one or all of the rounds would punch holes through his chest, disable or preferably kill him.

The first two missed; his body kept moving away from me in

reaction to shooting Katlyn off balance. The third round was a good clean hit. Pieces of bone sprayed out behind him like shrapnel; blood spattered the concrete and stonewall in a pattern like a thousand red spiders frozen by a quirk of time. His right arm dropped uselessly to his side, and the .44 clattered to the floor by his feet.

"I really don't think you're worth saving a second time, you fucking son of a bitch." I kicked his weapon across the basement with the side of my foot and watched the blood pumping from an arterial wound as if it was nothing more than yellow liquid spraying from a dog peeing on a street sign.

He sagged to his knees, eyes closed, and keeled over on his face. He passed out and lay dying alongside Katlyn, whose arctic-blue eyes hazed into death as I squatted, took her hand, and watched her final blink.

"Sorry, Katlyn," I said quietly. "I didn't mean for that to happen."

I thought of Dunbar, my promise to him, and found a handful of rags, grudgingly applied a wad of cloth and a tourniquet to Palmer's upper arm, tied it tight enough to stop or at least slow the bleeding, and realized what I'd accomplished. Once more, I gave him another chance to live, and maybe kill again.

After I untied Pamela, she smothered me with a rib-cracking hug, and I kissed her forehead gently, tasted her salty sweat.

"Do you know where he put your things?" I asked.

"No," she said. "He took them into the rear of the cellar. I think there's a storeroom or something back there." She used one arm to cover her breasts and the other hand to finger her gold cross.

Maybe she thought Jesus had saved her. I did not care to debate it and decided I would gladly be the agent of any power that gave me the strength to stop men like Palmer.

"Do you think he'll wake up?" she asked nervously.

"It's not likely; he's lost a lot of blood," I said, "but take this and use it on him if he tries to stand up again."

DEATH LEAVES A SHADOW

She looked at my .45 with distaste, but accepted it and used both hands to point it at the unconscious man.

The back room looked like a workshop, with two walls lined with old carpentry tools. Pamela's clothing lay neatly folded and piled alongside a bundle of small brown paper bags and an old Kodak box camera. The sight of them made me wonder if giving Palmer another chance to live could've possibly been the right thing to do.

When I lifted the camera to examine it, I nearly dropped it. Someone had etched Katlyn Twiggs' name into the metal base hinge that attached to the back where film was loaded. That verified that Twiggs shot the death photos, must have enjoyed her work, and meant more to Palmer than an unintentional accomplice. Katlyn was the blonde bimbo his wife cursed silently.

Carefully, I placed the camera where I found it, gathered up Pamela's clothes and shoes, returned, handed them to her, and relieved her of the .45. She dressed in a hurry and looked like she felt better after slipping into her shoes.

"Let's go," I said. "I'll stop along the way and phone the cops to let them know Palmer's here waiting for them to save his sorry ass." I took her hand. It felt sweat-slick and vibrated with fear.

Once outside, I said, "Okay, you're okay now. You acted brave in there, but I'm sorry he did that to you and I couldn't act sooner to stop him."

I have never been good at times like that, didn't know what to do or say. After turning the second corner, I parked on the side, pulled the handbrake, and threw the transmission into neutral, pulled her to me, put my arms around her, and felt her tears soak through my shirt.

"You're going to make it through this, doll," I said and truly felt that she might once she'd dealt with the raw feelings a woman must get after what she'd experienced.

"I thought he would rape me, Marlowe." She spoke into my chest, so her words sounded muffled, but I did not want to disturb her. I wanted to let her talk it out and help her by listening. I didn't really need her to inform me of what he did to her because that would tell me what he did to Lois too. But I held back and let her speak.

"He told me what he did to your fiancée, how he terrorized her when he broke into her house at 2 a.m." She choked up. "He locked her dog outside, and then woke her up. He made her get dressed first, which he said made her feel like he would not hurt her, and then he stripped her… I'm sorry. I shouldn't being telling you this."

"It's okay, doll," I said despite the fact that it was not, couldn't be, and I heard the knot I felt in my throat tangle my voice so it sounded brittle and hoarse as if I'd been screaming for hours. "You need to talk about what he did to you." I didn't want to hear what Palmer put Lois and the other twenty-four women through before he jammed the gun barrel in their mouths and pulled the trigger, or aimed it at an ear first.

Pamela had been talking while I remained locked in my head. I missed much of what she told me, but caught the end.

"He made her fold up her clothing, put them away, and put her underwear in a brown lunch bag. He showed me one like it. He said he promised her he wouldn't hurt her if she obeyed him, and then tied her up with strips torn from a silk slip from her dresser so she wouldn't bruise, and sliced off her ear before he…" She stopped again and I knew Pamela had finished reciting the story when the thought of his slicing off her ear became a vivid picture behind her eyelids.

She sat sobbing quietly, eyes clenched tight as if by not allowing the outside world in, she might erase the horrors residing in the putrid dark creases of humanity.

I knew the ending of what he did to my fiancée, but Palmer either lay dead in the basement or would be in police custody within a half an hour if I reached a public pay phone in time.

I hesitated, did not want to waste the nickel, but had made that goddamn awful promise to Paul.

"We need to find a telephone," I said and steered onto the street, drove until we came to a small section with stores lining the roads. At the corner, I saw the Morrisania Diner with a pay phone sign in the window.

"Lock the doors when I get out and keep them locked until I return." I parked and ran across the street, lifted the phone, dropped in a nickel, waited until I got an operator, and had her connect me to the local precinct.

The desk sergeant sounded grumpy, in need of coffee when he announced his precinct number and asked, "Can I help you?"

"Paul Dunbar, a homicide detective from downtown, told me to call and report a shooting," I said and gave him the address before he could respond. "Okay? You get that?"

"Yeah, pal, I got it. How bad is the victim shot?"

"He may hold on for a few more minutes, he may not," I said as if I reported nothing more important than the weather, and then hung up. There was no reason to wait around. Palmer either was or was not dead. However, I was finished with him. I didn't give a shit either way. The fact that I only got to put one round into his body felt disappointing, but now I could visit Lois' grave in Woodlawn Cemetery with a feeling that I'd served justice to her killer.

I knocked on the car window and Pamela jumped and pulled away as if I'd fired a gun in her face.

I watched her lean across the seat to unlock the door. After I slid in, she moved close enough that her hip pressed mine.

There was no way to know what she had on her mind, but I did not have a problem with her needing live human contact. I needed to feel it too. For too long I'd felt nothing much more than stinging emptiness, like steaming water was poured down my throat, boiling off any joy and warmth I kept to comfort me.

"I'll drive you home now," I said and glanced at her when she put her head on my shoulder. A sob welled into my throat. Swallowing several times drove it away, but that only buried the burning grief I battled to overcome.

Don't do this to me, I thought but, afraid of how I might sound, did not voice my feelings aloud. She looked desperately vulnerable, and I felt strangely detached from life, as if right then we drove through a town I'd never visited, at a time of night no different from any other moment on any other day after sunset. I could not have told you the hour, the day of the week, maybe not even the year.

I lifted my right arm, placed it over her shoulders, and felt a weight shift inside me, an emotional rock dislodged to expose a soul-deep wound, excruciating, with a red blaze rooted in the misery I'd experienced from the day I watched my first buddy die in Europe on up until I sat there with Pamela's fear pressing against my heart, her head on my shoulder as if I might be a man who could change fear into acceptance.

Then Pamela leaned off the seatback, and my arm settled around her waist. After a strong hug, I lifted my hand and grabbed the wheel. We drove like two strangers floating directionless in a lifeboat, wondering what happened to the ship we'd ridden, knowing that in spite of the odds, she and I had survived a hurricane worse than the one from 1938.

"Take me to where you're staying, Marlowe. I can't be alone tonight." Carefully, she examined my face while she talked. She lifted her hand and brushed her fingers gently across my cheek, touched my lips with a tenderness I knew I couldn't accept. I desperately wanted to kiss her fingers, but resisted.

I wrestled to keep my expression bland as I kept busy concentrating on driving. I truly wanted to be alone. The need to mourn Lois became brutally overwhelming and agonizingly raw.

When I finally glanced at her, her eyes glistened with unspent tears. My heart felt leaden and I fought to keep a sob of grief from exploding from my mouth. My teeth ground it down. My tongue pressed my palate as I nodded and murmured consent.

Sometimes, I thought, *all you have is the moment you're living*.

Chapter Twenty-Three

I drove down to the Battery and parked where we could see the water, the ocean. About then, the clouds seemed to fade, turned the lifeless sky into thinning shades of gray. Behind them hung a moon filled with craters and mystery perhaps easier to resolve than what I'd experienced that night.

I felt Pamela move as if she wanted a different type of affection, but I did not respond in a way that told her I understood her desire. Our situation reminded me of dates I had back in the day when I used my father's Hupmobile without his knowledge before war erupted and wiped the slate clean of all but the sharpest of childhood memories.

The bittersweet moments of new love, promises about forever, and nights long enough to become an entire summer evolved into a boy's concept of maturity.

Nothing died back then. The elderly passed on to another life, embraced the souls of lost pets and protected them too while they watched over the living as invisible winged guardians.

Then the final mushroom cloud of destruction over the Empire of Japan obliterated all human innocence forever. Death arrived with a new definition, created a new reality from the remnant ashes of our generation. We emerged like a badly damaged and crippled phoenix with the permanent thousand-yard stare of a dazed survivor stumbling out of Hiroshima.

I wondered how in God's name we could bring a new generation into the world we helped create. A world where their childhood innocence was spent, extinguished like a wooden match snuffed in a glass of stale beer before they were even born. We would pretend all was well again, but would know in our hearts that we did not feel the expression to be accurate or honest. However, at least we would attempt it as none before us had ever needed to try to do.

Pamela made a small sound. She lay tucked tight under my arm with her head on my shoulder as if she knew I would keep her safe from harm. Part of me knew I'd done far better with Pamela than I had with Lois. The rest of me knew I could no longer keep her or anyone safe without the delusional thinking of a 5 a.m. drunk, or heroin addict watching a wavering flame dissolve the juice he intended to jam into a vein to escape his dreaded reality.

The sound she made came again. I smiled wearily. She breathed evenly. I knew she slept, and decided to wait for sunrise before I drove back into town.

When the sun rose, it was with an explosion of red and yellow. I could feel its intensity, and tried to ignore what felt like a forewarning for the coming day as it dawned. As the colors faded into yellows, I started the car. Pamela yawned, lifted her head, and stretched.

With as much gentleness as I could muster, I kissed her forehead.

"Time to go," I said and backed onto the road.

The space in front of Irwin's building was empty. I parallel parked with more skill than I knew I had, shut off the engine, and sighed as I stepped out and into a light, cool drizzle.

Pamela came around the front of the Chevy and reached for my hand. We walked to the alley, I checked for unwanted company, found it empty, and went down the steps.

We landed in the bed without undressing, and both dropped into a hard sleep.

When I woke, it was to the sound of the telephone. The ring continued incessantly. I rolled on to my back and carefully extracted myself from Pamela's arms, went where the noise came from, found a red telephone in the main part of the basement, and lifted the receiver.

"Black," I said. "What do you want at this hour?"

"It's eleven thirty," Paul Dunbar said with a touch of humor. "Didn't know you ever slept late."

"Paul?" I asked. "How'd you get this number?"

"I called around and finally got Irwin. He gave me the number." He grew silent as if waiting for me to tell him something important.

I didn't want to tell him what happened last night, knew he'd be disappointed, but drew in a deep breath.

"Katlyn is dead, Paul. I'm real sorry, but Palmer caught me off guard and put one through her neck from three feet away."

"What happened to Palmer?" he said, now sounding all cop.

I explained everything, listening to his sounds of encouragement each time I paused, and finally finished with "I called the cops up in the Bronx and told them that Paul Dunbar said I should contact them."

"Well," he said, sounding more relieved than I expected, "at least we've got Palmer in custody if he lives."

"That tough bastard will live, but he might lose the use of his right arm if not lose the arm completely."

"Couldn't've happened to a nicer guy," Paul said with sarcasm. "When will you return to Lake Orange? We'd both like to get back to our normal lives."

Whatever the hell that means. I shook my head slowly, now ready for a strong coffee.

"I need to drive over and take care of Betty, and then I'll catch a train. When I get to the station, I'll hire a cab."

"I'll tell Stella you'll be here in time for dinner. Right now, I'd better go. I drove into town to pick up supplies and to try to learn how you made out. See you tonight, pal," he said.

"Right, Paul, and please tell Stella not to do anything fancy. A couple burgers on rye with ketchup will suit me, and two or three cold ones to wash it down." I hung up and found Pamela standing outside the entrance to the apartment. She looked a bit disheveled, sexy, and beautiful in her soiled and wrinkled dress with a dried bloodstain on one shoulder.

An hour later, I dropped her at her apartment with a promise that

I'd keep in touch, then went and took care of Paul's stinky cat and returned Irwin's car. It was early, so I walked to Grand Central, bought a ticket, and after lunch headed from New York and into the wilds of upstate.

The trip went uneventfully, until I arrived at the cabin and found the door locked.

Paul answered after I knocked. He looked past me as if he'd thought Bobby Palmer tailed me and was waiting to fire a second round into Dunbar's shoulder. Paul waved me inside and relocked the door.

"What the hell was that about?" I asked impatiently.

"We've got a serious problem, Marlowe." He looked worried. For Paul that was unusual.

What went wrong now? "What happened? Who died?"

"Nobody died yet. I went back to town about an hour ago and called my precinct to find out if Palmer survived surgery. Bobby Palmer walked from the hospital about two this afternoon. The cop at his door went to the john, so no one saw him leave and no one knows where the hell he's off to now. The only good thing about it is that the bastard got his right arm amputated." He rubbed his eyes with his palms and squeezed the bridge of his nose. "Damn it, nobody's that tough, Marlowe."

"Maybe he'll bleed to death soon. He can't be feeling too good, and he lost a lot of blood after I shot him. You're right, no man is that tough, but it doesn't matter. He's not going to be doing any more sniper work or firing a handgun for as long as it takes to retrain himself. I say he's dead or captured before that happens."

"Let's hope that you're right, friend," Paul said and patted my shoulder encouragingly.

We both turned to the kitchen when Stella called, "That you, Marlowe?"

"That's right, doll," I said.

"Right on time," she answered with a touch of amusement.

"She doesn't know?" I glanced at Paul with a frown.

"No, and let's leave it that way for as long as possible."

Since he knew I'd agree, he did not wait for my response, but walked to the kitchen and said, "Tomorrow we're all going home."

Well, isn't that just terrific, I thought, *now I've got Pamela, Stella, and Palmer to worry about*, and followed him into the kitchen for a warm hug from Stella and a great dinner. I looked forward to dessert, but not to our departure.

If not for the desire to visit Lois' grave in Woodlawn to leave her yellow roses and tell her how it all worked out, I might have stayed in the cabin forever. Well, not really, the city was my home, and I would've returned no matter what. Palmer could be damned.

That was the moment I decided that I would see to it that Melody Gibbson got a proper burial too, and planned to make the necessary arrangements to put her near Lois. What the hell, in the end a man is only as good as his word.

CPSIA information can be obtained
at www.ICGtesting.com
Printed in the USA
BVHW031641050919
557692BV00001B/171/P